"Compton writes in th
ists like Louis L'Amou
ries of Western legend

"Compton may very well turn out to be the greatest
Western writer of them all. . . . Very seldom in literature
have the legends of the Old West been so vividly
painted."
                                                    —*The Tombstone Epitaph*

A DIFFERENCE OF OPINIONS

As soon as the gunman collapsed, Paul went inside the
pantry. "Come along with me now," he said. "It's all
right."

Manuela was terrified. The commotion on the second floor was drawing closer to the top of the staircase,
so Paul kept Manuela in front of him and the stairs to
his back. He grabbed her by both shoulders, kicked
open the door, and shoved her outside. "Go to the sheriff," he said.

"Come with! Is too dangerous."

Before Paul could respond to that, two armed men
raced to the top of the staircase. One of them was a
short fellow wearing a brown vest over a white shirt
and chaps over filthy jeans. In fact, dirt covered everything he wore as well as the teeth he bared when he
shouted, "Hey! Where's Wes?"

Paul slammed the door shut and backed away. "I
don't know what this is about," he said, "but there's no
need for any further violence."

The short man raised his pistol to sight along the top
of its barrel. "I beg to differ, mister."

Ralph Compton

BRIMSTONE TRAIL

A Ralph Compton Novel
by Marcus Galloway

Ⓢ
A SIGNET BOOK

SIGNET
Published by New American Library, a division of
Penguin Group (USA) Inc., 375 Hudson Street,
New York, New York 10014, USA
Penguin Group (Canada), 90 Eglinton Avenue East, Suite 700, Toronto,
Ontario M4P 2Y3, Canada (a division of Pearson Penguin Canada Inc.)
Penguin Books Ltd., 80 Strand, London WC2R 0RL, England
Penguin Ireland, 25 St. Stephen's Green, Dublin 2,
Ireland (a division of Penguin Books Ltd.)
Penguin Group (Australia), 250 Camberwell Road, Camberwell, Victoria 3124,
Australia (a division of Pearson Australia Group Pty. Ltd.)
Penguin Books India Pvt. Ltd., 11 Community Centre, Panchsheel Park,
New Delhi - 110 017, India
Penguin Group (NZ), 67 Apollo Drive, Rosedale, Auckland 0632,
New Zealand (a division of Pearson New Zealand Ltd.)
Penguin Books (South Africa) (Pty.) Ltd., 24 Sturdee Avenue,
Rosebank, Johannesburg 2196, South Africa

Penguin Books Ltd., Registered Offices:
80 Strand, London WC2R 0RL, England

First published by Signet, an imprint of New American Library,
a division of Penguin Group (USA) Inc.

First Printing, February 2013
10 9 8 7 6 5 4 3 2 1

 REGISTERED TRADEMARK—MARCA REGISTRADA

Printed in the United States of America

PUBLISHER'S NOTE
This is a work of fiction. Names, characters, places, and incidents either are the product of the author's imagination or are used fictitiously, and any resemblance to actual persons, living or dead, business establishments, events, or locales is entirely coincidental.

The publisher does not have any control over and does not assume any responsibility for author or third-party Web sites or their content.

ALWAYS LEARNING   PEARSON

THE IMMORTAL COWBOY

This is respectfully dedicated to the "American Cowboy." His was the saga sparked by the turmoil that followed the Civil War, and the passing of more than a century has by no means diminished the flame.

True, the old days and the old ways are but treasured memories, and the old trails have grown dim with the ravages of time, but the spirit of the cowboy lives on.

In my travels—to Texas, Oklahoma, Kansas, Nebraska, Colorado, Wyoming, New Mexico, and Arizona—I always find something that reminds me of the Old West. While I am walking these plains and mountains for the first time, there is this feeling that a part of me is eternal, that I have known these old trails before. I believe it is the undying spirit of the frontier calling me, through the mind's eye, to step back into time. What is the appeal of the Old West of the American frontier?

It has been epitomized by some as the dark and bloody period in American history. Its heroes—Crockett, Bowie, Hickok, Earp—have been reviled and criticized. Yet the Old West lives on, larger than life.

It has become a symbol of freedom, when there was always another mountain to climb and another river to cross; when a dispute between two men was settled not with expensive lawyers, but with fists, knives, or guns. Barbaric? Maybe. But some things never change. When the cowboy rode into the pages of American history, he left behind a legacy that lives within the hearts of us all.

—*Ralph Compton*

Chapter 1

Arizona Territory

The town of Pueblito Verde was full of sinners.

So was every other town. The farther west a man traveled, the more sinners he encountered. When Paul Lester rode into town just over three years ago, he decided not to go any farther so as not to lose the faith that had caused him to wrap the white collar around his neck, stand in front of a room of bored and beaming faces, and try to shed some light onto troubled lives.

Paul had seen more than his share of sin before finding his calling and had seen plenty more since his arrival in Pueblito Verde. Of course, what he saw in a town that small lay mostly on the tamer side of transgression. What lurked behind the preponderance of the guilty faces in his congregation ranged from small acts of thievery to weaknesses of the flesh. While burdensome to the ones committing those acts and heartbreaking to the folks caught in the cross fire, they weren't the sorts of things that had caused Paul to start his westward journey in the first place. They were common acts of poor judgment committed by otherwise good people. And that, more than anything else, was why he stayed in Pueblito Verde.

Paul's faith gave him strength during a terrible ride through the desert as well as the dangers he'd faced when he'd first struck out from Louisiana. When he'd first arrived in Pueblito Verde, he had a dusty hat in hand, a hunting rifle in the boot of his saddle, an old Colt strapped to his side, and a Bible in his pocket. The little town didn't even have a proper church at the time, so Paul had suggested they build one. It had taken several months, in which time he'd become a genuine member of a community composed mostly of retired ranchers, shopkeeps, and tin panners, but he'd finally convinced them to erect a little building devoted to devotion. It was one of the proudest moments in Paul's life.

Even though the structure itself was smaller than a modest stable, it loomed like a monument thanks to the miles upon miles of empty desert behind it. As it was built on the western edge of town, Paul liked to think of it as the farthest he meant to go in that direction before planting any roots. Its steeple rose only slightly taller than the roof of a house with two floors, and its little bell tower was empty. Getting a bell to hang there was one battle Paul wasn't about to relinquish any time soon.

Folks in town mostly kept to themselves. That is, until Paul started organizing suppers, dances, and any other get-togethers he could justify. When he ran out of ideas, he drew from memories of similar events thrown by the church in the bayou town where he'd been raised. Although church was poorly attended at first, Pueblito Verde eventually came around to Paul's train of thought. Either that or they'd simply given in to his constant begging for people to join him in whatever merriment he'd devised. To date, the most popular gathering was Easter Sunday, when all the women put on their fanciest clothes, the children's faces were scrubbed, and everyone was stuffed full of ham by the time the sun went down. Men fired their guns in the air to celebrate most anything. That was something Paul had discouraged at first, but in the spirit of picking his battles, he relented and allowed a pleasant day to end on a rowdy note.

Folks generally took kindly to Paul's ministry. Rather than press too hard to enforce every single rule as decreed in the Good Book, he stuck to the broad strokes and filled in where he could. He'd learned long ago that dealing in generalities was the trick to preaching in the untamed West. With folks battling against hostile natives and even harsher elements, they generally didn't want to hear about another set of rules imposed upon them. When a man's life was already close to unbearable, threatening his next life didn't hold much water. Paul did his best to put as many souls as he could on the proper road, and the ones who were open to learning the finer details would come to him for more. One of those was a man by the name of Gar Kilner.

Gar was a big man with a penchant for speaking endlessly just to hear himself talk. Before Paul had come to town, he'd taken a stab at preaching the gospel, but his knowledge was limited to only the most basic of tenets. Only the most ignorant among Pueblito Verde's population bought any of what Gar was selling, and even that lasted only until that person was set straight by one of his neighbors. Gar had been resistant to accept Paul at first, but changed his tune in a turnabout that surprised even Paul himself. Once he'd admitted to knowing less than the new arrival in the white collar, Gar had become something of a permanent addition to Pueblito Verde's little church. He sat up front for every service, shouted loudest at every celebration, volunteered for every task, and oftentimes stopped by for no discernible reason whatsoever. This night's visit, from what Paul could tell at first glance, was one of the latter.

Midnight was swiftly approaching, and Paul stood outside the front doors of his church, hands clasped behind his back while gazing upward. Tattered clouds slowly roamed the starry sky, sometimes obscuring the moon's glow. Other times, the great pale orb could be seen in all its glory as if peeking through tears in flimsy curtains.

Carrying most of his weight across his midsection, Gar shifted to something of a waddle as he picked up speed to get to the church. His smile was earnest if not appealing. Raised eyebrows hinted at a desperation that drove him to this spot so often after he'd given in to the fact that he was nobody's shepherd. "Evening, Father!" he called out.

"Good evening, Gar," Paul said while shifting his hands so they were clasped in front of him. "Having trouble sleeping?"

"Afraid so," the big man said as he ambled up to Paul and took a spot beside him.

For the next few moments, both men stood in silence. Paul let his eyes wander from star to star while Gar picked out as many points of interest among the pebbles at his feet.

Finally, once the tranquility of the night was overpowered by the awkwardness of Gar's presence, Paul asked, "Is something troubling you?"

"Yeah," Gar chuckled. "You were always real good at telling what a man's thinking."

"I just pay attention, Gar."

"I'd like to confess something."

Paul drew a long breath, careful not to make it too obvious he was doing so to quell the impatience brewing inside him. Although he'd never asked his congregation to formally confess their sins, he made it known to them that he would be there if any of them wanted to unload some of their burdens. Every so often, someone would come in seeking advice along with the occasional request for absolution, but Gar Kilner felt it necessary to share every impure thought he'd had no matter when he'd had it.

Reminding himself of why he wore the starched collar in the first place, Paul turned to face Gar. It was always easier to be patient with someone after seeing the need in their eyes. "The last time you came along at such a late hour," Paul reminded him, "it was because of a dream you had involving one of the Hovey sisters. If this is along those lines, you don't need to confess. Your thoughts are your own. In fact, I believe the Lord gave us our thoughts as a way to savor the delights around us without actually partaking in them."

Gar's face twisted a bit as he tried to digest that. "You mean it's all right for me to think bad things?"

"Your dream about Miss Hovey wasn't bad. Inappropriate perhaps but not wicked."

"Plenty of folks might disagree with you on that one, Father."

"I realize that. It's really more of a practical matter. Men and women alike have had impure thoughts since before the Good Book was written, I'm sure. Trouble only comes when those thoughts consume a person or if he acts on them. Do you understand?"

"I did act on them," Gar said as he bowed his head. "Only, it didn't hurt nobody."

"How do you mean?"

"Where Miss Hovey was concerned . . . I watched her hang her laundry until the wind kicked up her skirts just right. Is that wrong?"

"You shouldn't spy on ladies, Gar. I've told you that numerous times. Any man can enjoy what he sees. By doing that, we are all simply enjoying the world God gave us."

"Does that include saloon girls?"

"They are God's creatures too," Paul said. "They have the same thoughts as anyone—"

"No, no," Gar interrupted, which was something he often did. "Watching saloon girls is what I meant. They're wicked women. Whores. Still, I . . ."

Placing a hand on Gar's shoulder, Paul said, "They are women. Someone's daughter. Someone's mother. Someone's sister. There is no shame in admiring them.

There is no shame in dreaming about them. There is only shame in shaming them. Do you feel you are disgracing any of these women by thinking about them?"

"Eh . . . sometimes."

"Then stop it."

Gar looked as if he'd just been ordered to clear the clouds from the sky with a wave of his hand. "That's it?"

"What more would you like?"

"Ain't there something I need to do to atone for what I did?"

"From what I've heard, you haven't actually *done* anything. The girls I've seen onstage at saloons are usually dancing or singing."

"You go to saloons?" Gar gasped.

Paul shrugged. "Only for a drink or to unwind after a hard day's work. There's nothing wrong with that."

"But bad things can happen at saloons. Them dancing girls . . . some of them are bad too."

"Bad things can happen anywhere," Paul said. "If we all focused only on a bit of restraint, think how much better this world would be. As for the dancing girls, there's no shame in admiring their craft."

"Some of what they do ain't exactly a craft," Gar said, sneering.

"True, but that speaks more of the sort of saloons you're visiting, now, doesn't it?" Before Gar hung his head any lower, Paul added, "We are men and it is within a man's nature to admire a woman. That is the way God intended it to be. You know well enough when you overstep those bounds, and I believe you are a good enough man to keep from going too far in that direction. As for the rest, try not to stare at the Hovey sisters or any other woman when it's inappropriate. Do I really need to tell you these things?"

"I suppose not. I just thought there was something I should do to make up for it."

"The best way to make up for a sin is to learn from it and not commit it again. If you're looking for something more than that . . ."

Gar's face brightened as if from the very prospect of being prescribed some sort of punishment meant to wipe his slate clean.

"You're to steer clear of the Hovey sisters on windy days and stop going to those saloons."

"Are you serious?"

Paul had spoken his words with a hint of humor in his tone, but the look on Gar's face when he heard them sapped every bit of lightheartedness from him. As always, Gar was in the market for salvation by the shortest road possible. His reaction to actually mending his ways as opposed to trying to erase them from the Almighty's sight was a sharp, stinging slap across Paul's face.

"Yes," Paul said in a carefully measured tone. "I am serious. You know what's right and what's wrong. Just do one instead of the other, and I swear if you ask me which one I mean, I'll put you through a penance more rigorous than you'd ever care for."

"Guess I'd rather just have my wicked thoughts and not make any lady feel uncomfortable by them."

"That's the spirit," Paul said while clasping his hands once more behind him. "Now, why don't you get some sleep?"

Gar took half a step forward and then stopped. "Mind if I ask you something, Father?"

"I've asked you and everyone else to just call me by my given name."

"Father is your given name," Gar replied simply. "Me and everyone else here in town gave it to you."

Suddenly feeling as if he were the one who'd transgressed, Paul shifted his eyes from the stars to the little town in front of him. Then he looked to the man who was always, no matter what the hour, looking to him. "In that case, I suppose you can call me what you like. What did you need to ask?"

"Why ain't you like other preachers?"

"What do you mean?"

"I've been to other churches in other towns, heard plenty of men in black spouting off about hellfire and telling folks what to do, but you're not like any of them as far as I can tell."

"I'll take that as a compliment," Paul said.

"You don't take proper confession."

"That isn't part of the practices of my belief."

"What is your belief?" Gar asked. "Are you Baptist? Catholic? Something else?"

"Does it matter?"

"To some . . . it matters a whole lot."

Paul didn't need to think for very long before conceding, "Yes, it does. I guess I've tried to learn what I can from as many good men as I could find."

"So you're not a proper minister?"

"Of course I am! I just believe that someone in my position should tailor his lessons to the needs of his flock. If you'd like me to answer for myself any more than that, you'll have to wait until morning. It's getting awfully late. Hopefully, you'll be able to sleep now that I've eased your mind a bit concerning those dreams."

Nodding happily, Gar said, "I don't expect you to answer for anything, Father. You've done a hell of a good job here and . . . oh no."

"I'll give you that one for free," Paul said. "Just watch your language in the future. Good night."

Gar started to walk away, but turned around again before Paul had a chance to open the church door and step inside. "I must be tired!" he said. "My mind's slipping. I never told you why I was here."

"It wasn't about a dream?"

"No, Father. That was the last time I came to see you. Seems like we both just got swept up in our philosophical discussion."

While Gar might have gotten swept up, Paul knew all too well that he'd pointed the conversation in a particular direction. In talking with Gar, such a tactic was a necessity. The alternative was to sign over hours upon hours in meandering debates and question after question that had no proper answer. Every now and then, those talks were refreshing. To excess, they were taxing beyond measure.

"You sure this can't wait until morning?" Paul asked.

Gar cringed, wrung his hands, and shifted from foot to foot.

Coming to terms with the fact that he wasn't about to get to bed any time soon, Paul asked, "Would you like to come inside?"

"Most definitely!"

Paul opened the church's door and allowed Gar to

step inside. Rather than close it, he stood beside the doorway to make it clear this would be a short talk. The interior of the church was currently only lit by two candles placed at the front of the chapel, which had two rows of pews that seated sixty people comfortably. The altar was a simple affair consisting of a long table covered in white linens embroidered with a beautiful crucifix surrounded by rays of light sewn in bright yellow thread. Candles were lined up along the table, framing a simple dais placed front and center between the long table and pews. Upon that dais were two things that had been with Paul since his first days preaching the Good Word: an ornate wooden cup and a Bible encased in a battered, dusty cover.

"What's troubling you, Gar?"

"It's something I overheard a few days ago."

"Overheard?"

"That's right. I was in the Red Coyote." When he mentioned the town's largest saloon by name, Gar's eyes drifted downward.

Not only did the Red Coyote sell liquor, but it also employed dancing girls as well as a couple of soiled doves who plied their trade in rented rooms above the bar. "There were a few strangers in town," Gar continued. "They were talking to Lydia about . . . well . . . you know."

Since Lydia was one of the soiled doves residing in the saloon, Paul nodded to show that he did indeed know.

"I think they were gamblers," Gar went on to say. "Or worse."

"Worse?"

"Yes, Father. They carried guns."

"That doesn't make a man worse than anything," Paul assured him. "If you recall, I carried a gun when I first came to town. In a land as rough as this, it would be unwise not to be prepared to defend yourself."

"These men carried pistols strapped to their sides. And they looked like they knew how to use them. But it wasn't just the sight of a gun that caught my interest. It was what they talked about. Before you say anything," Gar snapped, even though Paul hadn't even started to cut in, "you should know that I wasn't trying to listen in on a conversation that didn't concern me. One of the men was drunk and he was mighty loud."

Nodding while placing a hand on Gar's back, Paul gently moved the bigger man toward the door.

"He was saying something about riding with another fella," Gar said.

"I'm sure they spoke about plenty of things. That's what folks tend to do in saloons."

"One of the names he mentioned sounded familiar." Now that he was outside again, Gar looked around as if he wasn't quite sure how he'd gotten there. "I think it was the name of a wanted man."

"It's probably best you don't concern yourself with that sort of thing," Paul told him. "That could be dangerous."

"That's what I thought at first, which is why I didn't say anything. Not even to Sheriff Noss. And the more I thought about it, the worse I felt." Gar smirked and rubbed his hand flat across his forehead. "After all we talked about just now, I feel a little silly for getting so worked up about it. I suppose I didn't harm no one and it was just a bunch of talk."

"That's right."

"After all, ain't nobody heard a peep from Jack Terrigan for some time."

"Jack Terrigan?" Paul asked.

"I think that's the name that was mentioned. Then again, it could have been something else. I was drinking more than my share and I feel mighty bad about it. You got any way for me to make up for that, Father?"

Paul was quick to shake his head. "No need. It's just as likely you misheard what was said in the midst of all that noise inside the Red Coyote. Honest mistake."

"I suppose so. Good night, Father."

As Gar walked away, Paul felt an itch work its way beneath his skin like a single flea that had managed to crawl down the back of his shirt. He retreated into the church and closed the door, wishing for the first time since the church's construction that he could lock himself within the building.

Instead of going through the narrow door that led to the little room where he slept on a cot beneath a few blankets donated by a few kind families, Paul took a seat at one of the middle pews and prayed until the candles burned down to nubs.

Chapter 2

The following morning, Paul emerged from the church later than usual. His delayed appearance wasn't on account of oversleeping, because he'd only allowed himself to drift off for an hour or two. It was the middle of the week, which meant his absence wasn't noticed by more than a handful of folks along the route he normally took when getting his breakfast or running the errands that filled his day. The woman who served him his fried eggs and bacon smiled as he passed. She seemed to have a question for him, but didn't try overly hard to ask it as he tipped his hat to her and continued along.

Paul wore simple clothes without his white collar. Since most everyone in Pueblito Verde knew who he was, a uniform was hardly necessary. There would have been no way for him to sneak into the Red Coyote, so he didn't even try to cover his steps. Doing so would only have started some kind of scandal among the town's looser tongues.

The Coyote wasn't unlike many other saloons in many other towns. Its name was painted across a wide front window beside a door that opened into a large room containing a short bar, a few tables and chairs, as well as the stage that had no doubt captured so much of Gar's attention in recent days. At the moment, the stage was empty and a skinny old man played a piano that could very well have propped up one of the saloon's walls. The piano player stopped in the middle of a bouncy tune long enough to look over, toss a wave at Paul, and say, "Howdy do, Father Lester!"

There were less than half a dozen men drinking in the saloon at that time of day, and all but one of them turned toward the door as if they were afraid they'd be facing their final judgment then and there. Paul tried to allay their fears as best he could with a shaky smile and a friendly "Hello to you, Manny. Just stopping by for a quick drink."

Mentioning he was there for a sip of firewater was enough to make the local drunks cool their heels a bit. One man had barely glanced up to acknowledge Paul's entrance and seemed to have forgotten the door had even opened by the time Manny got back to his song.

Paul was no stranger to the Red Coyote. In fact, he often wondered why the saloon's regular customers still reacted the way they did whenever he entered. It was a simple, unavoidable repercussion for any man who stood at the front of a church every Sunday. No matter how human he tried to appear to his congregation, he would always be seen as something else. Something more.

Paul stepped up to the bar, leaning his elbows against a spot at the corner of the stained wooden surface that was close to the door but where he could see most everyone else inside the place. Before he could finish returning a couple of friendly nods from some of the other patrons, Paul was approached by a man with a medium build and a face sporting about two days' worth of light blond stubble.

"Sorry I wasn't at services this last Sunday," the barkeep said. "Had to stay here and keep an eye on the place. Not that I wouldn't prefer to close up on Sunday. I know that's the proper thing to do and all, but—"

Paul stopped him with a gently raised hand. "No need to explain yourself, Harrold. Every man needs to earn his daily bread. I'll have a beer."

Looking as if he'd been granted a reprieve, Harrold went straight to the beer taps located at the opposite end of the bar. It was a short walk that, Paul noticed, ended with the barkeep reaching for the tap on the right, which poured a brew that was much higher in quality than the cheaper swill he sold at the same price. One of the benefits attached to the strip of white around Paul's neck.

Harrold returned to Paul's end of the bar, wiping off the mug in his hand with a mostly clean rag. "What brings you by today?" he asked while setting the drink down. "Not that you need a reason, of course."

Sipping the beer helped calm Paul's jangling nerves. He'd been wound up tighter than a pocket watch ever since Gar's visit, and the only thing more difficult than spending a sleepless night in such a state was trying to look as if everything was right as rain. He leaned forward, prompting the barkeep to do the same. "I heard a bit of news that I find somewhat . . . distressing," Paul said in a whisper that was mostly drowned out by the piano music. "Could be nothing more than a rumor, though."

Harrold leaned in a bit more. "Plenty of rumors floating around any saloon. Usually not worth getting your feathers ruffled over. What did you hear?"

"Apparently, there was some . . . and I even feel a bit foolish for bringing this up . . . but what I heard involved a man named Terrigan."

The barkeep's eyes had shown hungry curiosity at the prospect of taking part in some juicy bit of news. That spark was immediately snuffed out when Paul mentioned Terrigan's name. Recoiling a bit, but dropping his voice to maintain their privacy, he said, "I heard something along those lines myself."

"What did you hear?"

"Not much. Just that . . ." Harrold sighed and his eyes darted toward the rest of his customers. Then he shifted his weight to lean against the bar so he was facing the shelves of bottles behind the bar and, to some small degree, Paul. If he'd been attempting to make his stance seem casual, he did a poor job of it. "Jack Terrigan is a cold-blooded killer. When it comes to men like that, it's best to just let them pass you by and hope they don't look in your direction. We may not get many of that sort around here, but I've run saloons in enough towns to know what I'm talking about."

"So someone here does know something about this Terrigan fellow?"

"Yes, but . . . like I already said . . . probably just some silly rumor."

Paul had always had a knack for reading people's faces, and his years in the ministry had only sharpened that skill. Hardly any such experience was needed for him to know that Harrold was certain whatever had been said in regard to Jack Terrigan was more than a silly rumor.

"Even if that's the case," Paul said, "I'd like to have a word with anyone who might know something about it and I'd appreciate if you could point me in the right direction." He took another couple of sips of his beer, giving the barkeep a chance to speak up on his own. When it became clear that Harrold intended to try to wait him out, Paul sighed and nodded slowly. "I suppose I'll just have to pursue the matter on my own. I was hoping you'd make this a little easier for me, though."

When Paul shifted his weight, Harrold reached out to grab his arm as if his favorite customer were about to be swept out through the front door. Seeing that he'd caught a few curious eyes, Harrold released the other man's arm. "What could you . . . Damn it, Manny! Who told you to stop playing?"

"Just taking a drink," the man at the piano replied.

"Take it quickly, then! I don't pay you to sit on your backside."

"Barely pay me at all," Manny grumbled.

Harrold wheeled around and stomped to the other end of the bar to fill a mug from the cheap tap. "Here," he said while slamming the beer down. "Come and get your free drink and play something to earn what I *do* pay you. Otherwise, you can be on your merry damn way."

The old man's grumping lasted until he crossed the room, got his beer, and took a sip. "Best in town!" he said while lifting the glass.

That brought a grin to both Harrold's and Paul's faces.

Turning back to Paul, Harrold waited for the lively music to resume before saying, "Sorry about the bad language, Father."

"Was there bad language?"

"I do my best to be charitable, but some kind just don't appreciate it. Know what I mean?"

Paul merely shrugged and took another drink.

"Who would talk to you about someone like Jack Terrigan?" Harrold asked in an urgent whisper. "It was Gar, wasn't it? That portly fool can hold his damn tongue about as well as he can his liquor, which is to say not at all. Sorry about the language again."

"You can stop apologizing and just tell me what I'd like to know," Paul said.

"I'd rather not."

"So do you mean to say that if I was any other paying customer, you wouldn't want to swap stories about some known gunman passing through these parts? I've been to some saloons in my day as well, and I know talk like that swirls around inside them thicker than cigar smoke. All I want to know is what is being said on this particular subject."

"First of all," Harrold said, "you're not a paying customer."

That sent a cold jab through Paul's gut, which showed plain as day on his face. He reached into a pocket, removed a silver dollar, and set it on top of the bar. "Here," he said evenly. "Since money is what you want, there it is."

If Harrold looked as if he'd gotten a reprieve before,

he now looked as if he'd just gotten news of his con-
demnation. "Tha-that's not what I meant," he sputtered while pushing away the coin as if it might burn
his fingers. "All I meant is that you're not just one of
the other cowboys or drunkards that walk through my
doors. You're a man of God."

"I may have chosen a path of faith, but I'm just a man."

"A man who does things differently than most others. For example, when most men want to hear about a
killer like Terrigan, all they want to know is gruesome
details of the last time he traded shots with the law.
They don't even care whose blood was spilled. Come
to think of it, they tend to like the stories where it's the
lawmen who were left in the dirt. Them stories are just
so much trash and ain't hardly the sort of thing I'd
want to tell to a preacher."

"I think there were more than just bloody stories
told about Terrigan in this saloon. Otherwise, I doubt
they would have created such a commotion."

Harrold slowly shook his head. "Damn it all to hell.
It was Gar who flapped his gums to you." After seeing
one of Paul's eyebrows raise, the barkeep winced and
muttered, "Sorry about the language, Father."

"Why don't you make up for it by telling me who
brought this news to Pueblito Verde?"

"I don't think that's such a good idea."

"All right, then, what if I settle for a different question?"

Breathing a sigh of relief, Harrold replied, "I'd like
that very much."

Paul leaned forward and said, "Tell me if the man
I'm looking for is that stranger right over there."

After checking to see which table Paul was nodding toward, the barkeep shuddered. "I really don't think this is a good idea."

"I'm right, aren't I?"

"Yes, but . . ."

"But what?" Paul asked while studying the stranger. He didn't have to be too careful about it because the man sitting at that table was the one who hadn't done more than cast half a glance in his direction since Paul had arrived. The stranger was dressed in a rumpled brown shirt and had a dark red bandanna tied around his neck. A filthy duster lay over the second chair at his table, which also had a battered hat hanging from its back. By the looks of him, he hadn't slept with a proper roof over his head in weeks.

Even though the stranger still didn't seem concerned about much of anything, Harrold was quick to put his back to him after glancing toward that table. "I'd rather you didn't approach that one."

"Why? He seems like a quiet sort."

"Yeah. The worst ones usually do."

"Now my interest is truly piqued," Paul mused. "Could that be Jack Terrigan himself?"

"No, and if you knew what was good for you, you'd stop tossing that name around like it didn't mean anything."

"I didn't think it meant anything anymore. It's been years since I've heard much about him."

"Word's been going around for some time," Harrold explained. "Most of it's been rumors, but it seemed there was something to them once the bounty was dusted off and put back on Terrigan's head." Seeing the scowl forming on Paul's face, Harrold quickly added, "Go ask the sheriff yourself if you don't believe me. Anyway, rumors and stories been coming and going just like they do for any other known gunslinger. Then the law started getting real serious about finding him. Sheriff Noss made it clear he was to be told the moment any news came along about Terrigan's whereabouts."

"I'm guessing he made it clearer to some than to others?"

"If you're talking about that whiny Gar Kilner, then yeah. Gar was here when Sheriff Noss said his piece, and he was sure to put the fear into Gar along with a few others who are known to stand about and poke their noses into other people's affairs. Gar took it to heart just like he does with just about everything." Harrold let out a breath that seemed to make his entire body smaller. "Gar's a good enough sort, but he tries my patience sometimes. Always bending my ear about some useless thing or other."

As much as he could sympathize with the barkeep, Paul just took a sip of beer and let the moment pass. He'd always known there was quite a bit of overlap between the duties of a preacher and someone like Harrold. On some occasions, Harrold might have had an easier time of it because of the fact that he was allowed to soften the blow to his parishioners with liquor.

"Anyways," Harrold continued, "it's a wonder you hadn't heard anything about it until now."

"The sheriff doesn't exactly share this sort of business with me. I swear sometimes it seems folks are trying to protect me from the outside world. Like they don't think I'm truly part of it."

The last portion of that statement had been a slip of the tongue on Paul's part. Harrold reacted with a shrug and said, "When people come to church, they're probably trying to put their own troubles behind them. Looking for enlightenment and spiritual . . . something or other. Know what I mean?"

"Yes. I do." Paul's beer glass was empty, so he moved it to Harrold's side of the bar. "I'd like a refill, please. And I insist you allow me to pay for it this time."

"Your money's no good here, Father," he said while walking down to the tap to fill his glass. "Just keep in mind what I was talking about before."

When Harrold returned with the freshly poured beer, Paul took a drink and set his glass down. "This conversation isn't over," he said in a quieter tone. "I'd like to know about Jack Terrigan."

Harrold grimaced as if he truly thought he'd diverted the preacher's attention enough to put the matter to rest. "All I know is what I already told you. He's supposed to be somewhere in the territory and is kicking up all kinds of dust along the way."

"He's in the territory? You didn't mention that before."

"Because it shouldn't be any of your business. All due respect, you're a preacher. Not someone who should be mixed up with the likes of these men."

"What type of men?" Paul asked. "Killers? Desperate, lost souls? Sounds like those are just the sort of men who need to hear from someone like me."

"Is that what this is about? You think you can have a chat with a man like . . ." Harrold paused before speaking the outlaw's name and shot a quick glance over to the stranger's table. "With a man like that and he'll just see the light? If that's what you're after, then I can save you a whole mess of trouble and tell you to forget it."

"My duty is to this town and the good people living in it," Paul said earnestly. "If there's something I can do in regards to a danger posed to Pueblito Verde or even this territory, it's my duty to see it gets done. If there's a chance I can talk sense into this Terrigan fellow, then that's something I should do. At the very least, I'd like to see if there's something I may be able to do to put an end to any danger that he may pose."

"You any good with a gun?" Harrold scoffed. "Because that's about all someone like that dog would understand."

"That is exactly why I feel I should help if I can. Every life means something and I won't stand by while one is wasted in sin or ended in a hail of gunfire. If that's not a duty worthy of a man of faith, then I don't know what is."

Harrold lowered his eyes as if he was catching up on the prayers he'd missed the previous Sunday. "You're a good man, Father. I knew that before, which is why I meant to spare you from getting involved with something like this."

"Well, I'm involving myself and you've done a fine job of trying to steer me in another direction. If I'm too stubborn to heed your advice, then whatever happens afterward is my fault. That," he added with a friendly grin, "is something I've learned throughout my years

of being the one who's usually handing out the un-
heeded advice."

"Unless you've preached the gospel in places a
whole lot more interesting than this one, I doubt you've
had many dealings with killers and bounty hunters."

Taking another look at the man sitting alone at his
table, Paul asked, "Which is he?"

"From what I can gather . . . both."

"Has he started any trouble since he's been here?"

"Not as such," Harrold replied.

"Then I doubt he'll start any with a man of the
cloth." With that, Paul slid the silver dollar he'd placed
on the bar earlier back toward Harrold and carried his
beer across the room.

Along the way, a few locals tipped their hats or
grunted short greetings before getting back to their
card games or whatever else occupied their time between drinks. Paul approached the stranger's table and
put on his warmest Sunday smile as he placed a hand
on the duster draped across the back of the only other
chair at the stranger's table.

After a few increasingly uncomfortable moments,
Paul asked, "Is this seat taken?"

"Yeah," the stranger replied. "By my hat and coat."

"Mind if I join you?"

The stranger looked up at him with cold blue eyes
set deeply within a face covered in scars that crossed it
like a crudely drawn map of intersecting railroad
tracks. His lips barely parted when he asked, "What the
hell would you wanna do that for . . . Father?"

Paul's smile was the same one he showed to the

eldest Hovey sister when she brought him one of her mixed berry pies. "I see my reputation precedes me."

"This is a small place."

"I can pull up another chair if that would be better."

When the stranger fixed a stare fully on him, Paul felt as if he were standing across from him in a dark alley. The other man's voice was a grating rasp that curled his mouth into a wicked sneer when he said, "It would be better if you turned around and let me be so I could enjoy my drink in peace. I don't need no god-damn sermon and I don't need to hear about ways to make my life any better from the likes of you."

This wasn't the first time someone had tried to in-timidate Paul Lester. Yet another advantage of being a preacher was that most folks didn't think they had to try very hard to get him to quake in his boots. "I'd like to ask you a few questions and I figured you might like to do so in a private conversation rather than in front of everyone here. If you can't do so in a civil tone . . ."

"Then what?" the stranger growled as he pushed his chair away from the table and got to his feet. "What will you do if I don't improve my tone?"

"Then I'll have to insist we talk outside."

A hush fell over the room.

Manny stopped playing his piano and turned around while reaching for the shotgun hidden near his feet.

Harrold placed both hands on his bar and declared, "There'll be no trouble in here!"

Amid all this tension, the stranger's face took on an amused expression. "I'm not looking for any trouble," he said. "Especially from a man with as much backbone and faith as this one's got. That's a mighty dangerous mix."

Paul nodded once. "It most definitely is." Without another word, he took another long pull from his beer, walked over to set the glass on the bar, and headed for the door. He didn't have to check behind him to know the stranger was following.

Chapter 3

Paul waited outside the Red Coyote, across the street, where he could watch the front door as well as the rest of the building. He traded pleasantries with a few locals who passed by on their way to one of the shops farther down the street or the stable on the other side of town. After a minute or two, the stranger stepped from the saloon while pulling his duster on. He stood near the door, stretched his back, and then put his hat on as if he meant to draw the process out for as long as humanly possible. Once it was clear he was on his own schedule and nobody else's, he crossed the street to stand beside Paul.

"So you're the town preacher?" he asked.

Paul did a good job keeping his voice level and patient. "That's right."

"No preacher I ever known would come into a saloon asking about the likes of Jack Terrigan."

"You heard that as well?"

"It's a small place."

Indeed it was, but Paul was certain the other man's ears were sharper than most of the ones inside the Red

Coyote's walls. Considering what he'd been told about the stranger, that wasn't much of a surprise.

"Then you must also know I've heard a thing or two myself," Paul said. "For example, the way you earn your money."

"And how's that?"

"You're a bounty hunter. Or . . . that's the rumor."

The stranger was quiet for a couple of heartbeats before saying, "That rumor happens to be true."

"Then why make me repeat it? If you think you're making me squirm just by standing there with two guns around your waist, then you're sorely mistaken."

"I wear these guns most everywhere I go. They're a part of me, and if they was enough to frighten you, then that says more about you than it does of me. As for the rest, I ain't the sort who makes someone jump through hoops. I have found I can learn a lot about a man just by watching how he talks about my line of work. Plenty of thoughts can cross his head when he says the words *bounty hunter*. Thoughts that can let me know if his tone will stay civilized farther down the stretch."

"I can understand that," Paul replied earnestly. "I've found much the same thing on people's faces when they talk about my line of work as well. My name is Paul Lester, by the way."

The stranger looked down at the hand Paul offered and shook it. "Should I call you Father?"

"Only if you forget my first name. I never caught yours, by the way"

That brought a grin to the stranger's face that was heartfelt, if unappealing. "Dave Sprole. Pleased to meet you. So, which line of work will this conversation lean toward?" he asked. "Yours or mine?"

"To be honest, I'd say it dips a toe into both."

"Just a toe? If you're looking to take on the likes of Jack Terrigan, you'd best be willing to commit more than that to it."

Clasping his hands behind his back, Paul started walking slowly down the street. When he was sure Sprole was following him, he asked, "Is it true that Terrigan is in this territory?"

"Could be."

"Surely a man in your line of work either knows or he doesn't."

"And for a man in your line of work, you're mighty anxious to get to an absolute answer in no time at all."

"Just because my faith does not rely on concrete answers," Paul replied, "doesn't mean that I do not search for them. In fact, because of the nature of my calling, you'll find I'm even more tenacious when I'm going after something that's within my reach."

"Jack Terrigan ain't even within *my* reach," the bounty hunter said. "What makes you think he's anywhere close to yours?"

"If he's on God's green earth, he's more within my reach than the questions I've devoted my life to answering." Paul came to a stop and turned on his heel so he was facing Sprole squarely. "I didn't approach you for a philosophical debate, although I'm certain you have some keen insights I'd like to hear. I want to know about Jack Terrigan."

"And here's the question that's got me stumped: Why do you give a damn about Terrigan?"

"Because I know him."

Sprole's eyes glinted like those of a wolf that had just spotted a fat, limping deer. "Do you, now?"

"I do and I want to find him so I can have a word with him."

"Perhaps he's the one you'd like to debate philosophy with?"

"That," Paul said without a flinch, "is not your concern."

"See, now, there's where you're wrong," Sprole said as he started walking again. This time, Paul was the one who had to rush a few steps to catch up. "Say what you want about my line of work, but if you know anything at all you must know that once I have a wanted man in my sights, every little thing he does or says, everyone he sees, and every place he goes is very much my concern. It's how I earn my daily bread while others take handouts after filling a bunch of simpletons' heads with nonsense about spirits and a bright, musical hereafter."

Paul had been baited enough times in similar ways to know when he was being set up. Weathering the attacks on his faith that had the subtlety of a fist wrapped around a brick, he said "You're trying to get me to lose my temper."

"Is that the worst you've ever heard on the matter? Folks around here really must be a good bunch of sheep. Sorry," he chuckled. "Lambs. Isn't that the proper term?"

"Folks around here aren't what we were talking about. I was talking about an outlaw who is close enough to send ripples through this very small pond.

That must be why you're here, and since I found you sitting comfortably in a saloon instead of preparing to ride out again, my guess is that you're not quite sure where to go next."

"Well, then," Sprole said through a grin that was still reminiscent of a wolf, "that would make two of us, wouldn't it?"

"I always know where to go next," Paul replied in a way that jabbed at the bounty hunter in much the same way Sprole had been jabbing at him earlier. "That is the advantage to someone in *my* line of work."

Sprole walked until the solid wall of a livery stable was to his back. Pivoting in a way that caused his duster to flap open and reveal the guns at his sides, he snarled, "What did you think would happen here, preacher? You'd stroll up to me, ask kindly, and I'd tell you everything I've worked so hard to learn about a killer who would put me down in a heartbeat? Even if I did decide to answer your questions out of pure kindness, I could lose a whole pile of money after you take your answers and spill them to the wrong person. Even if you do keep your mouth shut, what would you do next? Go running out to find him?"

"I doubt I could—"

Sprole cut him short with a swiftly raised hand. "Whether you're just a well-intentioned preacher or the smartest tracker in the country, it don't much matter. What does matter is that, whatever you did with the answers you got, Terrigan would catch wind of it. Knowing him the way I do after chasing him for as long as I have, I'd say only two things could come next. One," he said while ticking the options off on his fingers, "he guns you down and either kills you or makes you wish he had. Or two, he catches wind that someone knows where he's hiding and bolts like a jackrabbit. Either way, that just ain't acceptable." He then tipped his hat, showed Paul an empty smile, and stormed off.

But Paul wasn't about to let him go so easily. "If you have everything figured out, how come you don't have him in custody?"

"Having a plan don't mean it's been seen through all the way. Wheels are in motion, and I won't be thrown off course."

"I'm not interested in the price on his head. I just want to have a word with Terrigan."

"Best watch your mouth, preacher. You're spooking your congregation."

Although Paul's first instinct was to dismiss the bounty hunter's words, a quick glance toward the street proved they had some merit. Sure enough, two gray-haired ladies who organized the town's sewing circle were standing in front of a tailor's shop with bolts of fabric under their arms and horrified expressions on their faces. The elder of the two tried to regain her composure and speak to Paul, but was hurried along by the younger woman. A few men were scattered here and there along the street or boardwalk, most of whom stood quietly to watch what unfolded before their eyes. A few even had their hands resting on holstered guns.

"If they have questions," Paul said while shifting his focus back to Sprole, "they can ask them to my face. Right now I am asking you if you'll help me gain a moment of an outlaw's time."

"Which brings me back to what I asked you."

"You want to know why? Because it's my job, that's why."

Sprole grinned. When he placed a hand on Paul's shoulder, it was a surprisingly easy gesture. "Your job is to preach, so that's what you should do. Stay inside where it's safe . . . and preach."

Paul took hold of the bounty hunter's arm, gripped it tight, and removed Sprole's hand from his shoulder. "Did you hear what I said?" Paul asked. "I know Jack Terrigan."

"I heard, and if I were you, I'd keep it to myself. Plenty of men in my spot wouldn't just let you walk away after hearing something like that."

"If that's a threat, I'm not frightened."

"It's not a threat, but perhaps you should be a little frightened. Not by me," Sprole said, "but by the world around you. See, that's the problem with preachers or other wide-eyed folks like you. There isn't a healthy bit of fear in you that tells you to steer clear of men like Terrigan. Or me."

"Don't presume to know what's in my heart," Paul warned.

"All right, but I sure don't have to presume to know what's in your head. You've shown most of the cards you're holding. The ones that matter anyway. What would you say to Terrigan once you found him? Is it important enough to risk your life to get there?"

Paul closed his eyes, drew a breath, and was interrupted before he could reply.

"Let me guess," Sprole said. "It's your business. Well, you seem like a good man. Believe it or not, I've heard a few nice things about you in the short time I've been in town. That's why I'll let you go about your business while I go about mine."

When Sprole started walking again, Paul was tempted to let him go. It wasn't an urge to concede the argument or give up on what he'd started. It was too late for any of that. For a moment, he had to weigh whether or not there was any chance of getting what he was after. Wasn't it a foolish thing to keep fighting when a battle had already been lost?

Suddenly Paul felt shame in his heart.

Many folks saw him and others who'd been called as fools for holding on to their beliefs when a cruel, unforgiving world seemed to take pleasure in dimming the light that was at the foundation of faith. Whether any preacher was right or wrong wasn't the point as far as Paul was concerned. What people thought didn't matter. It didn't even matter if a thing could be proven or if it made sense. Paul Lester had chosen his path because, at the center of his very core, he believed it was the right thing to do.

Without another word or thought, Paul walked behind Sprole.

For several paces, the bounty hunter moved along silently. Perhaps he didn't know Paul was still with him, but he eventually turned to check over his shoulder to find the preacher smiling behind him. Sprole kept walking.

At the next corner, Sprole turned. The town's little church was at the end of that street and when he made another turn, Sprole looked behind him again.

Paul was still there.

"What are you doing, preacher?" Sprole asked.

"Following you."

"Is this supposed to convince me to change my mind?"

"Maybe. Maybe not. It seems to me you're good at your job, and if I continue to follow you, we'll both be led to the man we're after."

"You think you can keep on my tail that long?"

"Perhaps," Paul replied. "I believe I can hold on long enough to get where I need to go."

"I'm just headed back to my room at the hotel. If you think you're following me in there, you're sorely mistaken."

Paul remained silent. When Sprole put his back to him and walked faster, Paul kept him within his line of sight.

Sure enough, the bounty hunter went to his hotel. Sprole stepped inside the squat building that had once been the home of a miner who'd found just enough silver to pay for a wagon to take him to California. Paul stood outside, waiting for a few moments before circling around the corner of the building and waiting. Having lived in that hotel while the church was under construction, he was familiar with every inch of the place. For that reason, he knew exactly which window was at the base of the stairway to the second floor and which was at the end of the hall at the top of those steps. After a few more seconds, he shifted his gaze upward to the latter of those windows and was just in time to see the frilly curtains pulled aside so Sprole could peek out.

Paul smiled and gave him a friendly wave.

The man behind those curtains scowled and pulled the flimsy material back in place.

After that, Paul turned on his heel and marched down the street to the sheriff's office.

Sheriff Noss was a wide-shouldered man with arms that were thick with muscles forged from swinging an axe. Riding south from the Pacific Northwest put his logging days behind him, but he still kept the axe to remind folks what he was capable of. Even if the axe saw less use than the shotguns in his gun cabinet and the .45 strapped to his hip, Noss kept it nearby. It was hanging over the door that Paul pushed open to come inside and plead his case. After taking the time to place his signature on the paper he'd been studying during most of Paul's tale, the lawman gave him one simple word.

"No."

"Weren't you listening, Sheriff?" Paul asked. "I think Jack Terrigan is in this territory and I want to help you find him."

"How could you help?"

"I have resources. I have friends. I used to give last rites to condemned men at a jail in Tucson and got to know prisoners as well as turnkeys. Any of them could know enough to help narrow the search."

"As soon as Terrigan comes to Pueblito Verde," Noss said through a thin layer of stubble on his rounded face, "he'll be my problem. Until then, he's out of my jurisdiction."

"What about the reward that's been posted?" Paul asked, making a desperate plea to the other man's greed.

"If someone brings Terrigan in, I'll see he gets his money."

"Wouldn't it serve everyone's best interests if Terrigan was found before he came to Pueblito Verde? Maybe he can be captured without bloodshed. If there's violence, innocent people may get hurt. Good folks could be caught in a cross fire."

Noss set his pencil down and furrowed his brow. "You're really grasping at straws here. What's got you so riled up?"

"For one thing, I feel it's my duty to watch out for my flock when I can."

"Keep the peace, you mean?"

Paul brightened considerably. "Yes! Exactly."

"Keeping the peace is my job," Noss said. "I'll do mine and you do yours. Sound good?"

Paul might not have shied away from a difficult task, but he knew when it was the wrong time to take one on. Then again, he might also have been just plain tired, because he left the sheriff to the rest of his paperwork and stepped outside. "I have heard the word," he said to himself since there was nobody else around, "so I suppose I shall hold it fast so it may bear its fruit . . . with patience."

Even though he'd paraphrased from the Good Book itself, those words didn't go down easily.

Chapter 4

Three days passed and Paul remained mostly in his church, reflecting on unpleasant memories and doing his best to put together a sermon for Sunday's service. When Sunday came along, the turnout was a bit smaller than normal. Immediately, Paul's thoughts drifted toward the appalled expressions on the faces he'd seen while having words with Sprole in the street. It was very possible that the women from the sewing circle had spread some rumors of their own or perhaps the men who had been watching quietly weren't happy with what they'd seen.

On the other hand, it was just as likely that the people not in the pews were still in their beds stricken by a bout of illness or an unwillingness to interrupt their sleep. Paul went back and forth between not being concerned with the absences and feeling bad for the fact that he wasn't concerned. Finally he realized how silly that was and wound up right back where he'd started.

He hadn't heard anything from Sheriff Noss, which wasn't unusual since the lawman hadn't come to Sunday services for quite some time. Dave Sprole had fallen into a predictable routine. At least, in following the bounty hunter, Paul had become reacquainted with the breakfasts served at the hotel down the street from his church. Paul was on his way there this Sunday, planning how he wanted his eggs prepared, when he noticed a trio of horses tied to the post outside the hotel. He took note of the sheen on the animals' coats, which told him they'd been working hard not too long before finding themselves tethered to their current spot. Before he could reach for the handle of the hotel's front door, Paul was nearly knocked onto his backside when that door was pushed open by someone running outside.

The woman was in her late forties and had smooth, pale skin. Her green eyes were wide and focused on the street behind him, which explained why she didn't put a name to the face directly in front of her.

"Carol, what's wrong?" Paul asked.

It took a moment, but Carol finally recognized him. "Father, you have to get away from here! There's men inside. Men with guns!"

"Have you been hurt?" he asked while grabbing hold of Carol's arms to steady her.

"No, but there's going to be shooting. There's going to be trouble, I just—"

The rest of her words were swallowed up by gunshots exploding within the hotel. Bullets spat from those barrels shattered glass and preceded a stampede of heavy footsteps that Paul could hear thanks to a few open windows. "Who are they?" he asked. "What do they want?"

"I don't know! They just came in asking about the

man staying in Room Six and drew their guns while cussing up a storm. After that, I just ran!"

Realizing he was still gripping her arms tight enough to keep her from going anywhere, Paul angled her toward the street and let her go. "Fetch the sheriff!"

"Come with me," she pleaded. "I think those men mean to kill someone."

As if to emphasize her fears, more gunshots blasted through the hotel, followed by a scream that most definitely did not come from a man.

"Who else is inside?" Paul asked.

"Oh Lord," Carol moaned. "Manuela was in the kitchen last time I saw her."

"Can she get out on her own?"

"I don't know. I don't even know where she went after cooking for the last guest to come down for breakfast. I didn't mean to leave her. I just wanted to get out before . . . I'm so sorry."

Paul grabbed her again to give Carol a little shake as he said, "Pull yourself together. Go to the sheriff and bring him here. Try to remember as much as you can about what the men looked like or said when they came in so you can tell him whatever he needs to know."

She nodded. When Paul turned toward the hotel and took a step toward the door, she grabbed his sleeve and asked, "What are you doing? Come with me!"

More shots were fired, which only caused him to solemnly shake his head. "I can't leave Manuela inside. You did the right thing to get away. Go for help and I'll fetch her. Just go!"

His last words, combined with an insistent shove,

convinced her to run from the hotel. Paul didn't know for certain if she was following the directions he'd given since all of his attention was focused on the task at hand.

The hotel's lobby was only slightly more cluttered than normal. A few newspapers had been spilled onto the floor, and the ledger was askew on top of the front desk. What struck Paul most was the sharp, distinct scent of burned gunpowder hanging in the air. Rough, muffled voices drifted down from the second floor. Paul's first guess was that the men doing the talking were in one of the rooms closest to the top of the stairs. His hand drifted toward the spot at his side where a holster might be found if he'd been wearing one. As it was, Paul's fingers glanced only against the rumpled fabric of trousers that were badly in need of being stitched. He set his jaw into a firm line and used the lightest steps he could manage to make his way into the dining room.

Three of the four little round tables there were clean, and the fourth still bore a dish with the remains of someone's morning meal. A dirty napkin was balled up next to a glass with a few sips of milk left inside. Having stopped to search for any sign of the woman who'd cooked that meal, Paul darted his eyes to and fro while his ears strained to pick up any sound other than the argument going on above him.

Finally he heard it.

A trembling whimper came from the next room and was quickly stifled.

Paul hurried through the dining room and pushed open the swinging door to the kitchen to find no one in the narrow aisle flanked by shelves of ingredients, racks of crockery, and a stove connected to the ceiling by a wide black pipe. In the back corner, there was a narrow door to what had to be a pantry. Paul had taken two steps in that direction when someone backed out from the cramped room.

"You stay put, you hear?" the short man hissed. He wore a jacket, hat, and trousers that were all filthy with dust and sweat. His eyes were focused on something inside the pantry. A .38-caliber pistol was clutched in a tight grip.

The same trembling voice came once more from within the small storage space, sounding like a bit of steam forced through the stove's pipe.

"Answer me and be quiet about it," the gunman said. "Besides that other woman who ran out of here, who else is left?"

Paul recognized Manuela's voice, but she wasn't forming any words. Instead, she cried and fought to catch her breath.

Freezing in his spot, Paul felt every one of his muscles tense. As far as he could tell, the only reason he hadn't been spotted was that the gunman hadn't looked away from the pantry. Surely the other man could see some things from the corner of his eye, but he might not pay them any mind unless something moved. Since Paul knew he couldn't stay put for long before being discovered, he decided to make his inevitable movement count for something.

Paul lunged for the stove, stretching a hand out to one of the pots resting there. Almost immediately, the gunman turned to aim in his direction. The pot was heavy, so Paul used both hands to lift it up and angle it toward the gunman's head. Unfortunately, all the other man had to do to avoid the blow was lean back. There was no avoiding the contents of the pot, however, as the warm, lumpy oatmeal sailed through the air to splatter onto the gunman, the doorway, and several things inside the pantry.

"What the hell?" the gunman snarled as tepid water and some soggy oats ran down his face.

Although he was hoping for something much hotter within the pot, Paul swung again while shouting, "Get out of here, Manuela!"

The terrified cook was huddled in a corner of the pantry, peeking through her fingers while covering her face with her hands. She climbed to her feet and spoke in a quick, excited chatter. Even if Paul's Spanish was up to snuff, he wouldn't have been able to understand her above the pounding of his own heartbeat thrumming through his ears.

Lowering his shoulder, the gunman charged toward Paul with enough force to send him staggering back against the stove. Paul was thankful for the lack of heat from the stove as he brushed against the warm iron and pushed off to one side as the other man fired a shot at him. The gun exploded within the confines of the kitchen, its barrel throwing sparks into the air as a bullet glanced off the side of the stove.

Paul's thoughts raced inside his head, making him dizzier with every passing moment. If he'd been thinking clearer, he would have at least found something better with which to defend himself. It was too late for rationality now, however. All that was left was for him to try and make it out of that kitchen with his life.

The gunman was confused by Paul's appearance, but that didn't keep him from firing again. He took quick aim and fired a shot that punched a hole in the wall less than two inches from Paul's left shoulder. Before the gunman could take a moment to steady his aim, Paul swung his pot again with the intent of knocking the pistol away. Instead, the pot wound up encasing the man's hand like a large clunky glove with a long handle. Since the gunman couldn't get his hand free from the pot and wasn't about to relinquish his weapon, Paul tugged the pot up and toward the kitchen's back wall. With the gunman's hand still inside the pot, it as well as a good portion of his arm went along for the ride. The gun went off once more like a muffled dynamite blast, causing the man holding it to scream and twist away.

Paul was surprised at the amount of blood on the man's hand when it emerged from the pot. Then again, considering that the bullet had blasted through at such an odd angle, it must have ricocheted quite a bit before finding its way out. The man gripped his gun hand and clutched it tight against his chest while choking back another pained cry. Paul took that opportunity to hit him in the face with the pot and put an end to the scuffle right then and there.

As soon as the gunman collapsed, Paul went inside the pantry. He kept the pot in one hand and extended the other toward Manuela. "Come along with me now," he said. "It's all right."

She was terrified. There was still commotion going on above them, and when heavy steps thumped toward the general direction of the staircase, Manuela all but leaped to her feet and grabbed his hand so Paul could pull her out. While following Paul through the kitchen, Manuela rattled off an endless stream of panicked Spanish. He could pick out a word or two here and there, but the rest was just a frantic, breathless jumble.

The commotion on the second floor was drawing closer to the top of the staircase, so Paul kept Manuela in front of him and the stairs to his back. He grabbed her by both shoulders, kicked open the door, and shoved her outside. "Go to the sheriff," he said.

Manuela staggered a few steps before turning back around. "You come with me, Padre."

"Just go!"

"Come with! Is too dangerous."

Before Paul could respond to that, Manuela was proven correct in her assessment. Two armed men raced to the top of the staircase. One of them was a short fellow wearing a brown vest over a white shirt and chaps over filthy jeans. In fact, dirt covered everything he wore as well as the teeth he bared when he shouted, "Hey! What the hell you doing down there? Where's Wes?"

Paul slammed the door shut and backed away. His fingers were still clenched around the pot's handle as if it were a weapon that could answer any threat in front of him. "I don't know what this is about," he said, "but there's no need for any further violence."

Clomping down the stairs, the short man raised his pistol to sight along the top of its barrel. "I beg to differ, mister."

When a gunshot blasted through the air, Paul reflexively jumped. He hadn't been hit. He hadn't even been missed. The bullet that had been fired came from another gun entirely and hit the chest of the second man who'd been making his way downstairs behind the shorter fellow. That man winced while clutching the crimson stain now spreading across his shirt, crumpled forward, and fell toward the shorter gunman who'd descended before him.

The shorter gunman was looking up at something that Paul couldn't quite see. When pivoting to aim in that direction, the gunman was knocked off his balance by his wounded partner. "Get . . . offa me, Steve!" he grunted as he was forced to wrap his arm around the wounded man before both of them were sent down the stairs. Steve's head lolled forward and his shoulders trembled with a final gasping breath. Upon seeing this, Paul reflexively crossed himself and whispered a quick prayer for the man's departing soul.

The third man to walk down the stairs was Dave Sprole. In his right hand was the .44 revolver, and in his left was a smaller .38. Before Paul could finish his prayer with a quick amen, Dave straightened his right arm, squeezed his trigger, and blew a hole clean through the shorter gunman's shoulder. The gunman swore as he was knocked to one side. The impact of the bullet pushed him away from Steve's limp body, where he bounced off the banister and tripped down the rest of the stairs.

"Oh," Dave said as he caught sight of Paul. "What brings you here, preacher?"

"I—"

Paul was interrupted by the metallic *clack* of a pistol

hammer slapping against the back of a spent bullet casing. Dave calmly traded pistols so the .38 was in his right hand before pointing the gun's barrel at the shorter gunman's head. He pulled the trigger, adding another soul to those in need of a final prayer.

After that, the hotel was quiet.

Smoke hung in the air. Without a breeze to stir it, the gritty haze drifted downward like bits of mud on rain-streaked glass.

Paul held his breath, and the dead had none to spare.

Dave Sprole looked on, waiting patiently until he was certain it was all right for him to holster the .38. "What are you doing here, preacher?" he asked while emptying the spent casings from the cylinder of his .44 so he could replace them with fresh rounds taken from the loops in his belt.

"Actually I came to see you."

Sprole's eyes narrowed as he walked down the stairs. His feet moved around sprawling dead limbs and blood as if he were simply avoiding a puddle in the street. "You've seen me and plenty more. Seems like you're taking it fairly well."

"This isn't the first time I've seen bloodshed," Paul said. "I'm needed in the most desperate of situations."

"Most men would've run away faster than that woman you shoved out of here."

"You saw that?"

"I saw enough to put the pieces together. Ain't like she was being very quiet." Finished reloading the pistol, Sprole snapped it shut and dropped it into the leather holster at his side. "Anyone else in here we need to worry about?"

"I don't know. I just was told about Manuela. Are there other guests upstairs?"

"Not a one. That's why I was so happy with this arrangement." Sprole looked around and scowled. "Guess that's the end of my peace and quiet. About time I should move along." With that, he tipped his hat and turned to walk back upstairs.

Paul charged forward to rush up the stairs and slap a hand onto the bounty hunter's shoulder. Sprole stopped and turned as if his glare alone were enough to burn Paul's hand down to a smoking nub.

"Where do you think you're going?" Paul asked.

"Up to my room. What concern is it of yours?"

"Men have died here! You can't just go back up to your room like nothing happened."

"If it's the law you want, I'm sure the law will be around shortly. If you want me to look all pretty for the sheriff when he gets here, I'll need to go up to my room to freshen up."

When Sprole tried to leave, it was under the assumption that he would be able to pull out of Paul's grasp with little or no effort. Not only did the grip on his shoulder remain, but it became strong enough to pull him back a step or two. They were near the top of the staircase, which didn't leave much room to maneuver. Even so, Paul stepped up to the bounty hunter to stand toe-to-toe with him.

"Tell me what happened here," Paul said.

"Let go of me, preacher. I won't tell you again."

Paul let go. "Tell me what happened."

"The sheriff will be here any minute and I'll surely have to tell him the story. I ain't gonna spell it all out twice, so if you want to hear it, just be sure to stay close."

"No. You'll tell me now."

Sprole studied the man in front of him. "You got a whole lot of sand for a preacher. Maybe that's because you got this little pit of a town eating from your hand every Sunday morning, but none of that holds a drip of water with me. You want to step up to me, you'd best be ready to back your play. And before you say you've got the Lord on your side, you should ask yourself if the Lord will come down and stop me from doing this."

In a flicker of motion, Sprole drew the .44 from its holster and jammed the barrel against Paul's stomach. It dug in before angling upward to make certain it would do the most damage possible.

Sprole grinned. "Still feeling brave?"

"Tell me what happened here," Paul repeated.

Now Sprole appeared mildly confused. Although Paul didn't look down at the gun in the bounty hunter's hand, he could feel its barrel move away from his belly before he heard the brush of iron against leather. Sprole moved back half a step and slapped an open hand against Paul's chest. When Paul's backside hit the banister and he started to lose his balance, Sprole grabbed his shirt and pulled him back just enough to keep him from toppling to the ground floor. Leaving Paul there, Sprole climbed the rest of the stairs and walked down a narrow hallway.

"I was washing up when these men attacked me," Sprole said.

Paul climbed the stairs as well, noticing immedi-

ately that the doors to two different rooms were ajar
and one had been knocked completely off its hinges.
Gun smoke hung in the air even thicker up there, possibly because of the more confined quarters.

Sprole went to the room with the dislodged door
and stepped inside.

Following him, Paul asked, "Why did those men
come after you?"

"What do you care, preacher? Don't you have a sermon to write?"

Paul stood in the broken doorway, feeling every hair
on the back of his neck stand on end as if to warn him
of another attack. Watching as Sprole rummaged
through a small chest of drawers for some clothes,
which he then stuffed into a saddlebag, he asked, "Did
this have something to do with Jack Terrigan?"

"You really do have a one-track mind."

"Well, did it?"

Sprole looked up from his saddlebag, sighed, and
walked over to the single chair in the room. Once he
took the duster from the back of the chair and draped
it over one arm, a Spencer rifle could be seen propped
against the wall behind that chair. Hefting the saddlebags over his shoulder, he took the rifle and walked
toward the door. "I don't answer to no man, and I sure
don't answer to you," he said. "That means I don't
have to tell you anything."

"What about the law? Aren't you going to wait for
the sheriff to get here?"

"I said I thought the law would be coming here
shortly and I'd explain what happened. I never said I'd
sit around waiting for him to arrive. If he don't want to

stop what he's doing so he can look in on a shooting, that ain't my concern."

"He may not be here, but I am," Paul said as he planted his feet and crossed his arms over his chest. "You don't strike me as the sort who would leave through a window, and unless you want to move me, I'm not about to budge."

"Don't think I won't," Sprole growled.

"You can try."

Sprole eased the saddlebags off his shoulder, freeing his hands so he could hold the Spencer in a proper grip with one hand close to the trigger. For a moment, it seemed as if he was going to bring the weapon up to his shoulder, but then he set the rifle down so it rested against the footboard of the bed. "What's this burr under your saddle where Terrigan is concerned? Oh, that's right. You said you knew him."

"That's right."

"What is he . . . your brother?"

Paul's smile was tired in more ways than one when he replied, "For someone of my calling, every man is my brother."

"Spare me the sermon. It's been too long a day."

"I know Mr. Terrigan well enough to be concerned for his well-being. Until now, I have heard only a few passing rumors about him. Rumors I thought might be false or at least grossly overstated. But they are proving to be much more than that. If Terrigan truly is close enough to draw so much fire, that means he's close enough for me to look into his eyes and have a word with him."

"What do you intend on saying?" Sprole asked.

"Does it matter?"

"I suppose not. I was just curious, is all."

"Are you going after him right now?" Paul asked.

After taking a quick look at the state of the room, which included a broken mirror, a disheveled bed, a dresser that had been knocked askew, and a few bullet holes in the walls, Sprole replied, "Yes, I am."

"Then I want to come with you."

"Forget it. Now step out of my way."

Chapter 5

The small livery stable behind the hotel was just big enough to contain three horses and some gear. Sprole was leading his horse out of the stable by the reins when Sheriff Noss's voice bellowed through the air.

"And just where do you think you're goin'?" he asked.

"I've been in town for several days," Sprole replied. "And it's only now that anyone is so concerned with my welfare."

"It ain't your welfare I'm concerned about. It's the shots that were fired in that hotel."

"Well, go have a look for yourself, Sheriff. You can count the holes in the walls as many times as you want."

"Sure that's all I'll find in there is holes?" the lawman asked. "I hear some men may have caught some lead as well."

Several paces behind the sheriff, Manuela and the woman from the front desk strained to get a look at whom the sheriff was talking to. Sheriff Noss turned to Carol and asked, "That the man who did the shooting?"

She nodded.

"All right, Dave," Noss said as he made a show of placing his hand flat on the grip of his holstered pistol. "You know what that means."

"I was one of the men inside the hotel," Sprole replied. "That don't make me the instigator of what happened!"

"And what *did* happen? Perhaps you'd like to come to my office and inform me of the details?"

When someone else came around from the other side of the livery, Noss took a defensive posture and drew his pistol. "Whoever you are, you'd best throw down any weapon you're carrying!"

The figure stepping into view was also leading a horse by the reins. "It's just me, Sheriff. Paul Lester."

"Jesus, Father! Pardon the language, but what are you doin' here? There's been trouble, so you'd best get out of here."

"That is him!" Manuela said as she extended a shaky hand toward Paul. "He is the one!"

"That man right there?" Noss asked.

"Yes, yes! He saved me from the man that was going to shoot me," Manuela gasped. Unable to contain herself, she pushed past the lawman and ran all the way over to where Paul stood with his horse's reins in hand. She wrapped her arms around him and said, "*Gracias*, Padre. Thank you so much. You are more than just a padre. You are my angel!"

While Paul was flummoxed by the woman's overwhelming display of affection, Sprole was more than a little amused. The same could not be said about the sheriff, however.

"That'll be enough of that," Noss said while trying to pull Manuela away from her angel. "There's work to be done here and one big mess to clean up."

Tipping his hat to both of them, Sprole said, "Then I'll just leave you to it, Sheriff."

"The hell you will! You're not going anywhere! Pardon me again, Father."

"Quite all right," Paul said.

Once Manuela was pried away from Paul, she immediately latched on to Sprole. "This man was another one. The ones that try to hurt me also try to hurt him and he shot them first. He is a good man, Sheriff! Very good man."

The woman who worked behind the hotel's front desk was much quieter, which was how she managed to get closer without being noticed right away. "She's right," Carol said. "Those gunmen came in asking for Mr. Sprole and then they got rough. I barely got out before they got to me. I'm just so sorry I didn't think to make certain Manuela wasn't out as well."

"Is all right, Miss Carol," Manuela said in an accent that seemed to grow thicker the more worked up she got. "Father Paul was here to take care of me. He fought hard."

Suddenly Paul's eyes widened. "Oh! I almost forgot in all the excitement. The man who was holding this woman at gunpoint . . . I knocked him out, but I didn't kill him. He could be up and around by now!"

"Don't worry about that one," a young man shouted as he hurried around from the hotel's front porch. "We got to him right when he was startin' to wake up."

"Ah, good," Sprole said. "Then I can be off."

"Also found two dead men on the stairs," the young fellow continued.

"My deputies found some dead men," Sheriff Noss said. "That means I need to have a word with you. Now, are you going to draw this out some more or will you just come along peacefully?"

"That depends," Sprole replied. "Will I be answering your questions from behind bars?"

The lawman took one look at Manuela and got a fearsomely protective glare from her in return. When he looked over to Carol, the woman who worked the hotel's registration desk told him, "I ran away one too many times today as it is. I won't stand by and let you put an innocent man behind bars."

"Aw, for Chr . . ." Noss cut himself short and looked at Paul. "I'll watch my tongue, Father. If I ask nicely, will you come along with me?"

"Of course," Paul said.

"And could you convince your friend to do the same?"

When Paul looked over to him, Sprole rolled his eyes and let out a breath that seemed to deflate his entire body. "Why not?" the bounty hunter said. "It's not as if there's a gang of killers on the loose."

It was several hours later before Paul and Sprole got to have their talk with Sheriff Noss. They passed that time sitting in the sheriff's office, playing cards with one of the deputies and watching the rest of the town bustle past the front windows. Finally Noss came along to stomp into the office and plop into his chair behind his desk so he could start shuffling some papers that had been stacked on top of his ink blotter.

Since Sprole was in the middle of a poker hand with the deputy and Paul had more patience than all of the men in that room combined, Noss was the one to break the silence. "So," he said, "what's this I hear about a gang of killers? I'm talkin' to you, Sprole."

"You made us wait this long for an audience," the bounty hunter snapped. "How about you wait until this hand is over? I got money on this game."

"Don't make me get out of this chair," the sheriff warned.

Although the thinly veiled threat rolled like water off Sprole's back, it had an immediate effect on the deputy. The younger lawman threw his cards down and stood up from the empty barrel they'd been using as a card table.

"Don't make a reach for none of that money," Sprole said while pointing toward a small collection of pennies piled on the middle of the barrel's top. "You walk away from a game, you give up the pot. Everyone knows that."

"And if you're stupid enough to gamble in a sheriff's office," Noss said, "you're lucky to only lose the money in your pockets. If you didn't know that before, you do now. Take that money, Kyle, and clear them cards away so I can have these men's undivided attention."

Kyle scooped up the pennies, collected the cards, and pushed the barrel back against the wall to the spot where he'd found it. Sprole was left sitting on a stool in the middle of the floor with his hands propped on his knees.

"Seems like you've had a busy day," Sheriff Noss

said as he settled into his chair. "Busted apart the second floor of a hotel, killed two men, and knocked another one senseless."

"To be fair," Paul said, "I was the one who knocked out that man."

"Right." Noss leaned forward to place his hands on his desk as he said, "I already heard the story from them ladies who rushed over to heap their praises on you two. To be honest, they're the biggest reason both of you are on this side of the bars in that cell I got over yonder."

The cell in question was a large cage built into the back corner of the office. Bars set into the floor stretched up to the ceiling, broken only by a narrow door. Having visited plenty of prisoners requesting solace for one reason or another, Paul was very familiar with it. The prospect of spending time inside that cell made him look at it in a different light, however.

Sensing that he'd struck a chord in at least one of the two men in front of him, Sheriff Noss removed his hat and tossed it onto the coatrack behind him with a well-practiced flick of his wrist. "I've heard from everyone else. The mess is mostly cleaned up and the bodies are being fitted for coffins. That leaves you two."

"Glad to see we're so high in your pecking order," Sprole grunted.

"Why should I let you roam free in my town?"

Since the lawman's eyes were leveled squarely at him, Sprole said, "Because I wasn't doing anything wrong. Those men came looking for trouble and I defended myself."

"Who were they?"

Sprole shut his mouth and shrugged.

"Were they part of Jack Terrigan's bunch?" the lawman pressed.

Another shrug from Sprole.

"Why don't you ask the one that's still alive?" Paul asked. He didn't flinch when every eye in that office turned toward him. "The man that I knocked cold. He's still alive, isn't he?"

The sheriff nodded toward one of his deputies.

"He ain't sayin' much, but he's up and about," the deputy replied. "I got him chained to a bed at Doc Chandler's place, so he ain't exactly up, but he's awake. Wasn't saying much of anything that bears repeating."

"Then make him talk," Paul said. "That's your job, isn't it, Sheriff? Get to the bottom of why they're here."

"That's mighty tough talk from a preacher," Noss said.

Sprole chuckled. "I've been noticing the same thing." Just when Paul thought the bounty hunter was going to repeat what they'd talked about at the hotel and outside the Red Coyote, Sprole let out an exasperated breath. "Those men were with Jack Terrigan. I can tell you that much."

"How can you be certain of that?" Noss asked.

"Because I've been chasing the son of a . . ." Casting a quick glance over to Paul, Sprole chewed back the words he'd been about to say and continued with "I've been chasing Terrigan for months. He's riding with anyone who can fire a gun, surrounding himself with men he can use as bait or fodder for any bullets that have his name on 'em."

"You know it's Terrigan?"

"Yeah," Sprole replied without hesitation. "I've seen him plenty of times with my own eyes. Now, you can question that man you got chained to a sickbed all you want, but he won't tell you anything I can't tell you. In fact, you shouldn't believe a word that comes out of his mouth. He'll try to throw you off the trail of the rest of Terrigan's gang so he can wait for them to come and bust him out of here."

Noss straightened up as if his honor had just been smeared. "Ain't no one's ever busted out of my jail."

"That's just because you've never had custody of a man who rode with the likes of Jack Terrigan. One of the men I killed back at that hotel was named Hollister. Of the three that came sniffing around for me, he was the one that's been riding with Terrigan's bunch the longest. If Jack were to come back and bust one of his men out of a jail cell, it would be Hollister. The one the preacher knocked out was just some kid who started riding with Terrigan less than a month ago. That's why he was sent to watch over some woman in a food pantry."

Slowly digesting what he'd heard, Noss looked once again in Paul's direction. "What about you, Father? Why were you at that hotel?"

"I went to see Mr. Sprole."

"What for?"

"To try and convince him to let me ride with him when he goes after Jack Terrigan."

"I thought you were smarter than that. You truly think you can save every man's soul?"

"That's my job, Sheriff," Paul replied.

Although that caused Sprole to shake his head, it

was enough of an explanation to placate the sheriff for
the time being. "I've met plenty of bounty hunters in
my day," he said to Sprole. "Usually they're just interested in collecting money or figuring out who would be
the juiciest target to track down next. I hardly ever seen
one as cooperative as you."

"That's funny," Sprole said. "I didn't think I was being particularly cooperative."

Looking toward the deputy with the pocketful of
pennies, Noss asked, "Did this one try to skin out of
here before I got back?"

The younger lawman shook his head. "Nope. He
just sat there playing cards."

"That's because he wanted to stay here to see if the
man chained to his sickbed had anything to say," Paul
said. Despite the venomous stare coming from Sprole,
he went on. "Since the young man is new to the gang,
he would probably let something slip. Something that
could be used in tracking down the rest of them. Since
he's not saying anything at all, sitting around here is
just a waste of time."

"That's mighty insightful of you, Father," Noss said.

"We've stayed put long enough for you to check on
our story," the preacher said. "Since you don't seem
overly interested in hearing what else Mr. Sprole or I
have to say on the matter, I'm guessing you've already
pieced together enough to know that what you were
told was the truth."

The lawman nodded. "Seems pretty straightforward
all right. Those men came in looking for trouble and
they found it. I recognize one of them as a no-good
horse thief, so there's no reason to think any better of

the company he kept. All I got left is a bounty hunter, the town preacher, and two women who swear both of you are saints."

"It all adds up," Sprole said impatiently. "Are you gonna cut us loose or not?"

"I don't see any reason why I shouldn't."

"Good. Then I'll have my guns back."

Upon hearing that, the two deputies in the room put themselves between Sprole and the cabinet in the corner where the weapons were kept.

"You can have them tomorrow," the sheriff told him.

For a moment, it seemed the bounty hunter might lunge at any of the men in his sight. "Why keep me until tomorrow?" he asked.

"Because I can see your temper is frayed," Noss said. "And a man in that frame of mind don't need a pair of pistols at his side."

Sprole shifted his gaze. "Just had to open your mouth, preacher. Next time you feel the need to stick your nose into my affairs, you'd best remember this moment because it's when you wore through my last bit of patience. Bible or no, I won't have you get in my way again."

Drawing in a breath, Paul steeled himself so as not to show any sign of nervousness. "This is a small town, Sheriff," he said. "News doesn't leave here very quickly. What happens if Terrigan comes looking for this Hollister person under the assumption he's been captured?"

"I'm counting on it," Noss said.

Sprole shook his head. "Terrigan ain't stupid. He must have sent someone else along with them other three to ride back and let him know what happened."

"Ain't nobody left town once the shooting started," the sheriff insisted.

"How can you be so sure?"

"I know who to ask, that's how!" the lawman snapped as he pushed his chair back and got to his feet. "I know how to do my job! Me or my men already got wind that Terrigan might be coming along, so we were watching the trails leading away from town."

"Right," Sprole sighed. "That's why you and your deputies were right there when I was attacked in that hotel."

"If you must know, the shooting started soon after we were in position. Those gunmen must have already been in town by the time I heard Terrigan was nearby. We were on the lookout for trouble outside town, which is why we were late in getting to the hotel. Since then, I've had lookouts posted and would have known if anyone had left."

"So they could still be here?" Paul asked.

"No," Sprole said. "If Terrigan was here, he would have led the charge or taken a shot at us while we were all outside the hotel. There's no reason for him to hang back and watch them other three walk into a hotel for what should have been a simple shooting. He ain't here."

"And nobody's left town to send word out to anywhere he might be camped," Sheriff Noss said with absolute certainty.

"Which puts us in an excellent position," Paul said. "Terrigan should be waiting for word from his men. It's been long enough and he might be getting anxious. He may even come into town searching for answers himself."

Noss and his deputies exchanged a few nervous glances. Sprole picked up on that right away and was quick to say, "Terrigan's gang has spent a lot of time on the trail. I know because I've been hot on their heels for some time. It wouldn't be strange for those men to take some time for themselves in town once their job was done, so Jack may not think much if they're not back just yet. If he doesn't see them soon after sundown, he may start getting anxious."

"Then I best try to get some useful talk out of Doc Chandler's patient," Noss said.

"In the meantime, perhaps you should turn me loose," Sprole offered. "If I find Terrigan, I'll bring him straight back here for my reward and you can take all the credit you want for seeing he gets what's coming to him."

"And if you don't find him?"

"Then you're rid of me. It ain't as if I got any reason to stay here."

Paul could tell the sheriff was teetering on the brink of a decision and just needed a gentle nudge in one direction. "Either way," he said, "you win. You could always ride with him to make sure the job gets done properly."

The sheriff grinned widely. "I like the sound of that."

Sprole, on the other hand, was far from amused.

Chapter 6

Dr. Chandler's office was slightly smaller than the sheriff's. It contained a single row of cots on one side and a little rolltop desk on the other. The young gunman Paul had hit with the pot was chained to the bed farthest from the door. His shirt was soaked through with sweat, and the one leg he hung over the side of the cot was shackled to the frame. His right hand was wrapped in a thick bundle of bandages. His left was stretched back and cuffed to the thick iron arch where a headboard would have been on a proper bed. When he noticed the sheriff and Paul had stepped inside to have a few words with the physician, he began grousing loudly.

Doc Chandler was in his late forties and had a long face with sunken cheeks. Despite looking more like a patient than a healer, he was a friendly sort who always had something for the collection plate when it was passed his way during services. Paul shook his hand and got a warm smile in return.

"How has our young visitor been?" Paul asked.

"Apart from the wound in his hand, he's got one

beauty of a goose egg on his head. Says you gave him both. Could that be true?"

"Could be," Paul replied with a smirk.

The doctor stifled a laugh and knocked a fist against Paul's shoulder. "It's like we always say, never underestimate the quiet ones, right?"

"That's right."

"What about him?" Chandler asked as he nodded toward Sheriff Noss. The lawman hadn't been interested in any of the other two's banter, so he'd walked straight past them to approach the gunman's bed.

"He's just here to ask some questions," Paul explained. "Didn't you think he'd be back for his prisoner?"

"Sure, but . . . do you think I should oversee the questioning?"

"I think the sheriff can handle himself."

"Yes," Chandler replied, "but that young man hasn't exactly been easy to get along with. He's tried my patience, and I'm someone sworn to heal."

As if to prove the doctor's point, the gunman grunted something that Paul couldn't quite make out before snapping his head forward to spit a large wet mess at the sheriff. Almost immediately, Noss snapped his fist out to punch the outlaw in the face. It wasn't a vicious blow, but landed hard enough to send the outlaw's head straight back into the bed's frame. Skull met iron with a dull *clang* and the outlaw went limp for the second time that day.

Sheriff Noss turned around, walked back to the front portion of the room, and said, "Might want to have another look at your patient, Doc. He seems to have had another bout of unconsciousness."

As Dr. Chandler rushed to the outlaw's bed, Noss wiped off his cheek using a handkerchief.

"That didn't get you very far," Paul said.

"I wouldn't be so sure."

Seeing a faint glimmer of hope, Paul asked, "What do you mean?"

"When I walked up to him, he was full of himself and ready to tell me where to go. When I told him his two friends were dead, he lost his confidence real quick. All he had left was that desperate little display you saw in order for him to try and feel like a big man. He was scared. Real scared. And that didn't start until he knew them other partners of his were gone."

"Which means Terrigan or any of the rest of the gang aren't here in town with them!"

The sheriff motioned for Paul to keep quiet, but he nodded all the same. "That's exactly what I mean. If there was someone here that we missed, that young fella back there would have some thread of hope to hang on to. Someone would either be coming for him or would skin out of town to tell Terrigan what happened here. When I told him about the other two being dead, he turned white as a ghost. There ain't no way for a man to put on a show that good unless it's the truth."

"Perfect!" Paul had to rein himself in when he saw the doctor glance back at him. Lowering his voice, he put his back to the rest of the room and asked, "Where does that leave us?"

"It don't leave *us* nowhere, Father. You did your part. More than your part, to be certain. You can go back to your church and write up a good sermon for Sunday with my thanks. I've got a job to do, and I'd appreciate it if you didn't mention anything you heard to anyone other than me or my deputies. No need to spread another rumor or stir up commotion. There's been more than enough of that already."

"Is Mr. Sprole still in town?"

"He's being watched closely by my deputies," Noss replied. "Nothing against my men, but I should probably get back to them sooner rather than later." With that, the sheriff tipped his hat and strode out the door.

Paul followed him outside. "You should consider working with Mr. Sprole," he said. "That man can help you track down Mr. Terrigan."

"I've done a good spot of tracking in my day. I don't need the help of some bounty hunter."

"But Terrigan needs to be found! He'll get suspicious when those other men don't come back, and he's bound to ride into town looking for them. There could be trouble and more innocents could be hurt!"

"You're preaching to the choir, Paul." When the lawman smirked at his own joke, he gave the other man a calming pat on the shoulder. "You did well with all of this and I don't intend to let an animal like Jack Terrigan get anywhere near my town. Go back to your church and rest easy. I'll be rounding up some men to head out to find that outlaw's camp."

Paul brushed the sheriff's hand from his shoulder and said, "I want to go with you."

"What good could you do on a posse?"

"I've met Jack Terrigan before. I can help you find him."

The lawman's brow furrowed. "When did you meet Jack Terrigan?"

"Some time ago. If I see him, I think I can help convince him to give up before anyone else gets hurt."

"If Terrigan or his men get hurt, it's because they brought it on themselves. Some might say they got plenty of hurt comin' after all that they've inflicted upon so many others. Isn't it in the Good Book? Eye for an eye and all that?"

Paul shook his head solemnly. "The lessons taught in the Bible are there to learn from and use as guidance. Anyone who's read the entire book and has taken it to heart knows the intention of the passage you mentioned isn't for it to be . . ."

"Sorry I brought it up," Noss was quick to say. "But you ain't gonna convince me otherwise. You're a preacher and your place ain't riding out on the trail of an outlaw. I'm the law in this town and it's my job to get my hands dirty. You get in the way of me or my men and I'll lock you up just to keep you safe."

"Be serious, Sheriff," Paul said with a forced chuckle. "I hardly think such drastic measures would be necessary. Besides, how long will it take you to round up a posse? A few days?"

"Maybe less."

"That's too much time wasted. You need someone to go *now*, and those young men you deputized aren't up to the task."

"And you are?" the lawman scoffed. "Just stay somewhere it's safe and I'll let you have a word with Terrigan once I bring him in."

"You'll bring him in alive, then?"

"If I can," Noss replied. "But I wouldn't hold your breath. From what I've heard about this one, he ain't exactly the sort who comes along quietly. You have my word that I won't put him down unless he leaves me no other choice. That good enough for you, Father?"

There were times when Paul felt as spry as a man in his prime. Although his prime years were behind him, he wasn't an old man either. If he let his whiskers grow long enough, a few strands of gray might be seen, but at least they would cover the wrinkles that had become etched into his face over the last few years. There were times, however, when he felt every day of every one of those years as if they were kindling piled onto his shoulders and he was forced to carry it all from one end of the day to the other. Listening to the coddling tone in the lawman's voice, knowing he had to swallow it down and act as if he liked it, Paul felt like the helpless old man he feared he might someday become.

"I can help you find him," Paul said before he could stop himself.

Showing him a patronizing smile while patting his shoulder, Noss said, "It sure is good of you to offer, but Terrigan probably doesn't even know his boys are hurt. Odds are, he's thinking they're wetting their whistles at a saloon or keeping company with one of the working girls here in town before getting down to their business. By the time he suspects anything and decides to ride in to do anything about it, my men and I will be surrounding his camp."

"So you know where Terrigan is making camp?"

"Not just yet, but it shouldn't be hard to find. Since we'll be catching him by surprise, it should be even easier."

"You might want to take Mr. Sprole with you, then," Paul said. "He seems quite skilled."

"Actually, I was thinking about that very thing."

"You were?"

Instead of patting Paul on the back, Sheriff Noss gave it a heartfelt slap. "And it does me good to put a surprised look onto the face of a man like you! Yes, I was going to ask if Sprole wanted to come along with me, but I doubt he would think the offer was anything more than me trying to keep an eye on him."

"Is it?"

"I'm a lawman, Father. I keep the peace. That's always been my strong suit. At their root, bounty hunters are trackers. It's what they do best. Between the two of us, I'd say we got a pretty good chance at finding Terrigan and bringing him home in time for breakfast. Also, I sure don't want him getting close to that gunman with the wounded hand. My deputies are on short supply, and frankly I think you're right about there not being enough time to organize a posse from the men in town. That means your Mr. Sprole is a natural choice."

"I still think I should go with you."

"Tell you what," Noss said in a resigned tone. "I have every intention of bringing Terrigan back alive. If I'm going through all this trouble, I want to make sure there ain't more members of his gang out there waiting to undo everything that gets done. Soon as I do bring him in, you'll be the first one to have a chat with him. All right?"

Paul wasn't a stupid man. After the time he'd spent in the professions he'd chosen throughout his life, he'd become adept at reading people's faces and gauging the sorts of things going through their minds. He would never profess to reading anyone's thoughts, but he could get a general feel for what was going on between their ears. Most of what the lawman told him was true. More than anything, however, the sheriff was just trying to get Paul to stop talking and leave him alone. Not a big surprise, actually, since he did have a lot of work to do. To that end, Paul nodded and said, "I'm sure you've got this well in hand. Probably best if I just leave you to it."

"Glad to see we're reading from the same page, Father. Now, if you don't mind, I've got a posse to organize." The lawman had started walking back toward his office when he stopped and turned partway around so he could say, "There is something you could do for me. You spent some time with Dave Sprole. You think you could help grease the wheels where getting him onto my posse is concerned?"

"I don't really—"

"Tell him there'll be a fee for his service and that he should meet me at the stable just down the street from my office in an hour. I've got to get a few things in place before we leave. Thanks, Father."

And then the sheriff was gone. Noss strode down the street at a pace that made it clear he would make it difficult for anyone wanting to catch up to him. Knowing the lawman would only speed up or cut through an alley if he knew he was being followed, Paul didn't bother trying. Instead, he walked back to the sheriff's office, where he found Sprole standing outside smoking a cheroot.

"You're still here?" Paul asked.

Sprole nodded and patted his empty holster. "Ain't about to leave without my guns. What's your excuse?"

"The sheriff is forming a posse to go after Terrigan. He wanted to know if—"

Grabbing the cheroot and holding it almost tight enough to crush it, Sprole said, "You need to get me on that posse. It would be better if it came from you because you already know him and . . . well . . . he trusts you. I'd ask him, but he'd probably just think I was trying to get my guns back or that I might try some sort of double cross, even though that wouldn't get me anywhere. Just see what you can do for me, will you?"

Paul had earned a mighty good reputation for mediating between people who couldn't see eye to eye. Whether those people were parents and children, husbands and wives, or neighbors or siblings, bridging gaps between folks was a major portion of any preacher's duties. Rather than show the bounty hunter how similar he and the lawman truly were, Paul took a more self-serving route by sighing and telling Sprole, "The posse will be meeting in an hour at the stable right down the street from here. I'll go have a word with the sheriff to convince him to let you ride along with him. Just be at that stable and don't give any of the others a hard time."

Clamping the cheroot between his teeth, Sprole grinned around the narrow cigar and vigorously shook Paul's hand. "I owe you one, preacher."

"That's right, you do. Just don't forget it."

After Sprole turned and marched back into the office, Paul retraced his steps to Doc Chandler's place. In the short time it took for him to get there, he could feel an excitement crackling through the air. Word was spreading about the shoot-out at the hotel, the bodies being prepared at the undertaker's parlor, and the steps that the sheriff might or might not be taking to answer back for all that had happened. Looks were being cast at Paul as well, most of which were wary or surprised. While the lawmen and even the bounty hunter had done what was expected of them, the preacher wasn't playing his accepted role.

The people of Pueblito Verde were looking at their preacher in a different light. That wasn't necessarily a bad thing, but it wasn't altogether good. After all the work he'd done to sink roots into the little community so he could go about his tasks in peace, Paul felt more uncomfortable with every boisterous word of praise he received. By the time he got back to the doctor's office, he was glad to shut the door behind him.

Dr. Chandler was at his desk across from his only patient. When he saw Paul, he stood up and crossed the room to meet him. "What brings you back so soon?" Chandler asked.

Paul looked over to the gunman. "Is he awake?"

"I don't think so. He's either still out or playing possum. Either way, I can't blame him. Sheriff Noss knocked him pretty good. He needs his rest, so I wasn't about to try and wake him up. Was there something else you needed?"

"No. I thought I could keep an eye on him."

"Shouldn't one of the deputies be doing that?" Chandler asked.

"One probably will. A posse is being organized and a guard will be assigned."

The doctor let out a breath. "That's a relief. I know he's shackled and all, but it makes me a little nervous having a dangerous outlaw here who'll be awake and raring to go before too long."

"Well, I'll be here to lend a hand until a deputy gets here." With that, Paul pulled up a chair and sat down beside the outlaw's bed. Once the doctor stepped outside, Paul said, "I know you're awake."

The gunman sat up fast enough to rattle the chains connecting his arm and leg to the cot's frame. "What do you want?"

"I'm here to listen to what you have to say."

"Like what? A confession?"

"If you'd like."

"I got nothin' to say to you," the younger man growled.

Paul settled into his chair. "Then you shouldn't mind if I ask you a few questions."

Chapter 7

The posse consisted of four men. It was late afternoon when they broke into two pairs and rode out of town. Sheriff Noss insisted on partnering with Dave Sprole so he could keep an eye on the bounty hunter, and they rode toward a rocky stretch of trail to the south. Two of the sheriff's deputies hung back for a while and then took a wider trail to the north. The idea was to sneak at least one of the pairs past any lookouts that might have been posted by the outlaw gang to keep watch for riders leaving Pueblito Verde.

When Sprole and the sheriff rode away from town, both were ready to be ambushed at any moment. There wasn't any reason to believe the outlaws were poised to bushwhack anyone so quickly, but the anticipation of forming the posse and putting together a strategy for capturing a man as dangerous as Jack Terrigan put all of the men on edge. After a few hours of riding with nothing but dust in their teeth to show for it, that edge was dulled a bit.

"How much farther should we go before doubling back to check on your deputies?" Sprole asked.

Noss shook his head while letting his eyes wander along the horizon. He shifted in his saddle and looked along the other horizon while saying, "I thought for sure we would have found them by now."

"How? By riding out and waiting for them to jump us? I'm glad I didn't know that was your only plan when I signed on."

"Well, you're the tracker!" Noss shot back. "Where are all of your great ideas for hunting him down?"

"It's not like I can just lift my nose to the wind and sniff him out! There's more to it than that, and you should have let me do this my way if you wanted it done right. When the four of us met at the stable, I told you we should have done it properly."

"There isn't time for that!" Noss replied. "We had to ride out while we still had surprise on our side. If someone was watching the trails leading from town, this was the trail they would most likely have been watching. There's plenty of higher vantage points up in them rocks," he said while sweeping his hand toward an outcropping to one side of the trail. "I know this terrain better than anyone, and we've already ridden past every good spot someone could have made camp."

"Well, maybe Terrigan don't know this territory as good as you do," Sprole pointed out. "Could be he and his gang just picked the first spot they found. Or maybe they came in from the north."

"That's why I brought you along! You've been tracking this killer for so long, why couldn't you tell me which direction he was coming from?"

A rifle cracked somewhere in the distance. The sound of the shot was faint compared to the hiss in

Sprole's ear as the bullet whipped past his head. Finely honed instinct brought his hand down to the pistol at his side so he could draw the .44 that he'd been entrusted with as part of riding on the posse. Unfortunately, he didn't have a target.

Sheriff Noss reacted in a similar manner, but drew his rifle from the boot of his saddle instead of the pistol strapped to his hip. "High and to the right," he shouted while levering a round into the rifle's chamber.

Following the directions he'd been given, Sprole sighted along the top of his pistol until he picked out the bump at the top of a rock outcropping that could have been the silhouette of a man's head. When he saw the sunlight glint off a rifle's barrel, the bounty hunter fired a shot up at the rocks. Knowing he was too far away to put the pistol to its best use, he told the lawman, "Try to keep him pinned down. I'll get around behind him."

The sheriff nodded before taking aim and squeezing his trigger. The sound of that shot mingled with the pounding of hooves as Sprole rode down the trail toward a spot where he could steer off the path to circle around the back of the outcropping. Trees that grew in a territory containing so much rugged terrain were tougher than ones found in thick Oregon forests or even at the foot of the Rocky Mountains. The crooked trees blocking Sprole's line of sight as well as his horse's progress barely swayed in any breeze, and they withstood the shots that were fired back and forth with a minimum of bark flying from their trunks when hit. Brushing against one of them as he urged his horse to ascend the rocky slope, Sprole felt unforgiving wooden claws scrape at his shoulders and arms. A few branches even slashed his cheek when he attempted to navigate the shortest route to the rifleman's hiding spot.

Fortunately, those trees were just as much of a hindrance to the sharpshooter. After one more shot that clipped a thick branch without severing it, the man at the top of the outcropping swore loudly and began scrambling down another part of the slope.

"He's on his way down!" Sprole shouted, hoping the sheriff was able to hear him. "There's gotta be a horse tied somewhere nearby!"

Through the trees, Sprole could see a narrow figure making his way down the slope. He fired one shot that was too rushed to hit much of anything and another that might have come within a few inches of its target. The sharpshooter was a gaunt man with a pale face covered in dirt. The rifle he brought to his shoulder was a Winchester, and he squeezed off a round that whipped through the branches between them to graze not only the bounty hunter's leg but the horseflesh pressed against it. Sprole let out a pained grunt as his horse twisted around to reflexively move away from the source of its pain.

Sprole fired his last round wildly as the world teetered crazily around him. He tried to maintain a grip on his reins, but the horse was already skidding down the slope. Even if he managed to stay in his saddle, Sprole knew he could still be in a world of trouble.

The horse whinnied and fought to keep its footing. Its rider cut his losses and launched himself from the saddle at his first opportunity. It might not have been the most favorable option, but Sprole preferred to take his chances with gravity and a hard landing than gambling that his horse wouldn't crush him beneath its weight. While the horse might have been moving awkwardly, it hadn't built up much steam and Sprole was able to swing his leg up and over its back so he could jump toward a patch of ground covered in coarse grass near the base of the slope. From there, he could see Sheriff Noss charging around the other side of the rise just in time to meet the sharpshooter.

Sprole might not have broken anything on his landing, but he did end up on his back with most of the wind knocked from his lungs. He kept his eyes on the other two men while his hands rushed through the familiar motions of reloading his pistol.

"Stop where you are and toss that rifle!" Noss shouted.

The man with the rifle fired a quick shot before retreating into the sparse trees along the side of the slope. Noss wasn't about to let him get to cover and pressed his advantage by snapping his reins to catch up to him. Before the sharpshooter got very far, the sheriff was on him. Noss fired once, forcing his target to change direction, and then brought his horse around to cut him off as he exploded from the trees.

Thundering around to get in front of the fleeing man, Noss reined his horse to a stop and pointed his rifle down at him. "I said toss that gun, mister!" he roared.

The skinny man's narrow shoulders rose and fell with every labored breath. Although he must have had plenty of heat in his furnace, he did as he was told and tossed the rifle.

"That's good," Noss said while climbing down from his saddle. "On your knees."

The rifleman did that as well and even clasped his hands on top of his head before he was asked to do so.

Holding his rifle to his shoulder, Sheriff Noss glanced over to the bounty hunter and asked, "You all right?"

"Just a little bruised," Sprole replied. "Be there in a second."

Focusing on his prisoner as he walked toward him, Noss asked, "What's your name, boy?"

The sharpshooter lowered his head as if every bit of fight chose that moment to leave him.

Sprole got to his feet and approached the other two. He'd barely taken two steps when the prisoner surged into motion.

The instant Noss was close enough, the man on his knees looked up and reached out to grab the barrel of the sheriff's rifle with both hands. He twisted the rifle, causing Noss's finger to become trapped beneath the trigger guard. When both men struggled for possession of the weapon, a shot was accidentally fired that thumped into the ground several yards away from either of them. The sharpshooter got one foot beneath him and then rose to stand on both, all while he continued twisting the rifle to bend Noss's fingers and elbow in the wrong direction to drive the sheriff to his knees.

"Hold it right there!" Sprole shouted. "Put your hands up or I'll shoot!"

But the sharpshooter was already committed to his course of action. One more vicious tug was all it took to wrest the rifle from the sheriff's hands. He levered in a fresh round and fired it in Sprole's direction, forcing the bounty hunter to dive to one side. Making sure to keep the sheriff between him and Sprole, the sharpshooter ran over to the lawman's horse and jumped into the saddle so he could pound both heels against its sides. The horse kicked up a cloud of dust as it raced away from the slope to a small cluster of nearby trees.

Sprole could see another horse tethered to those trees. The two shots he fired weren't enough to knock the rider from his commandeered saddle. After that, he knew the other man was out of range. By the time Sheriff Noss had gotten his hands on his .45, he was too late to prevent his target from snapping his reins and riding away.

Sprole ran to his horse, trying to calculate how far ahead the other man had gotten thanks to his head start. Fortunately, Sprole's horse had already made its way to him so he could pull himself up and ride after the sharpshooter. Even so, the bounty hunter knew he wouldn't be able to catch his prey without a prolonged chase.

Then, like an answer to his unspoken prayers, two more horses rode in from the north to converge on the sharpshooter. One of them kept after the fleeing man, while the other broke away to approach the outcropping of rocks. "We heard shooting!" one of the deputies shouted. "Is the sheriff hurt?"

"He's fine," Sprole replied. "That's the man that fired at us! Don't let him get away!"

Once he saw an irritated wave from the sheriff, the deputy pointed his horse's nose toward the sharpshooter and snapped his reins. Sprole was gaining speed as well, and even though the other men were still a ways ahead of them, he felt a pang of hope that the three of them could catch one outlaw who had to be low on ammunition by now.

Beyond the trees near the slope, the terrain opened to a field of thick-bladed grass. The sharpshooter rode across the field, and the deputy who had kept after him was closing in fast. When the sharpshooter slowed after the younger lawman fired at him, Sprole wondered if the deputy had scored a lucky hit. Instead, the sharpshooter turned in his saddle and extended his arm to fire a pistol that had either been at his side the whole time or stashed somewhere in his saddlebags. Wherever the gun had been before, it spat a single round now, which knocked the deputy from atop his horse. The younger man fell backward amid flailing arms and legs. Sprole might not have been able to see the deputy's landing, but he knew it couldn't have been pretty.

Sprole was getting close enough to see that the fallen deputy was still moving where he'd landed. "Check on him!" he shouted to the second deputy who rode alongside him.

The young lawman didn't need to be told twice, and he veered away to circle back around and tend to his wounded partner.

Swearing under his breath, Sprole watched the outlaw pull ahead of him. No matter how many times he snapped his reins, Sprole was unable to coax more speed from his horse. When he considered tapping his heels against its sides, he felt a jab of pain from the scratch he'd been given by one of the sharpshooter's bullets. Then he recalled the same bullet had grazed the horse as well, prompting Sprole to ease back on the reins and allow the animal to slow to a walk.

Reaching down, Sprole didn't have to search for long before his hand found a warm, slick patch on the horse's coat. Sure enough, when he examined that hand he found it to be covered in blood. He reined the horse to a stop, rubbed its neck, and glared at the reward that had slipped through his fingers.

Chapter 8

Most nights at the Red Coyote Saloon were filled with bawdy laughter and music from the piano next to the small stage. Tonight, it was almost full but not quite so festive. Manny sat at the piano, letting his fingers tap out a slowly meandering tune as it came to him. The working girls who made their rounds to the gamblers seated at the card games being played were careful to steer clear of the table at the back of the room. Even Harrold the barkeep waited to be signaled before he went over to refill the glasses of the men sitting there. When he got the summons this time, he grabbed a pitcher of beer and plastered on a wide smile.

"How's Allen doing, Sheriff?" the bartender asked.

Sheriff Noss sat at the table with Sprole and the other young man who'd ridden with them earlier that day. Upon hearing the name of the deputy who'd been knocked from his saddle, he nodded and replied, "Still haven't heard much of anything."

"He's a good boy. I bet he could even be sheriff someday."

"Yeah, maybe."

"Give him my best, Sheriff." Looking at the other two men in turn, Harrold asked, "Can I get anything else for you men?"

Sprole nodded his head and shifted in his seat. "I'll take a whiskey."

"Glass or the whole bottle?"

"What do you say, Sheriff?" Sprole asked. "Want to split a bottle with me?"

The lawman's face was colder and sharper than the point of an icicle as he replied, "Watch what you drink tonight. We're not just going to let that man get away. Not after he shot my deputy. You'd best be ready to ride come sunup, because if you're not, I'll drag you along anyway."

"Just a glass, then," Sprole said. "I need something to ease the pain in this leg."

"Coming right up," the bartender said as he hurried away from the table.

Once Harrold was out of earshot, Sprole winced and rubbed the portion of his leg that had been stitched together a mere few hours ago. "I think that doctor of yours has something against me. The way he sewed me up, you might have thought he was putting together a pair of britches."

"He had more important matters to tend to," Noss said. "Like your horse, for one."

Sprole nodded at that and accepted the drink that was put in front of him by the returning barkeep. "I guess it's a good bit of luck the town doctor don't mind tending to man as well as beast. Here's to Whitewater!" he said while lifting his glass high. Upon seeing the confused expressions on the lawmen's faces, he added, "The horse, you ignorant wretches."

When the sheriff lifted his glass, the deputy did the same. All three men downed their drinks and shook the table when they set them down again.

"We should be out there right now," the deputy said. "That coward shot Allen and just ran away. We can't let something like that pass."

"And we won't," Noss assured him. "Charging out in the middle of the night won't do anyone any good. By the time first light comes along, Dave and I will be ready to go. That yellow back-shooter won't have been able to get too far ahead. Now that we know where to start looking, a real tracker will be able to hunt him down. Ain't that so?" the sheriff asked as he slapped Sprole on the back.

"Sure," the bounty hunter replied. "It might take a few days, but we'll find him."

"A few days?" the deputy groaned. "What kind of tracker are you?"

"One that knows it takes time to get the job done right. Unless you're careful, you could just as easily wind up following tracks left by any other horse that passed along the spot where you're looking while the man you're after takes off in the opposite direction. If you thought you were gonna hunt down Terrigan and his gang quick enough to be home for supper, then you really don't know much of anything, boy."

The deputy pushed away from the table and got to his feet. More than once, his unsteady movements almost ended with him hitting the floor. "Watch who you call boy!"

"Sit down before you make an ass of yourself," Noss snarled.

After a short period of deliberation, the deputy decided to sit.

Noss glared at the younger man until any semblance of a fight left the deputy's eyes. After that, he clapped him on the back and said, "I need you to keep your head on straight, since you'll be the one watching the store when I'm gone."

The deputy's eyes widened. "You mean it?" he asked.

Sprole took a drink. "You have a store?"

"I mean the town," Noss snapped. "He'll be watching over it while I'm gone. While *we're* gone, that is."

Although starry-eyed at first, the deputy quickly shook it off and asked, "I'm not going with you?"

"I've got to go, and with Allen resting up, that doesn't leave me much choice."

"There's Daniel."

"Like I said," Noss sighed. "Not much choice. You're the only one for the job, and I know you can do it. Dave here is right about this being more than a ride back out to that hill. Tracking a man ain't no easy thing. It'll take days and even after we catch up to Terrigan, it would be foolish of us to just charge in like we got an army behind us."

"You could round up some men in other towns. This territory is full of folks who got good reason to want to see Terrigan hang."

Noss gripped his glass as if he meant to shatter it in his hand. "Terrigan may come back for that fella we got locked up at Doc Chandler's. Even after we move him to a jail cell, there could still be men looking to cut him loose. One of my deputies was already shot. I ain't about to let that pass, and I sure ain't about to let them animals ride into Pueblito Verde like they own it. No, sir," he said while slamming his glass down. "I won't let one more drop of blood get spilled on account of those mad dogs."

Although the deputy was quick to agree with the sheriff, Sprole wasn't so anxious to join in. He wore an unconvincing smile as he downed the last of his whiskey and set his glass on the table.

"We ride out tomorrow, so you'd best get your sleep," Noss said to his deputy. "I'll look in on Allen before I go and will have a chat with my prisoner soon as I finish this drink."

Grudgingly, the deputy said, "I appreciate you leaving me in charge, Sheriff. I won't disappoint you."

Noss nodded. "I know." After the deputy was gone, he looked over to Sprole and asked, "What's eating you now?"

"I've been after Jack Terrigan for the better part of a year," the bounty hunter said. "There were times when I thought for certain I'd gotten him, only to have him squirm away."

"You were alone when you came to town. I take it you usually work that way."

Sprole held on to the empty glass as if he was trying desperately to collect enough whiskey inside to compose at least part of another sip as he said, "Only after one of Terrigan's men killed my old partner. They've been sloppy since they got into the Arizona Territory, but that won't last long. When Terrigan or his men fire at someone, they usually draw blood."

"They have drawn blood," Sheriff Noss said. "More than I've seen in a while."

"You don't see many gunfights in this town, do you?" Sprole chuckled.

"No, sir," Noss replied in a sober tone that was colder than the rocks in a desert night. "Why do you think that skinny fella with the rifle got away from me today?" Although he forced a tired grin onto his face, it was obvious that he wasn't in a joking mood. When he spoke again, it was in a rumble that was barely loud enough for Sprole to hear. "I've worked plenty of towns, make no mistake about it. I've handled my share of cowboys with loud mouths and quick trigger fingers, but—"

"You don't need to explain any more to me," Sprole said. "I saw what I needed to see when we were out there. What happened wasn't nothing to be ashamed of. That sharpshooter had higher ground and was waiting for trouble. He got the drop on us. It ain't pleasant, but it happens."

"He got away. That don't set well with me."

"It don't set with me either," Sprole told him. "But you're right about a couple of things. That outlaw may have gotten a head start, but he ain't going much farther tonight. Wherever he is, he's holed up until morning. Also, we know where to pick up his tracks and I can find them once we get back to them rocks. That is, if you were serious about me coming along with you."

"I said you were coming, didn't I?" Noss snapped.

"Sure, you said it. It's just that lawmen ain't usually anxious to work with a bounty hunter."

"I never said I was anxious to do it. Let's just say I

had to make the best decision as quick as I could. That's the one I made and I'll abide by it." The sheriff stood up and picked up his hat from where it had been resting beside his glass. "We're heading out at first light. If you're not saddled up and ready to go by then, I'll drag you from your bed and toss you onto your horse myself. Speaking of which, will your horse be ready to go?"

Sprole winced. "He would probably do fine if I didn't push him too hard. . . ."

"I'll arrange for a horse for you to use. Just be at them stables closest to my office when I told you to be there."

"Here's to first light," Sprole said as he raised his glass and waved for Harrold to come fill it. Almost immediately, the barkeep averted his eyes and turned back around to place the whiskey bottle back on its shelf behind the bar. "What are you doin'?" Sprole grunted.

"What I told him to do," Sheriff Noss replied. His hand was still in the air after motioning for Harrold to put the liquor bottle back.

"And why would you tell him something like that?"

"Because you've had enough. In case you're either deaf, stupid, or forgetful, we're riding at first light."

"I recall that part, but first light ain't happening for a while. In the meantime, I'll do what I please."

"You want to ride on my posse? You'll do what I say, just like any of my men. I'm off to get some sleep and suggest you do the same. There'll be time for drinking later."

"There's other saloons in this town, Sheriff. Just as I'm sure I can find a bottle of whiskey somewhere else."

Noss eased his hat back onto his head so the brim

didn't knock Sprole in the face when he leaned down and told him, "I so much as catch a whiff of liquor on your breath in the morning and I'll lock you up."

"Lock me up for what?"

"Killing two men in that hotel for a start. Defending yourself or not, I got every right to put you in a cell for a while after you send two men to their graves. And if you don't like that reasoning, I'll come up with something else. I'm the law in this town and nobody's about to argue on your behalf." Straightening up and easing his hat back into its normal spot, Noss added, "You're a smart man, Dave. Riding on this posse will be good for you. Help me bring in Jack Terrigan and the reward on his head is yours . . . minus expenses while we're on the trail, of course."

"Expenses? That's—"

"Only fair, since you'll have a much easier time getting the job done with a duly appointed lawman at your side."

After taking a moment to consider it, Sprole asked, "Will there still be a posse fee coming?"

Noss walked toward the door. "So long as you pull your weight, you'll get your fee. It isn't much for a big-time bounty hunter like yourself, but it's an honest wage."

Still holding his empty glass, Sprole waited for the sheriff to walk away before grumbling, "A wage that should offset them expenses you'll tack on." He waited a few more seconds before trying one more time to signal for a drink. Harrold shook his head as if the Grim Reaper himself had cut the bounty hunter off for the night.

Sprole repositioned his chair so he could get a better look at the stage. Every so often, one of the girls would stand up there to sing along with whatever Manny was playing on his piano. The girls had soothing voices, but not soothing enough to make up for the distinct lack of whiskey in his system. Sprole glanced at the banister along the upper portion of the saloon that ran alongside the second-floor rooms. One of the soiled doves picked him out and gave him a tired wave. Just then, Sprole didn't have the steam to climb all those stairs to get to her.

"Must be gettin' old," he grunted while pulling himself up from his chair. He walked over to the bar and knocked to get Harrold's attention. When the barkeep didn't look at him, he knocked harder.

"Not supposed to serve you no more tonight," Harrold said with the quickest of glances over his shoulder.

"How much do I owe for what you did serve me?" Sprole asked.

Still trying to look busy polishing the same beer mug he'd been working on for the last minute or two, he replied, "Nothing. Sheriff Noss settled the bill."

"Really? Well, at least he's good for somethin' other than giving me tired lectures. Guess I'll be on my way."

Harrold spun around then, wearing an anxious expression on his face. "Be sure to come back to the Coyote after you bring in that killer! The girls love to show their appreciation to peacekeepers."

"I'll just bet they do. Will I get a discounted rate?"

"Not as such, but the first beer will be on the house!"

"Sounds like a good enough reason to put my neck on the line." Sprole tipped his hat and strode toward the door. "I'll see you again when them prisoners are locked up. Keep those girls warm for me."

Outside, it was several degrees cooler than it had been when Sprole entered the Red Coyote. While the Arizona Territory could feel harsh and unforgiving during the daylight hours, they could be just as cold and desolate at night. When Sprole walked back to his hotel, he didn't have much trouble imagining he was the only living soul in the territory.

A crisp breeze rolled in, bringing with it scents of open, dusty spaces he inhaled gratefully. The touch of the wayward winds on his face was better than a splash of cold water to wash away the effects of the liquor he'd drunk. He wanted to close his eyes to savor a few steps of his walk, but the instincts he'd acquired throughout years of hunting wanted men wouldn't grant him such a dangerous indulgence. As if to reinforce those barbed fences he put up between himself and the rest of the world, a figure separated itself from the darkness.

Sprole slowed his pace a bit and allowed his swinging arm to brush his jacket aside and clear a path to his holstered .44.

The figure was moving at a brisk walk before, and could have been going in one of several different directions. Now that Sprole had focused on it, he could tell the figure was coming straight toward him.

No longer caring about appearances, Sprole placed his hand on his .44 and took a solid dueling stance with his feet planted shoulder-width apart and his body turned sideways so as to present a narrower target. Like any bounty hunter worth his salt, Sprole knew

plenty of men who wanted to see him dead. Every outlaw, no matter how cruel or heartless he was, had
friends and family. Some bounty hunters themselves
weren't much better than the men they tracked for a
living and wouldn't be above gunning down their
competition if they thought it might put them one step
closer to a hearty reward. Knowing how many killers
were slithering around in these parts and the sizeable
prices on their heads, Sprole knew the figure could
have been any number of unwelcome visitors from his
recent and distant past.

The figure drew closer, perhaps taking a moment to
size the bounty hunter up. Blood rushed through
Sprole's veins in expectation of a fight, only to freeze
there for a moment when he finally got a look at the
figure's face.

"That you, preacher?" he asked.

Having walked past a torch posted to illuminate the
corner of Third and Main streets, Paul Lester rushed
toward the bounty hunter. His hair had been tousled
by the wind, and his face was pale, leaving him looking
several years older than normal. "Where's the sheriff?"
he asked.

"He just left. Why?"

"Where did he go?"

"I don't know. Probably home. He said he wanted to
get some sleep. What's wrong?"

"It's the prisoner," Paul said. "The one being kept at
Doc Chandler's office. He's gone."

Chapter 9

Where Sprole had been hesitant to approach Paul before, he rushed at him now. "What do you mean he's gone?" he asked while grabbing the preacher by both shoulders.

Paul was quick to pull away when he told him, "Get a hold of yourself! You won't do anyone any good if you carry on that way." Leaning forward, he asked, "Is that whiskey on your breath? Have you been drinking?"

"I already got a talking-to from the sheriff and I won't stand still for another one. What's this about the prisoner being gone?"

"It's like I said," Paul replied while straightening the sleeves of his thick white cotton shirt. "He's not there. I've been sitting by his bedside for most of the day, but had to tend to some of my other duties. When I came back just now, he was gone."

"Why were you going back there at this hour?"

"I've been talking to him all day long, trying to learn anything that might help find the rest of his gang."

"Did he tell you anything?"

"Would you really like me to try and recollect everything he said?" Paul asked. "Or would you rather try to find him before he gets too far away from town?"

Sprole shifted his gaze toward the end of Third Street as if he could see all the way to Doc Chandler's office. Sniffing the air, he narrowed his eyes and said, "He's not getting far tonight. Not on foot anyways. Apart from the stable near the sheriff's office, how many other places in town are there where he could get to a horse?"

"There's a livery at the other end of Third and any number of horses kept by folks at their homes, behind the hotel, or anywhere else."

After cursing under his breath, Sprole said, "You say he was at the doc's office last you saw him?"

"That's right."

"How long ago was that?"

"No more than two hours ago," Paul said. "But the doctor's been there as well. He probably saw him sometime after I left."

"You don't know for certain?" Sprole asked.

The preacher shook his head. "I saw he was gone and just asked if the doctor had moved him. Once Doc Chandler told me he'd stepped out just before the prisoner escaped, I rushed to find the sheriff."

Sprole's mind raced a mile a minute. His heart pounded an excited rhythm against the inside of his ribs, causing every one of his senses to become sharp and hungry for any hint of his prey. "All right, this is what we're gonna do. You know where the sheriff lives?"

"Yes."

"Good," Sprole said. "Go fetch him and bring him to the doctor's office. I'll head there right now and have a look around. Unless he got a hold of a horse, that outlaw's probably holed up somewhere in town or real close."

"And what if he did get a horse?"

"Then he probably still didn't make it very far. There's not much of a moon out tonight, which means he'd have to know every inch of this terrain like the back of his hand to build up any kind of speed."

"Maybe you should—"

Sprole was already hurrying down the street. "Go on, preacher. You want to be a part of this so badly, here's how you can pull your weight. If I find a reason to leave that office, I'll let the doc know so you and the sheriff can come after me."

If Paul had anything to say to that, Sprole didn't stand still long enough to hear what it was. As he picked up speed tearing up Third Street, his eyes soaked up every hint of movement along the way. A few stray dogs lurked in the alleys, and a drunk slept against a dry goods store. Sprole slowed just long enough to make sure the drunk wasn't the man he was after and then hurried the rest of the way to Doc Chandler's office.

As he drew closer to the narrow building, he drew his .44 and moved so his boots made as little noise as possible crunching against the dry ground. His eyes darted back and forth between the office's front door, its windows, and either side of the building itself. Before stepping up to the door, he ducked into the alley beside the office and made his way to the other end.

There wasn't much to see along that shadowy corridor between the office and Chandler's neighbor. Apart from a short stack of small crates and some old newspapers rustling in the breeze, there was just a pair of large rodents scurrying toward a loose board at the base of the building next to the office. Sprole timed his steps so the sound they made blended with the scraping of the rodents' feet. Even if it wasn't enough to fully mask his approach, the sound could confuse anyone who might be listening for a hint that someone was coming down that alley.

Sprole could sense the desperation of the escaped prisoner as if it were a wisp of perfume drifting through the air. His fingers flexed around his .44 in anticipation of putting it to work. When he reached the back of the office, he looked in both directions to see if anyone was waiting there for him. Chances were slim that the prisoner would be so close, but the gunman had been laid up in a sickbed after being knocked out twice and was probably bleeding again after forcing his way out from his cuffs. Wounds like that had a tendency to stack up, making it even less likely that the fugitive had gotten very far at all.

Grinning at the thought of the prisoner lying somewhere in plain sight, Sprole dropped to one knee so he could get a better look at the ground. As he'd already pointed out to Paul, there wasn't much light and unfortunately there also weren't enough tracks in the dirt to give him a hint as to which direction the prisoner might have gone. The chase was young, however, and Sprole knew better than to get disheartened now. He circled around the building, made his way down the other alley, and pushed open the front door so he could walk inside.

Upon entering the dimly lit room, Sprole found himself at the wrong end of a shotgun.

"Drop that gun!" the shotgunner barked.

Sprole didn't even begin to panic as he lowered his .44 and inspected the floor near the front door. "It's just me, Doc. David Sprole. I'm working with the sheriff. Remember?"

Dr. Chandler angled the shotgun down just enough for him to get a better look at the man hunched in front of him. "Oh, that's right!" he said while setting the shotgun against the wall. "Sorry about that. One of the deputies left that weapon. Didn't think I'd ever pick it up, but after today's events, I've been nervous. I trust you heard about what happened?"

"The preacher told me you lost your patient. Any idea how long he's been gone?"

"Has to be less than an hour," Chandler replied. "Father Paul was here all day. He left after feeding the patient his supper and then came back to tell me he had other matters to tend to. He was here for a while and then left. I checked on the patient one more time before I had to go across the street for some supplies. I have an arrangement with the owner of that shop and he lets me—"

"How long were you gone?" Sprole interrupted. "That's all that matters now."

"Right. Of course. I couldn't have been gone for more than fifteen minutes. The patient was sound asleep and chained to his bed just as he'd been all day. Considering how much he struggled against those shackles, I know they were strong enough to hold him."

Sprole made his way toward the back of the room where the prisoner had once been. Now all that was left to mark the gunman's time there was a mess of rumpled sheets and two sets of shackles. Sprole took his time approaching the cot so he could soak up any important details that could have been left behind. "If them shackles were so strong, then how did he get away?"

The doctor stopped walking and tucked the shotgun's stock under one arm like a hunter. "I honestly don't know."

Having arrived at the cot, Sprole picked up the iron cuff that had formerly been secured around the prisoner's wrist. "This ain't busted, which means he didn't break loose from his chains. He unlocked them."

"What?" Chandler gasped as he hurried forward to get a look for himself.

"Who has a key to these?"

"The sheriff, of course, and me. I insisted on being given one in the event that I had to perform a procedure or get him away from the bed."

The suspicion in Sprole's eyes matched the tone of his voice when he looked at the doctor and asked, "Why would you have to do that?"

"What if he needed to be moved for some sort of procedure?" Chandler replied defensively. "What if there was a fire? I don't have to explain myself to you! What I do is in the best interests of my patients no matter who they are or what they might have done!"

"I ain't turning the screws on you, Doc. I'm just trying to figure out what happened. If he got a hold of a key, that's a whole different story than if someone came along to pick the lock."

"I doubt those locks could be picked," the doctor chuckled.

"Then you don't know much about my line of work. Where's your key?"

Dr. Chandler seemed supremely confident when he patted the breast pocket of his shirt, which lay beneath a plain black vest. "I kept it right here where I could be certain it was . . ." Suddenly his confidence fell away like so much dried mud. "Oh, dear lord."

"Your key's gone," Sprole sighed. "Was his hand still bleeding the last time you checked it?"

"Yes," Chandler replied as if he'd just taken a punch to the stomach. "He was always difficult and . . . pawed at me or tried to push me away."

Sprole stepped up to the doctor and tugged at the front of his vest. Once he got the scant amount of light in the room to shine on the vest at the proper angle, he could see there was smeared blood near his pocket. The few smudges on his shirt were much easier to find. "Looks like he picked your pocket, Doc."

"I'll be damned," Chandler groaned. "But . . . that could also have happened when I was working. I've done a lot of stitching today, including you and a horse!"

Turning his attention back to the cot and the floor on either side of it, Sprole asked, "What kind of condition was the prisoner in the last time you saw him? Was he bleeding badly? Was he strong enough to run?"

The doctor was clearly flustered while continuing to

pat himself down as if the missing key would somehow turn up elsewhere on his person. "What's all of
that matter now? The damage is done."

"But the hunt has just started," Sprole said with a
grin. "How far could he make it tonight in the condition he's in?"

Stopping with his hands still pressed flat against his
pockets, the doctor furrowed his brow and mulled a
few things over before replying, "All the struggling he
insisted on doing was a strain on his stitches. I tried to
redo them once, but he wouldn't have it. I just kept
changing his bandages, and to be honest, even that was
a chore, so—"

"Doc," Sprole snapped. "Was he up to speed or
not?"

"In small doses," was the doctor's response. "When
he got himself worked up, he could go for a while, but
between the loss of blood and the knocks to the head,
he wasn't in any condition to ride. Even on foot, I'd say
he'd be stumbling more often than running."

"Now, that's the sort of thing I wanted to hear,"
Sprole said. "What about the bleeding?"

"That was mostly under control. If he broke another
stitch or two, there could be some, though."

Standing in front of the bed now, Sprole dropped to
one knee and touched the floor with a fingertip. He
rubbed that finger against his thumb, and then scooted
to another spot. His eyes took on an excited sparkle as
he hurried to the window. After a quick examination of
the sill, he dabbed another spot and then held his hand
out for the doctor to see the crimson stain he'd found.
"Looks like he busted a stitch or two after all."

"Oh my," the doctor sighed. "Considering everything else he's been through, he could be passed out somewhere to bleed out even more."

Sprole slid the window open and drew his pistol before sticking his head outside. "I should be so lucky," he grunted while waving a hand outside to test the waters. It was unlikely that a man in the prisoner's situation would stay in one place for very long after catching such a lucky break and even less likely that he'd stick around to stage an ambush. The blood wasn't dried all the way, so it hadn't been too long since the man had gotten away, and if he was still outside watching that window for some reason, his nerves were most likely frayed. Even though he'd already circled the outside of the building earlier, Sprole looked out there again before climbing through the window.

"What are you doing?" the doctor asked as he rushed toward the open window.

Having already dropped to the ground beneath the window, Sprole crouched down to examine the dirt. "Considering he's still bleeding, how far would you say he could have gotten?"

"There's no way for me to know how badly his stitches have been compromised. I'd need to examine him to know for certain—"

"Take a look at your floor to see how bad he's bleedin'!" the bounty hunter snapped. "Just make a guess so I'll be able to round him up."

The doctor looked at the sill and shook his head. "If he tore through all of his stitches, I suppose the bleeding could be much worse."

"Now you're thinkin'," Sprole said as he let his eyes

adjust to the darkness so he could search for more drops.

"Most likely, he's feeling light-headed. He was unsteady on his feet before. All of this exertion would have made that worse. He was probably fairly excited when he started running."

"I'm looking for a short answer, Doc."

"He couldn't have gone far without either falling over or needing to rest. I'd say he's somewhere fairly close by."

"So he couldn't have grabbed a horse and ridden out of town?" Sprole asked.

Judging by the expression on the doctor's face, Sprole might as well have suggested the wounded man had won an election for the presidency. "Heavens no! He was barely able to remain upright the last time I saw him earlier this evening, owing to the knocks he took to the head. Being jostled on a horse—"

"Thanks," Sprole said as he walked toward a dark spatter on the ground nearby. "That'll do just fine."

The last time he'd examined the grounds outside the doctor's office, the blood drops hadn't caught his eye. Without knowing what he was looking for, the dark patterns could very well have been mud or any number of things. As Sprole bent toward the little dark spots on the ground near his feet, his senses stretched past all the impediments being heaped upon them. The darkness seemed just a little brighter. The cold didn't bite into his flesh as it had when he'd walked to the Red Coyote Saloon. Even the whiskey he'd drunk when he'd been at that place wasn't clouding his head as it had before.

He was in his element now.

A predator with the scent of fresh meat in his nostrils. The animal he was after was not only on the run, but wounded. That made the hunt even sweeter.

"Hey, Doc!" Sprole shouted.

The doctor hesitantly approached the window, wincing as if a gun battle were already under way. "Y-yes?"

"Bring me a lantern."

While all too eager to leave the window, Chandler was even more cautious when he returned and extended his hand outside. He gripped the handle of a small lantern that had previously been sitting on his desk. Sprole took it from him quickly, not wanting to move his eyes from the spot he'd found. He scowled through an angry grimace that came to him when his eyes adjusted to the light source. With the lantern in hand, he could now see the patch of ground much better.

His intense expression shifted to one of pure glee when he caught sight of the imprints that had been made in the earth. They were deep and long, like two wide grooves that had been cut by a pair of fence posts. Sprole looked to either side of them and found smaller lines to the left of the pair of wide ones. Looking back up to the window, Sprole had no trouble imagining the escaped prisoner climbing down from the window in such a rush that his feet skidded in the dirt to leave those two wide imprints. When he'd stumbled, the wounded man had reached out with one hand to push himself up again, using desperate fingers that carved out those smaller scrapes.

With a bit more sniffing around, Sprole found an im-

print that was almost as wide as and much shorter than
the skidding tracks closest to the window. There was
one deep track that pointed him to another. The next
one was deeper toward the front and more rounded.
Sprole grinned, picturing the escaping prisoner stopping there and twisting back and forth to try and decide where he wanted to go next. It would take a bit
longer in the dark, but Sprole went through the motions of finding the next imprints.

There was no telling what could happen between
now and daybreak. Even if the doctor was right and the
prisoner wasn't about to go much of anywhere right
away, high winds could tear through town or a quick
spot of rain could make tracking someone very difficult. There was no reason for the prisoner to get even
more of a head start than what he'd already gotten.

Bounty hunters' lives weren't easy. Some men condemned them for being nothing more than bloodthirsty
gun hands, while others tried to shoot them on sight.
Lawmen didn't care for them much, and the lawless
benefited only when a man like Sprole was six feet under. Whiskey provided some bit of comfort, and sharing company with the occasional woman with low
standards provided a bit more. Like any other predator
on God's green earth, a bounty hunter only found true
joy when he was hot on the heels of someone doing
their level best to get away from him. It was what David Sprole was born to do.

He inched forward with lantern in one hand and .44
in the other. Part of his attention was focused on the
ground in front of him, and the rest was committed to
looking for any hint that the prisoner might try to get

the jump on him. A quiet breeze stirred as Sprole picked out another set of tracks. The imprints were shallower than the previous ones, and the next set were even shallower than those. The more tracks Sprole found, the farther apart they became.

The fugitive had decided where he was going and had started running to get there.

"Ready or not," Sprole muttered through a wicked smile, "here I come."

Chapter 10

After finding Sprole and breaking the news to him about the missing prisoner, Paul went straight to the sheriff's house. Noss lived on the opposite end of town from his office in a little cabin that, as near as Paul could tell, had been purposely placed to be as far away from town matters while still being within the boundaries of Pueblito Verde. It was a sturdy structure built by every one of the sheriff's family members who had resided in it. Now the sheriff was the only one who called the cabin home. No light shone from any of the windows. No smoke rose from the chimney. When Paul knocked on the door, the sound of his knuckles against the door echoed within.

After a few seconds, Paul knocked again. He waited and was about to try a third time when a haggard voice roared from deep inside the cabin like a bear growling from the depths of its cave.

"Who the hell is it?"

"It's Paul Lester."

As Paul stood on that narrow porch with his hands clasped in front of him and his head bowed, he was a picture of patience. With a bit of effort, he could hear the heavy shuffle of feet on the other side of the door, followed by grunting breaths as the door was pulled open.

Sheriff Noss didn't look as if he'd just gotten home. In fact, he looked as if he'd been asleep for about three days before answering the door and blearily saying, "Sorry about the turn of phrase, Father."

"Nothing I haven't heard before," Paul said. "I take it nobody else has come for you yet?"

"Why?" he asked as if he already knew what was coming. "What happened?"

"That prisoner escaped."

"Which one?"

Paul scowled and drew a breath. That single deep inhale was enough for him to detect the scent of liquor wafting from the lawman. "The prisoner that was taken from the hotel."

"You mean the one whose hand you blew off before knocking him out?"

"Yes. That's the one."

"I thought he was strapped down and barely able to move," Noss said.

"He's a desperate man, Sheriff. And now he's loose."

"Aw, for Chr . . ." Noss paused and turned around on the balls of his feet, leaving the door open. "Might as well come in while I throw on some clothes."

Paul stepped inside and shut the door behind him. "Where are your deputies?" he asked.

"If you're looking for them around here, you're in the wrong place. And if you ain't seen 'em yet after that prisoner got away, they must be in the wrong place too."

Inside, the cabin was only slightly more inviting than it was on the outside. It contained a heavy oak rocker, a small square table with a few dirty plates on it, and a little stove in a far corner. A food pantry stood beside the stove, along with a rack where two pots and one pan hung from hooks. The air smelled of burned coffee and blackened toast. Rather than examine the kitchen any further, Paul walked over to a window next to the rocker that rested beside a short bookshelf. The sheriff stomped into one of two bedrooms. The second door next to his was not only shut tight but dusty and encrusted with cobwebs.

"It's been a while since I've paid you a visit," Paul said. "Maybe a bit too long."

"Nah," Noss said from the next room while pulling on a clean shirt.

"If you'd like, I could have a word with one of the women in the congregation. Perhaps she could come by and help you clean the place."

"Thanks, but no."

Paul stood at the window, staring out at a row of simple wooden crosses planted several yards from the side of the cabin facing away from town. The markers had a clear view of a sprawling patch of land that seemed to stretch all the way out to the farthest reaches of creation. Not only did those crosses mark the darkest time in the lawman's life, but the day they'd been driven into the ground was the last time Sheriff Noss had set foot in Paul's church.

"You don't seem overly concerned about this prisoner escaping," Paul mused, watching the lawman's reflection since Noss didn't turn around to look at him.

"And you seem overly concerned with how clean my house is. You came here alone, so I'm guessing someone is already out trying to find that one-handed gunman."

"Yes. Dave Sprole went to have a look."

"Just what I thought," Noss grunted. "I need a couple new deputies. Them boys would rather let that prisoner run away than miss a meal or two while trying to bring him back."

"It's the middle of the night," Paul pointed out. "I doubt anyone will be going very far until morning."

"Best let me be the judge of that." Dressed in the clothes he'd had on at the saloon, apart from the addition of a clean shirt, Noss buckled his gun belt around his waist and reached for the hat hanging on the hook beside the front door. "Who was the last one to see that man with the shot-up hand?"

"That would be me and Doc Chandler."

"Tell me what happened as best you can while we go see the doc."

The two men strode out of the cabin. Even though the sheriff's line of sight would naturally have swept over the crosses beside the cabin as he turned toward Third Street, Paul noticed the lawman's eyes dip downward. Only after he was several paces past the markers did he break into a stride toward Doc Chandler's office. "How long has it been since you've been to church?" Paul asked.

Without hesitation, the lawman replied, "Sixteen months or so."

"Ever since you lost Martha and the boys."

"That's right. Now tell me what happened with that prisoner."

"Facing up to what happened to them might help you make peace with it, you know."

Sheriff Noss stopped as if he'd hit an unseen wall and wheeled around to face him. "I have to face up to what happened every day I wake up and they don't. Have you lost an entire family?"

"I've lost plenty. Most every man has at some time or another."

"But unless you can tell me you know what it's like to be content and surrounded by them that you love one day and digging their graves the next, don't try to act like you understand."

Paul reached out for him while saying, "A lot of time has passed and—"

Noss slapped away Paul's hand as if someone were trying to take the gun from his holster. "It ain't a wound that just heals over!" he snapped. "I'm moving along and that's all you need to know on the subject."

"It's my job to try and ease suffering when I can."

"And it's *my* job to keep the peace in this godforsaken little patch of dirt, so just tell me what you know about that prisoner escaping or stand aside so I can talk to someone who's more cooperative."

For a moment, Paul considered pressing on with his previous concerns. Once he reminded himself of how little could be accomplished when two men are dead set on locking horns instead of speaking earnestly, he nodded and let the matter rest. As he and the sheriff resumed their walk toward Doc Chandler's office, Paul told the lawman everything he'd told Dave Sprole. When he was done, the doctor's office was in sight and the sheriff looked as if he'd walked ten miles to get there.

"Is that all you got to say?" Noss asked before climbing the two steps leading from the street to the doctor's front door.

"On this matter . . . yes."

"Good. It's late, so you can go back to bed or tend to whatever business you tend to at night."

"I'd like to stay, if that's all right."

Noss shook his head and stomped up the stairs. "Whatever I say probably won't make a lick of difference. Just keep out of my way."

The hand that Noss extended toward the doctor's door went immediately to the gun at his hip when he heard the sound of quick footsteps crunching against the gravel. Both he and Paul turned toward the sound to find Sprole circling around the building to meet them up front. The bounty hunter raised his hands while wearing an excited grin.

"You lookin' to get yourself shot?" the sheriff groused. "Sneaking up on me like that's a real good way to go about it."

"And if you're looking for the prisoner that escaped from here when you or your men were supposed to be watching him," Sprole said, "then following me is a real good way to go about it!"

"What are you doing out here? This is town law business."

"Then the town's lawmen should have been here to deal with it," Sprole shot back. "As it turned out, I'm here and it's my business to track down men that don't wanna be found."

"Since you were deputized to be part of my posse, I suppose that's all well and good. What have you found?"

Some of Sprole's grin faded when he said, "That posse was disbanded. I'm not taking orders from you or anybody else."

"Fine. Just tell me what put that sloppy grin on your face."

Paul could tell the bounty hunter still had his nose bent out of shape, so he stepped in before that could be expressed any further. "I met up with Dave when I was on my way to get you, Sheriff," he said while putting himself between the two men. "He's had a bit of time to look at what was left behind after the prisoner got away."

"Did he, now?" Shifting an angry glare at Paul, Noss added, "And I can only assume that you spoke to this bounty hunter first because you also figured he was duly deputized to deal with such matters?"

"I figured he was qualified to track the prisoner down before he got too far," Paul said. "And then I went straight to you. Now that we're *all* here, why don't we tend to the business at hand instead of bickering amongst ourselves?"

Jabbing a finger against Paul's chest, Noss said, "Go home, Father. Now."

Much to Paul's surprise, Sprole walked right up to the lawman and shoved him back while saying, "Leave him be. This preacher's been doing your job better than you or your men so far."

It was a surprise, albeit not a pleasant one. Paul started to reassert himself, but was kept back by both of them.

"Don't proceed to tell me how to do my job," Noss growled.

Sprole lifted his chin so he could look down his nose at the sheriff when he replied, "Seeing as how you seem to have an aversion to getting off your lazy rump and lifting a finger to do anything around here, perhaps someone else *should* tell you how to do your job! One of your deputies was hurt when we were ambushed. Wouldn't it have made sense to leave him in there with the prisoner instead of letting him go back to his own bed for the night after the doctor patched him up?"

"How about I wound you so *you* can stay in the doc's office for a while?"

"Now, hold on," Paul said. "Both of you! It's been a long day and we're all working with frayed nerves."

"Keep out of this, Father!" Noss barked.

Just then three of the sheriff's younger deputies hurried over to the small group that had gathered in front of the doctor's office. To add to the commotion, Doc Chandler himself stepped from his office to see what was going on.

"What happened here?" one of the deputies asked at what had to be the worst possible time for that question.

"You!" Noss said to the deputy. "Get inside and have a look at what that prisoner left behind!"

The assistant lawmen all stood and blinked at the doctor's office as if they expected to see something awe-inspiring appear on the walls. "Left behind?" one of them asked. "Isn't he still tied to his bed?"

The sheriff balled up his fist and strained to keep himself from using it.

Meanwhile, Sprole was straining to keep his smirk from turning into outright laughter.

In a voice that came awfully close to being a hiss, Noss said, "Yes, the prisoner got away. I want you boys to spread out and search this town from top to bottom to find him. Look for anyone that might be missing a horse. Look for any broken windows that might show where he could have ducked in to hide. Look for anything at all that might let you know where he got to."

"Probably don't have to worry about the horse just yet," Sprole said.

Glancing sideways at the bounty hunter, Noss said, "You keep out of this."

Once again, Sprole raised his hands in mock surrender.

"And *you*," Noss said as he shifted back to his deputies, "start searching every inch of this town until you either find the man you were supposed to be guarding or find some hint of where he might have gone."

The deputy who had done the talking thus far sputtered, "But I—I mean, we all were—"

"No!" Noss snapped. "I won't hear any excuses! Just do what you're told and find that prisoner. He's dangerous and I won't have him running loose in my town. You hear me?"

Rather than say another word, the deputies all nodded. Sprole leaned over to one of them and said, "You might want to start inside the doc's office. Looks to me like your prisoner skinned out the window and then headed back into town. If you want, I can show you the tracks."

"Ain't it a bit dark to be looking for tracks?" the deputy asked.

"You're right," Sprole said. "Best just go about it the

way you normally do." Even though he kept any other smart comment he might have added to himself, the sheriff looked as if he knew exactly what was running through the bounty hunter's mind. At the moment, however, Noss was more perturbed at his own men than at Sprole.

"Why don't I show you what Mr. Sprole has discovered?" Dr. Chandler offered.

Although it pained him to do so, the sheriff replied, "That would be a good idea."

As one deputy followed the doctor inside, the other two started walking toward Third Street. One of them said, "We'll start searching the rest of the town."

"Good idea," Sheriff Noss said through gritted teeth.

The two younger lawmen muttered to each other while hastily putting some distance between themselves and Noss.

"Real good boys you got working for you there, Sheriff," Sprole said.

This time, it was Paul who stepped up to the bounty hunter and hissed, "Unless you've got something helpful to say, keep your remarks to yourself."

"Stay out of this, Father," Noss said.

Sprole nodded and reached out to place a hand on Paul's chest so he could push him aside as if he were opening a door. "He's right, preacher. It's probably best for you to keep your distance."

"And why's that?" Noss asked. "Are you planning to do something stupid? You planning to show everyone what a bad man you are by taking a stand against me?"

"I sure am thinking about it right now," Sprole told him.

In what was already becoming a tiresome habit, Paul moved forward to get between the other two. This time, before he could try to negotiate some sort of peace, he was shoved back with even more force than before. His response was pure instinct when he knocked aside the bounty hunter's hand.

Sprole chuckled in much the same way as if a child tried to lay down the law of the land. "You don't know what you're doing, mister. Just go home and polish your Bibles."

"No. I have something I want to say."

"Save it for Sunday," Sprole grunted. "We got real business to discuss." With that, the bounty hunter pushed Paul aside so he could strut directly up to within an inch of Sheriff Noss's face. Before he could take his stand, Sprole was spun around by Paul to face him one more time. When Sprole grabbed the front of Paul's shirt, his hands were swiftly knocked aside. When Sprole started to speak, a fist cracked against his jaw so quickly that he didn't even see it coming.

The punch didn't do any real damage, but it stunned both Noss and Sprole into silence.

"Good," Paul said as he rubbed his knuckles. "Now that I have your attention, I'd like to politely ask you two to refrain from talking to me like I'm a child. I am not a child and I do *not* appreciate being pushed around like some sort of dog."

Although anger was showing in his eyes, Sprole took a breath and forced it back. "All right," he said with a nod. "You made your point."

Looking over to Noss, Paul said, "This hasn't been an easy night . . . for any of us. There's work that still needs to be done, and the way I see it, we're the ones best suited for the task."

"Wouldn't be so much work if them deputies weren't such an incompetent bunch of . . ." Seeing the way Paul glared at him, Sprole stopped himself in midsentence and closed his mouth.

"There is work to be done," Noss said in a tired voice. "I'm just trying to do it. No offense meant, but chasing after an escaped prisoner ain't exactly your concern, Father."

All Paul had to do was raise an eyebrow to get one of the men chuckling.

Sprole shook his head as he laughed and propped his hands on his hips. Suddenly he looked as if the entire day's events had caught up to him.

"What's so funny?" Sheriff Noss asked.

"Didn't the padre here come to you about something involving the man who sent your escaped prisoner into town in the first place?"

"You mean Jack Terrigan? What does . . ." Noss closed his eyes and clenched his jaw shut so tightly that the muscles in his face flexed beneath his cheeks. "I told you before, Father, and I'll tell you again. You ain't about to come along with me or anyone else who goes after that killer. I don't care whether you knew him or not. It ain't your place and you'd only be slowing us down."

"I can ride well enough to keep up with anyone," Paul replied.

"We already looked for the rest of that gang and only got ambushed for our troubles. The only person who knew anything to help us look in the right spot for

Terrigan or who might even know if Terrigan is still in the territory just climbed out Doc Chandler's window!"

"He's still in town," Sprole said. "I'd stake my life on it."

The sheriff sighed. "Good. Then we'll find him."

"I've seen men lose hope," Paul said. "I've seen plenty of men who thought they had nothing to live for. I've also seen plenty of men resign themselves to their fate, no matter how bad it may have been, simply because they figured they didn't have anything better lined up for them."

Stomping toward the open door leading into the office, Noss grunted, "What's that got to do with anything?"

Paul followed closely behind with Sprole bringing up the rear. "That man," Paul said as he pointed toward the bed that was once occupied by the prisoner, "hasn't resigned himself to anything. He still has hope that he can escape his punishment, which means he's got some sort of plan of what he aims to do or where he aims to go next."

"Could be he's just desperate to get away from here," Noss said as he approached the bed with the shackles still attached to its frame. "Ever think of that?"

"Yes," Paul replied patiently. "But if the three who shot up that hotel came into town under Terrigan's orders, the rest of his gang must be camped nearby. It only makes sense."

"That it does," Sprole said.

"And you said yourself, Sheriff, that you could find

those others if you could only narrow down the possibilities for a search."

"I know what I said," Noss snapped. "But our best bet in finding that outlaw camp was the man who slipped away from here when he was not only chained to his bed but supposed to be under *some*body's watchful eye." Before anyone could say what was on their minds, the lawman added, "And I *do* realize my eyes were some of those that should have been doing the watching."

Paul's voice lost all the edge it had had a few moments ago. "Whatever mistakes were made are in the past. All that's left is what we're supposed to do about it now."

"He's got a point there," Sprole agreed.

Having gotten to the bed, Noss examined the empty shackles and immediately found the blood trail on the floor. Glancing toward the bounty hunter, he said, "I've had about enough from you."

Paul made certain to give the sheriff room to maneuver. From that minimum safe distance, he said, "It could be a blessing in disguise that this man escaped."

"I'd like to hear how you arrived at that," Noss grumbled.

"Because there's a man here who can track him."

When Noss forced himself to look over at Sprole again, the bounty hunter nodded and told him, "I already found enough to give me a good start. Soon as I get some light to go by, I should be able to figure out where he went. Since he's wounded, catching up to him shouldn't be too difficult."

"I'm saying perhaps you shouldn't catch up to him," Paul added. "At least, not right away."

Straightening up, the sheriff scraped the side of one finger along the lower portion of his rounded face. "If there's a camp hidden somewhere nearby, he could lead us straight to it."

Sprole grinned as if he were about to lick his chops. "Even if he found the strength and the means to get moving tonight, I shouldn't have any trouble picking up his trail. That trail could lead us to Jack Terrigan himself."

"All right, then," Noss said. "I'll bring Dave along to track our escaped prisoner. Did you think I wasn't about to do that anyhow?"

"I know you intend to do whatever you can, Sheriff," Paul said evenly. "I'm just asking that you do so in the proper frame of mind. Holding on to anger won't help you. We all need to work together to find these dangerous men and make sure they are dealt with."

Noss approached Paul as if he were on the lookout for another quick right cross. "There you go with saying *we* all the time. You truly think *we* are going after these outlaws?"

"Yes, sir, I do."

"And why might that be?"

"Because I can help you," Paul told him.

"Apart from blessing our meals around the cooking fire, how do you intend to help us?"

"In the event that they aren't still in a camp somewhere or Terrigan isn't with them after all, you'll have to figure out where to go from there. I might know where Jack Terrigan is headed and what that gang may be doing next."

Once again, both other men were silent for a moment. The sheriff let out a short, nervous laugh before asking, "How would you know something like that?"

"Because," Paul replied, "I heard the prisoner's confession."

Grudgingly, Noss nodded his head. "Meet me at sunup. Be ready to ride and if you get in my way, you'll need whatever grace the good Lord can spare because I won't have any for you."

Chapter 11

The sun was just making its presence known by sending a few streaks of purple into an otherwise inky blue sky as Paul and Sheriff Noss rode out of Pueblito Verde. Neither man had gotten much sleep the night before, which didn't deter them from getting such an early start. Paul rode a gray mare that had spent almost as much time in a stall as it had hitched to the cart that he sometimes used to bring supplies to his church or travel to neighboring towns for the occasional funeral or wedding. The horse seemed more anxious than any of the others to be out and about at that particular moment.

Sheriff Noss sat atop his white, spotted gelding. Both he and the horse hung their heads low and moved as if they were about to fall over. "You're a real piece of work, you know that?"

Paul looked over to the lawman and asked, "What do you mean?"

"If I didn't know any better, I'd say you were full of beans where this whole confession thing is concerned."

"Why do you think that?"

"Because . . . I didn't even think you heard confessions. That is, unless you built some confessionals into your church since the last time I was there."

"It's been a long time since you came to church," Paul pointed out. "Lots of things have happened since then."

The lawman fixed a stern gaze onto him before flicking his reins to coax a bit more speed from his horse.

"Since you brought it up," Paul said, "I didn't have any confessionals built. That's not exactly a part of our church. I believe that practice is something done by other faiths."

"I know. Martha used to talk about confessing when she was a girl. Her side of the family was Roman Catholic. Still is, I suppose."

"Perhaps you could visit them sometime. Might do you some good. It might even do them some good to see you after Martha's untimely passing."

A familiar shadow crept across the lawman's face. It was the same shadow that came whenever he spoke the name of his departed wife. It became even darker if he thought about his two departed children. Before that darkness claimed him, Noss looked over to Paul and said, "If you're trying to distract me, it won't work."

"Distract you from what?"

"From the fact that you're only along on this ride on account of some confession you heard even though you just told me that you don't take confessions."

"Not as a general rule," Paul corrected. "That doesn't mean I won't listen if one is offered. You see, in some faiths, confessions are a required practice. In others, they're simply encouraged. For all faiths, however, confession is always good to unburden a troubled soul."

"There you go again," Noss grunted. "More fast talk and distraction. Sometimes it seems like you use more smoke and mirrors than a magician. I must've been overly tired or just plain loco to let you talk me into letting you come along on this hunt. Come to think of it, since we ain't that far along, it's probably best if you turn around right now and go home."

"I wasn't lying to you about what I was told the other night, Sheriff," Paul said gravely. "I may not have brought up the notion of confessing to that prisoner, but I sat at his bedside so I could be there if I was needed. Eventually he needed to get some things off his chest and he decided he wanted to tell them to me."

"Probably because he figured he could trust a preacher not to go off and flap his gums to the law. Guess he was wrong about that."

"You're tired and bitter," Paul said. "You've been that way ever since you lost Martha and the boys. Lashing out at me or anyone else won't ease your suffering." After a few silent moments, Paul shifted in his saddle. "Of course, I could see why you'd be suspicious. Just so you know, I intended to keep what I was told to myself. He is a dangerous man, though, and when he escaped, I knew he intended to harm others as soon as he was reunited with the rest of that gang. That's why I mentioned it at all."

"So just tell me what was said so I can find that gang and put them all behind bars," Noss said.

"That wasn't the deal and you know it."

"Ah, that's right," Noss mused. "You don't take con-

fessions regularly, but you do go on crusades. Interesting faith you got there, Padre."

"I asked to come along with you before and you
would have none of it. I asked again when you decided
to retrieve this prisoner and you still wouldn't have it.
And since you are so fond of pointing out the inconsis-
tencies of what I do, why is it that you decided to ride
out after this man when you normally don't like ven-
turing out of your jurisdiction?"

"The law's the law," Noss replied. "That man was
my responsibility and I won't just sit back to let someone else deal with him."

"Which is exactly why I wanted to come along. I can
help not only him, but Jack Terrigan as well. And if I
help him, I can keep other folks from being hurt by him
or his men."

Continuing as if he hadn't even heard Paul's last few
sentences, Noss said, "And there's also the matter of a
bunch of armed cowboys riding into my town and
shooting it up without a care in the world. If I let that
pass, I might as well hang a sign outside Pueblito Verde
that welcomes that sort of behavior."

"You could have asked for help."

"I did. My deputies are watching the town and
Dave's riding ahead looking to where that fugitive has
gone."

"No," Paul said, "I mean help from another lawman.
It seemed wise to leave your deputies behind to take
over your duties while you're away. The lot of them
should be able to keep things in line for as long as we're
gone. But you could have sent word to another town.
There's always that marshal in—"

"I already told you," Noss cut in. "This is my mess and I'll clean it up."

Paul looked over at him and nodded. "It's good to see you taking pride in something again."

"What's that supposed to mean?"

"You haven't been the same . . . for some time now."

The lawman chuckled and watched a small cloud of dust being kicked up by Sprole's horse in the flat stretch of terrain alongside the trail. Since there wasn't much else out that way apart from a whole bunch of scrub and jackrabbits, the horse stirring up that dust couldn't exactly hide. It was getting closer now, so he watched to make sure the rider didn't have any trouble getting back to the trail. "I haven't been the same and you've never changed," he said.

"I believe I've changed a lot since I arrived," Paul said in his own defense.

"You never could just come flat out and say something. Always beating around the bush, holding out until somebody deciphers whatever clue or hint you decide to drop for them. I suppose that little habit could just come with the collar, eh?"

For a good portion of the last day or two, Sheriff Noss had done a lot of muttering to himself and shaking his head. Now it was Paul's turn and he kept himself busy that way until Dave Sprole rode up close enough to be heard without shouting.

"Looks like I was right," Sprole said. "After that prisoner stole a horse from them folks on the outskirts of town this morning, he headed this way."

"Was he still bleeding?" Noss asked.

"There's plenty more ways to track a man," Sprole

replied. "Especially if we know where to start. Between me and the preacher, we've been able to narrow it down even further. It ain't a quick process, but I'd say the man we're after only got a few hours' jump on us. Good thing we knew he was headed south."

With that, both of the other men looked over to Paul.

"Yes," the preacher said without flinching. "It is good that we knew which direction he was headed."

"*We* didn't know, Father," Noss said. "*You* did. And it's all because of that confession you refuse to tell us about."

"If I told you everything, you wouldn't have let me come along."

"You're already along," Noss pointed out. "Might as well spill the beans on the rest."

Paul shook his head. "I know you well enough to know you wouldn't hesitate in the slightest before sending me back to town as soon as it suited you."

"Then go over what you *would* like to share."

"Yeah," Sprole said as he removed his hat and used the back of his hand to wipe some of the sweat that had been beading on his brow. "Now's a good time for that, seeing as how the tracks get harder to follow less than a quarter mile off this trail."

"The first thing he told me," Paul said as if reciting the words from memory, "was that he needed to get into the desert. I think he was delirious when he started saying that, but I could tell he believed it."

"Makes sense," Noss said with a nod. "Plenty of outlaws take to the desert when they need to lie low for a while."

"He told me he'd meet up with the rest of the gang a day's ride south from Pueblito Verde."

"That's what you told us before," Noss said.

"Then why make me say it again?"

"Because we need more if we're gonna get the jump on these men! The drips you fed us before were enough to get us on the scent, but letting us ride much farther without any more help than that won't do us much good. At the least, it'll take away any advantage we might have had, and at the worst, it'll cause us to ride into another ambush. This time, we may not ride away from it without getting a whole lot of holes blasted into our hides."

Paul looked over to the bounty hunter, who'd been a surprisingly good ally the previous night. He knew it wasn't going to be an easy row to hoe, but after letting the others know about the confession he'd heard, Paul had been raked over the coals for hours on end. It had been a tedious battle of wills and words, ending with an uneasy stalemate. Paul knew just enough to make his presence valuable, and with the information he'd promised to them, the other two had agreed to let him ride along.

It seemed Sheriff Noss had limitless strength when it came to refusing Paul's request. Sprole had stuck by Paul's side, however, coming up with a few good reasons why the preacher should be allowed to join them. His position was that, so long as Paul's information panned out, they could gain an advantage that would allow a smaller group of men to bring in what was left of Terrigan's gang easier than if a larger posse attempted the same task. The bounty hunter had been after the outlaws for long enough to know that Terrigan never traveled with more than half a dozen other men at any given time. Sprole had captured one member of the gang a short time before arriving in Pueblito Verde and had killed two of them at the hotel shootout. Since Terrigan hadn't been given much time to catch his breath and recruit other gang members, that only left one or two still traveling with him and the fellow with the wounded hand who had escaped from Doc Chandler's office.

When Paul looked to him for support now, the bounty hunter said, "We can sure use this fugitive as a quick way to find them others, but it would make things easier if we could gain some ground. Otherwise, there's always the chance that he could meet up with Terrigan and leave us in the dust before we get a chance to have a word with them face-to-face."

"You told us you just needed to know what direction he was headed after leaving town."

Sheriff Noss let out an exasperated breath. "I must have rocks in my head to have gone along with any of this. I've thrown in with a silver-tongued preacher and a bounty hunter who can't even track a man who leaves a trail of blood behind him."

"I already told you plenty of times," Sprole said while pointing at the lawman as if he meant to stab a hole through his shoulder. "That blood trail led me back into town, and after that it was gone. Besides, it ain't like you can track a man in town the same way you track him out here. Anyone who's hunted down any fugitives would know that much."

"East Raynor," Paul said.

Both of the other men stopped in midtirade so they could point their eyes in his direction. "What was that?" Sprole asked.

"I said East Raynor. That's where Wes said he was going."

"Who's Wes?"

"The man with the wounded hand," Paul replied. "The escaped prisoner."

"How'd you learn his name? Did he confess that too?"

As the riders had been bickering, the animals beneath them had drifted to a stop. Paul flicked his reins to get his horse moving again. "No. I asked his name and he told me. Perhaps that's one of the reasons he thought I'd listen to anything else he had to say."

"Right," the sheriff scoffed. "I reckon he was just lonely."

Sprole wore a smirk similar to the sheriff's as he said, "That's why plenty of gunmen kill folks. They just want someone to care about them."

"It's not your business to be there to soothe anyone else's suffering," Paul said. "It's mine. I was there at that bedside while you men were out doing your jobs. How about you trust that I did my job?"

Noss came alongside Paul's gray mare and said, "Pardon me for thinking so, but even you gotta see why we're frustrated. You're holding out on information that we need. Out here, where there ain't a thing standing between us and a bunch of outlaws looking to do us in, one little mistake can be the death of us. And believe me when I tell you that Jack Terrigan and the company he keeps won't give two specks of dirt about how good your intentions are. They'll kill you, just like they'll kill me and Dave."

"I know. That's why I'm telling you about East Raynor."

"I've heard of a place called Raynor," Sprole said. "It's a little mining town that was half deserted about six months ago. I'd be surprised if there was anything worth stealing out there."

"I heard about Raynor too," Noss added. "And it ain't deserted. I rode down that way in the spring to lend a hand with some claim jumpers that were making life miserable for the marshal living there. That town's built itself up again in recent days. From what I recall, the east part of town has always been the roughest."

"Rough enough to attract the likes of Jack Terrigan?" Sprole asked.

"If Father Paul swears that's what he was told, then I believe him." When the lawman looked over, it was clearly a chance for Paul to make a confession of his own if he needed to.

"He told me he had to get to East Raynor," Paul said. "That's all he said on the matter."

"What about other matters?" Sprole asked.

Paul's lips formed a tight line across his face. The sun had been blazing down on them all day long, but it seemed especially hot now. "He . . . also said the rest of the gang might be camped about a day's ride outside Pueblito Verde."

"Right," Sprole said. "They're headed for the desert. That's what you said before."

"Go on, Father," Noss urged. "We all came this far. I ain't about to make you turn back now."

"You swear?"

"I swear."

"He's only expecting to meet one or two others," Paul said. "Terrigan and the others should already be in Raynor, scouting out what they intend to steal next."

"And what might that be?" Noss asked in what was clearly a strained tone.

"He didn't say," Paul admitted. "All he told me was that the job was going to be rough and he expected it to get bloody. That's what he wanted to confess to me. That . . . as well as some other thing he did in his past that probably has no bearing on what we're doing now. I hope that helps you."

Reluctantly, Noss looked over to Sprole.

The bounty hunter scratched his chin and stared out at the rough stretch of ground he'd covered to get back to the trail a few minutes ago. "It helps to know where we're headed. That is, if they'll even go to Raynor once they know one of their gang already spilled his guts to a preacher."

"Preachers are supposed to be the best kind of counsel a man can keep," Sheriff Noss said. "No offense, Father, but you coming to us with this confession you heard ain't exactly how men of the cloth are supposed to operate."

"No offense taken," Paul replied. "I've always been more apt to choose my path according to how good it feels to walk it instead of following all the signs along the way."

The lawman's thoughts raced within his head, causing him to stare at the open terrain in front of him as if he was examining equations scrawled on a school-teacher's board. "If Terrigan is already at Raynor or at least on his way there, the rest of the gang will want to meet up with him there. Even if they decide against whatever job they got lined up, they won't want to leave Terrigan swinging in the wind waiting for them. What else did you hear at that bedside, Father? And I don't mean confession. I want to know about that man's injury."

Sprole was quick to answer that one. "It isn't enough to hold him back. I spoke to the doctor about it myself. He told me wounds like his will probably make him light-headed or sick to his stomach after a short while of riding."

"Which means he'll probably want to get to his camp sooner rather than later," Noss said. "Do you think he knows he's being followed?"

"I've found enough tracks to point me in the right direction," Sprole said. "But it's been slow going. Even if he is light-headed, he's still getting ahead of us. Since we're talking right now, he's getting even farther away."

While the bounty hunter was growing impatient with every second that passed, Noss settled into his saddle a little easier. "So, strictly speaking, my fugitive ain't exactly being followed yet. He probably doesn't even know there's anyone after him. What would you do from here, Dave?"

Without needing much time to think about his an-swer, Sprole said, "Since the man we're after has gone off the trail, it makes things a bit easier in some respects and a bit harder in others. Easier because any tracks I find will most likely come from him and harder because I'll have to look a bit harder to find them tracks."

"It's pretty open country that way," Noss said as he looked in the direction from which Sprole had come. "We may even catch sight of him if we find some high ground."

"And when night comes along, if we're anywhere close to him and them others, we should be able to spot any campfires they make from miles away."

"Good!" Paul said joyfully. "Everything seems to be working out after all!"

Both men stared back at him, and this time, neither seemed to be enthusiastic.

As the day wore on, Paul wasn't pressed for more information about the confession he'd heard. The few times the subject was broached, it was treated as a delicate matter. Paul knew he would be skating on thin ice by withholding information the way he had, but simply couldn't think of a better way to make sure he rode along with the other two to confront Jack Terrigan. It was a necessary evil, which didn't make it feel any better at the pit of Paul's stomach.

Although the terrain was mostly flat, the lack of a trail made Paul feel disoriented. It wasn't the first time he'd strayed from the beaten path, and he'd never much cared for it. Having a road laid out for you always made it easier to mosey along at a decent pace. So long as he knew the trail beneath his horse's hooves led to a particular place, a man could relax and just follow it to where he needed to go. There were plenty of advantages to blazing a trail of his own, but expediency wasn't one of them.

Sheriff Noss took it upon himself to watch for any hints of the fugitive's tracks while keeping an eye on Sprole using field glasses he'd brought along with him. The bounty hunter had sped out to the farthest point he'd scouted so he could resume following the tracks he'd discovered, leaving the lawman to find whatever he could on his own. Apart from the rare imprint left in a patch of clay or dirt, Noss examined scrapes on bare rock, horse droppings, and overturned stones. Those things were few and far between, but seemed to provide the lawman with enough to convince him he was headed in the right direction. Paul could only imagine what Sprole was doing farther ahead.

The preacher's day consisted of much more menial tasks. The only weapons he owned were a hunting rifle and an old Colt revolver, both of which he'd brought along with him for this journey. He put the rifle to use after spotting a brace of jackrabbits scurrying across open land late that afternoon. He brought one of them down along with a pheasant for supper that evening. The pistol proved to be useful when a snake had slithered up to him while he'd been loading the rifle at a watering hole. As much as Sheriff Noss encouraged him to keep the snake for its meat, Paul wouldn't have it.

"We are hunters by nature," Paul had explained. "Not savages."

"Even a savage would make use out of somethin' he killed," Noss said while refilling his canteen from the same water that his horse was enjoying.

"If I have to answer for casting aside that snake instead of eating it, then so be it. Hopefully the good
Lord will understand."

Having slaked their thirst as well as their need for
philosophical distractions, the horses and riders moved
along.

It wasn't until nightfall that Paul and Noss caught up
once more with Sprole. They were crossing a long
stretch of rough, rocky terrain that looked as if dirt had
been blown into uneven layers and turned to stone.
The bounty hunter stood beside his horse, holding the
reins in one hand so as not to allow the animal to stray
too far from the cluster of rocks beside them. Hills had
started to form, like larger versions of ripples within
the ground itself, giving the terrain the appearance of a
slowly roiling ocean that built to higher peaks the farther out it went. Once the sunlight had faded, Paul
could truly feel the loneliness of the desert.

Coyotes howled in the distance.

Wind blew without much of anything to get in its
way.

Stars emerged from the depths of a vast, endless sky.

Despite feeling dwarfed by the vastness of his surroundings, Paul couldn't help feeling closer to the
heavens themselves.

Before Noss could call out to him, Sprole motioned
for them to dismount and be quiet about it. Paul and
the sheriff led their horses to where the bounty hunter
stood. The grin on Sprole's face was almost bright
enough to make up for the loss of sunlight.

Pointing at Paul, Sprole said, "That smile on your face means you probably already saw what I did."

"I was just admiring the sky," Paul said.

"Well, peek around them rocks and you'll find something else to admire."

All three men went to a pile of boulders that looked small from a distance simply because there wasn't much of anything to compare them to. The largest rock was about the size of an overturned dinner table, and the others ranged from the size of melons all the way down to pebbles. While not very large in itself, the pile stood at the upper slope of a rise that swept all the way down into a desert basin. In the dim glow of moon- and starlight, Paul could see other choppy stone surfaces broken up by scrawny trees, scrub bushes, and more rocks.

At the edge of a wide expanse of desolate landscape, there was a line of trees that were all bent as if by a strong wind blowing to the north. The dark scrub thinned out there, making way for a few larger rocks as well as what looked to be a fairly deep gorge that was about as wide as a creek. Paul squinted to try and see things as they truly were. Between a sky that seemed to absorb what little light there was and shadows that made any ditch look like a chasm, it was difficult to discern what truly awaited them down there. What wasn't hard to see was the flickering glow of a campfire burning like a single candle in a vast, dark room.

When Paul straightened up to get a better look, Sheriff Noss grabbed him by the elbow to pull him down. Sprole was nearby, hunkering down to stare at the distant fire as if it was the only thing on earth he cared about.

"Hey, Father," Noss whispered. "Remember all that talk about you leading us in circles and wasting our time on a wild-goose chase?"

"Yes."

"You're forgiven."

Chapter 12

Noss and Sprole hurried back to their horses and got busy making preparations. Paul checked his rifle and pistol to make sure both were loaded and then stuffed his pockets full of spare ammunition.

"Just where do you think you're going, Father?" Noss asked.

"With you two. I came this far, so I'm not about to turn back."

"Nobody's asking you to turn back. You just can't come along for this."

"You don't even know who's down there," Paul said.

The bounty hunter and lawman both chuckled at that one. "This ain't exactly a stretch of land many folks ride across," Sprole said. "I already got enough of a look at the men down there to see that there's only two of them and they're both armed."

"That doesn't say much," Paul said. "We're armed too. Anyone riding out here with a lick of sense is carrying some sort of firearm."

"One of them's got his hand wrapped up in a whole

mess of bandages," Sprole said. "His right hand. You think that's a coincidence?"

"No. I just—"

"Take it easy, Padre," Sheriff Noss said as he gave Paul a friendly slap on the shoulder. "You spent the first part of the day trying to justify why you're here and how good your information was, and now you're gonna spend your night trying to prove us wrong when we find our fugitive?"

"We shouldn't go off half-cocked, is all I'm trying to say," Paul told them. "The last thing you two should do is storm in on some innocent person's camp with guns drawn, frightening him out of his skin!"

Sprole snapped his .38 shut and then drew his .44 so he could hold it at an angle that allowed him to check the cylinders in what little light was available to him. "I make a good living tracking men like this one, and that don't happen by leaving important things to chance. Once a man's in my sights, I'm very particular about making sure he's the right one. Those men," he said while snapping the pistol shut and then dropping it into its holster with a quick flourish, "are the right ones."

"How close were you able to get?" Noss asked.

"I crept a ways down into that basin," Sprole replied while hooking a thumb toward the flat expanse spread out below them. "It wasn't as dark as it is now, so I didn't risk being seen. Caught a pretty good glimpse of 'em through my telescope. The one with the bandaged hand is definitely the one that scampered out of that window back in town. I'd stake my life on it."

"Well, I don't like you two going down there," Paul said.

Still clapping him on the back, Sheriff Noss eased up so he was patting instead. Somehow the lighter impacts twisted Paul's face into even more of a scowl. "It's good of you to worry," the lawman said, "but there's no need to fret. This is what men like me and Dave do. If there's trouble, we'll know how to handle it."

"Besides," Sprole added, "how are we supposed to bring these men in if we don't confront them?"

"I realize all of that," Paul said as his patience strained like piano wire. "What I meant was that I don't like you two going down there in *that way*." When he said those last two words, Paul pointed toward the side of the rocks where Sprole and Noss were preparing to go. "We've all been real careful to keep our heads down, and I'm sure we haven't skylined ourselves up here. Even if we had, it's dark enough so all anyone would see is a few rough shapes. Still, if anyone down there did catch sight of any movement . . . even from our horses . . . they'd be watching this spot pretty closely."

Both of the other men still had the condescending looks etched onto their faces, but there was no longer the self-righteousness that had backed them up before. Finally, after a few tentative glances, Sprole said, "He's got a point."

Noss removed his hand from Paul's shoulder and snatched up one of the shotguns he'd brought along with him. "If he's so worried about drawing undue attention, he wouldn't talk so much." Despite that complaint, the lawman walked around to the other side of the rocks and started looking for an alternative way down into the shallow basin.

The bounty hunter walked past Paul and stopped

before beginning his descent. "You know how to use that rifle?"

Looking down at the weapon he'd brought, Paul nodded. "I've fired it plenty of times."

"Can you hit anything?"

"Yes, sir."

"Something that moves?"

Paul nestled the rifle's stock under his arm so he could cradle the weapon while pointing its barrel at the ground. "I put the meat in tonight's stew, didn't I?"

"Hitting a rabbit or bird is one thing. Hitting a man is another."

"One's a much bigger target."

The quickness of that response caught the bounty hunter off his guard, but Sprole wasn't flustered for more than a second before saying, "Joke all you want, preacher. But if things start to go bad while me and the sheriff are down there, it would be good to know the man watching our backs isn't afraid to pull a trigger."

"I said I'd help you two," Paul replied. "That's what I intend to do."

"I don't give an ounce of spit about your intentions. I'm after Jack Terrigan, and you seem to have some information that will get me to him sooner instead of later. That's all well and good. You've even had some good suggestions along the way. Fine. A fresh set of eyes is always a good thing. But if you're the sort of man who'll hesitate to fire a gun on account of some fear of besmirching your spit-shined soul, then I'd like to know right now. It wouldn't be the first time I've waded into dangerous territory on my own."

Paul's eyes had narrowed and had taken on a fiery glint. "If I'm raising questions now, it's only because I'm trying to keep the two of you from rushing in when there's no need. The plan was to follow that fugitive so he could lead us to the rest of Terrigan's gang. If there's only one other man down there, I doubt that's the rest of the gang."

"But we know where the gang is headed, right?" When Paul didn't answer right away, Sprole asked, "Isn't that right?"

In the time Paul took before answering, Sheriff Noss reappeared from around the rocks. "Are you coming or aren't you?" he asked in a harsh whisper.

Without taking his eyes from Paul, Sprole said, "I'm just making sure our preacher friend won't turn out to be the anchor that sinks us both once we're down there and it's too late to turn back."

"You don't have to do anything, Father. Just wait up here and be quiet."

"I don't see why you insist on going down there now," Paul said. "We've spotted them and they don't know we're here. Why not just let them lead us to Terrigan?"

"Because this is about more than just Jack Terrigan," Noss replied. "It's about the entire gang. We know they're headed to Raynor, don't we?"

Paul nodded.

"Since Raynor isn't too far from this spot as the crow flies, this could very well be a broken trail leading there a hell of a lot quicker than the ones used by the handful of stages that go out that way. But that doesn't hardly matter as much as the fact that the rest of the gang will be waiting there . . . unless you're trying to throw us off their trail."

Paul straightened up to meet that challenge and was immediately shoved down again by Sprole before he could present a silhouette that might be spotted from a distance. "I most certainly am *not*."

"I guessed as much," Noss said. "You've been too wound up to get to Terrigan for you to start sabotaging us now. But there's only three of us . . . one of whom ain't about to gun down no outlaws. Once we get to Raynor, things will be a lot easier if we've already weeded out two of Terrigan's men. That would leave . . . how many?"

"Counting Terrigan himself," Sprole replied, "two or three. Depends on if that other one down there is one of the ones I saw before."

"The point is, there are fewer of them killers down there now than there will be in Raynor." The sheriff turned toward the basin as if he could see through the cover provided by the rocks all the way down to the little campsite. "We stumbled upon a nice little situation here and we actually got a leg up on the man that's been giving us the slip for too long. I say anyone that don't take an opportunity when he's given one don't deserve a second opportunity. I know you're a man of God, but do you understand what I'm talking about, Father?"

Sprole impatiently shifted on his feet until Noss motioned for him to keep quiet. The bounty hunter wasn't happy about it, but settled down.

"I understand," Paul said. "I would just hate for anyone else to get hurt."

"Your friend Jack Terrigan is the one causing folks to

get hurt," Noss said. "Aren't we all out here to put an end to that?"

It didn't take long for Paul to nod.

"Stay here and keep quiet," Noss said. "Dave, you're with me."

The bounty hunter picked up the Spencer rifle that he'd propped against a rock earlier and circled around their cover to make his way into the basin. Before he was out of earshot, he grumbled, "Preacher should've stayed in his church where he belongs."

After giving them some time to gain some ground, Paul carried his hunting rifle around to the side of the rocks where the other two were originally going to make their approach. He leaned over so as only to show a sliver of his face while bringing the rifle up to his shoulder. The Henry model .44 didn't look like much anymore, but it had seen him through plenty of hard days. Its familiar weight in his hands and its stock against his shoulder were a comfort amid so much that seemed to be spiraling out of his control.

Control.

Paul had always found humor in the concept that any man truly had control of his destiny. Even in the years before he'd started preaching the gospel, he'd been all too certain that he didn't control much of anything. Sometimes all a man could do when he found himself atop a bucking bronco was hang on as best he could and ride it out. This might not have been what he'd hoped for when he thought about tracking down Jack Terrigan, but Noss and Sprole made some good points. Paul was out of his element. He never liked to admit that, but there was no denying it now.

"No turning back," he said quietly to himself. "I started this mess and I have to see it through."

Staring along the top of the Henry's barrel, Paul lowered himself to one knee and rested the side of the rifle against the rock. That way, with one eye blocked by the stone, he could only see through the rifle's sights. His body was planted firmly in place, and his hands were steady. The longer he stared down at the scrub-filled basin, the clearer it all became.

"Lord," he whispered without moving his line of sight or allowing his hands to falter, "this felt like the path I needed to take, but now I'm not so sure. From the moment I heard Terrigan's name, I knew he was close. If that man is close, it's my duty to get to him and steer him away from the path he's chosen. Should I have ridden out on my own? Have I put these good people at risk just to achieve my own ends?"

Paul had never gotten a direct answer to his prayers, but that wouldn't stop him from voicing them. He'd heard others talk about signs they'd been given or divine inspirations they'd received. For him, faith was something quieter than all of that. It was something that was always in the center of his heart, even when he'd spent so many years swallowing it down or denying it was even there. Instead of a great, luminous hand from above guiding him to the righteous path, his faith was a gentle nudge when he found himself at a crossroads. A persistent reminder of what part of him always knew to be the proper direction. A single rope thrown to him when he was sinking in the most turbulent of waters.

Paul Lester hadn't always had faith, but it had always been there waiting for him. It had steered him away from the shadows only a few short years ago, not with a bolt of inspiration, but with a second of clarity telling him the way he'd spent his life to that point was wrong. He'd served time in purgatory, unsure of what he was supposed to do next, and when he'd emerged from that, it was because he'd followed the quiet, undeniable guidance from within.

This is wrong.

That is right.

No matter what anyone said or how dark the world around him might have been, Paul relied on the little nagging instincts that were too pure to have simply sprouted by chance. They'd been put there, maybe from the moment of his birth or perhaps from the moment the first man had been birthed, but they were a part of him. And no matter how hard he might have tried throughout his younger years to crush those instincts that prodded and needled him, they never died. They were the true voice of his faith.

They were not convenient.

Oftentimes, they were painful to hear.

Unfortunately for Paul, they were never very loud. And yet, somehow, they could still be heard.

"The sheriff is right," he whispered. "And so was I in bringing these men here. This may not have played out exactly as I'd hoped, but we're here all the same. Those killers are away from Pueblito Verde. It's a miracle we found them at all out here in this desert. And soon we'll stop the rest of them from harming another soul. This was my only chance to find the leader of this gang, and I won't turn back until I've had a chance to speak to him. Above all else, I need to do that. Right now, though," he said as he tightened his grip on the Henry rifle, "I need to shepherd these good men through the valley of death."

The shallow basin wasn't exactly a valley, but the preacher smirked at how the phrase applied to his situation. Just like that, his doubt was lifted. No longer did he question his motives or the actions he'd taken thus far. As always, the thin strand of faith at the center of his being was there and it held strong.

Paul's vision was clearer.

His heart was no longer heavy.

His hands were steadier.

As he reached for his hat so he could move to a better position, Paul felt as spry as he had when he was younger. "Thank you, Lord. I won't let you down."

It didn't take long for Sprole to follow Noss through the sparse trees scattered along the side of the basin. Although there was plenty of scrub at the bottom, the knee-high bushes were covered in enough dry leaves to make a loud scraping noise whenever they were disturbed. While that made sneaking through them a difficult prospect, there was enough of a breeze to get plenty of those branches scraping against each other without anyone to help them along. Unless someone knew better, they could easily guess that the scrapes created by Sprole's footsteps were caused by the wind. But Sprole did know better and he could easily discern the sound of Noss's footsteps close behind him.

Sprole also knew how easy it was for a man to lose the element of surprise. All it took was one step that was just a bit heavier than the rest, one breath that was just a bit too loud, and a fight was on. If this went well, there wouldn't even be a fight. If it went badly, the whole world could come crashing down around the bounty hunter's ears.

Those cheerful notions occupied Sprole's mind as he inched toward the campfire. The sheriff was beside him now, keeping pace as they stayed low and crept onward.

After several minutes that felt like just as many hours, they were close enough to the fire to hear the voices of the men around it. Sprole strained his ears to pick out specific words, but all he could make out was two distinct tones. The men at the fire seemed relaxed and making small talk. Even so, it galled Sprole that he couldn't discern any more than that.

Noss tapped him on the shoulder. When Sprole looked over, the sheriff pointed to him and then swept his finger in a semicircle around the right side of the little campsite. Then he tapped the same finger against his own chest and made a similar gesture around the left side. Sprole nodded in agreement and the men separated so they could flank the camp from opposite sides.

Keeping his ears focused on the voices and his eyes pointed at the ground directly in front of him, Sprole looped out a short ways to put some distance between himself and the camp before coming around to his assigned angle.

Suddenly the voices stopped.

Even the wind took a moment of silence, leaving the sound of Sprole's last step to echo in his ears like a gunshot. Soon he heard some rustling, which he assumed was the sheriff on the opposite side of the camp.

Then he realized those sounds had come from somewhere closer than where the sheriff should have been. On top of that, the camp was still unusually quiet. There was a chance that the two outlaws had simply decided to get some sleep. Another possibility was that they'd realized what was happening and were searching the darkness even now for a trace of the men who had pursued them this far. Without anything else to go by, Sprole could only try to rein his thoughts in as best he could and keep moving.

The wind picked up, giving him some degree of cover as the dry brush started swaying once more.

The campfire was weak enough that Sprole couldn't quite see past the couple of trees surrounding it. He could see the flickering light from the flames, but the last time he'd caught sight of the outlaws, they'd been sitting with their backs to the trees and their feet stretched out in front of them. The fire was dwindling, making it even more difficult for him to get an easy glance at either of the men using it for warmth.

Sprole remained still, craning his neck to take another look at the camp, and had to suppress a snarling curse when he saw one of the outlaws' horses stood in his way like a thick wall of dark flesh. As he maneuvered slowly and carefully to a better vantage point, he got the sinking feeling that he was no longer at an advantage. The camp had grown too quiet for his liking. Not one scrape of a body shifting against the ground could be heard above the crackle of the fire.

Not one cough.

Not one sigh.

Nothing.

The effort of keeping his body low while moving so slowly strained every muscle below Sprole's waist. When he was finally in a better spot, the bounty hunter's worst fears were realized.

The camp was empty.

Chapter 13

Sprole crouched down and stayed there as if his entire body had been petrified into another of the crooked lines sprouting from the dry, rocky ground. As he listened for any hint of movement nearby, he eased the Spencer rifle down so he could place his hands on the pistols holstered at his sides. It felt like a long wait, but when he finally got his fingers wrapped around the familiar grips, he allowed the breath he'd been holding to slip quietly from between clenched teeth.

Once the beating of his heart slowed to a steady thump, the subtle brushing of a body against dry branches could be heard. He narrowed his eyes into slits, curled a finger around the trigger of his .44, and waited for the next step to be taken.

Sheriff Noss was circling around to the left of the camp. His steps were quiet but could still be heard. The movement Sprole had detected came from the opposite side, and when he concentrated a bit harder, he could tell the steps were lighter than anything a man the lawman's size could attempt to make.

Every muscle in his body tensed as he waited for that next shoe to drop. The harder he listened to every sound the night had to offer, the more of them he found. Leaves scraped against each other. Trees creaked. Animals called out. Birds flapped their wings. In fact, several birds took flight after abandoning their nest in a clump of scrub bushes not too far away. One bird could have been restless. Two taking flight at the same time could have been a coincidence. More than that led Sprole to believe they'd been spooked. Without pondering the matter any further, the bounty hunter turned on the balls of his feet toward the general direction from which those birds had come. The bushes where the birds had been flushed into the open were slightly taller than the ones near Sprole. Even so, they weren't nearly enough to hide the man who'd been moving behind them.

The figure in the darkness stood up straight and raised a shotgun, which he propped upon the mass of bandages wrapped around his right hand. Even though the gunman was clearly struggling to take aim, the scattergun didn't exactly need precision to do a whole lot of damage. Pulling its trigger caused the shotgun to roar, illuminating the bushes like a glimpse of daylight that lasted less than a second.

It wasn't the first time Sprole had been on the wrong end of a shotgun, and he dived for cover the moment he saw it in the fugitive's hands. He wasn't stupid enough to expect any protection from the dry branches scraping against his legs, so he opted to drop as quickly as he could and press himself as flat as possible against

the ground once he got there. Buckshot filled the air
above him, shredding through the back of his jacket
like sets of hot claws.

"Drop the gun!" Noss shouted from the other side of
the camp.

By now, Sprole had gotten a good look at the man
holding the shotgun. All he'd really needed to see was
the bandaged hand, but he could tell for certain by the
face behind the shotgun that he'd found the man who
had climbed out of Dr. Chandler's window. When the
gunman swung the shotgun around to fire its second
barrel at the lawman, Sprole lifted his .44 and fired a
shot of his own. It was taken from a peculiar angle,
which didn't bode well for its chances of finding its
mark. Whether the fugitive was hit or just as spooked
as the birds that had exploded from the bushes not too
long ago, he ran back to the campfire, firing along the
way.

"Watch yourself, Sheriff!" Sprole hollered. "There's
still another one out here I can't account for!"

"Ain't nowhere to hide," Noss shouted to Sprole as
well as to anyone else within earshot. "Best way to stay
alive is to toss your weapons and surrender before
things get a whole lot worse."

Another shot was fired, which didn't come from the
fugitive, Noss, or Sprole. The bounty hunter didn't
even see a muzzle flash before the round hissed
through the air a few feet from him. Judging by the
obscenity that escaped Noss's lips in a sharp yelp, the
bullet had gotten a whole lot closer to him.

"I think I saw where that shot came from!" Sprole
shouted.

The lawman stood up with his shotgun gripped in both hands. The first barrel belched a plume of fiery smoke amid a thundering roar. Along with a bunch of critters that had been residing in the bushes in front of him, a larger figure emerged from hiding and scampered deeper into the shadows.

"Leave him to me," Noss said. "Just make sure you get the fella with the wounded hand."

Sprole had a thing or two to say about that, but decided not to argue since the man he'd been assigned was less than twenty yards in front of him. Wes hunched over while loping away from the camp in a pathetic attempt to circle around and flank the bounty hunter. When Sprole shifted his aim toward him, the fugitive raised his left hand and started firing his pistol.

The shots might have been wild and aimed from his off hand, but they were coming from close enough range to cause Sprole some concern. He pushed off with both feet and hit the ground on his belly. Hot lead continued to blaze above him, and the final shot was dangerously close to drawing blood. Seeing as how that was the sixth round to be fired from a man who could use only one gun at a time, Sprole stood up and raised his .44. "Live or die," Sprole said. "Choose now and be quick about it."

The one-handed fugitive grunted a string of filthy words as he threw his gun to the ground.

Sheriff Noss moved away from the campfire. Not only did the shadows provide a bit more cover, but his eyes were given a chance to adjust to the darkness a little more than when he'd been closer to the flames. Instincts honed from keeping the peace in several towns over more than a decade served him better than his eyes or ears. He only needed to feel a shiver run down his spine for him to drop to one knee and lower his head. A fraction of a second later, a rifle shot cracked through the air.

As the bullet whipped past him, Noss could still see the afterimage of the sparks that had flown when the shot had been fired. He took quick aim with his shotgun, pulled the trigger, and gritted his teeth as the weapon unleashed its fury into the dark mass of bushes in front of him.

Noss strained his eyes to catch any hint of movement on the outskirts of the campsite. Without shifting his line of sight, he let the empty shotgun fall from his hands so he could draw the .45-caliber pistol strapped to his hip. The sky was a dark, inky black accented by glittering pinpoints of starlight. Shadows were everywhere, most of which were just parts of the horizon. When one sliver of a shadow moved on its own accord, Noss pointed his gun in that direction and fired.

"Run for it, Theo!" the one-handed fugitive shouted.

Glancing over toward Sprole for half a second, Noss was able to see that the bounty hunter was still wrangling his fugitive. Although Sprole loomed over the other man, he suddenly had a fight on his hands as Wes caught his second wind. If the shouted command was a distraction, Noss didn't want to play into it any more than he already had. The shadow he'd spotted dropped down and darted toward a pair of horses tethered to a few sickly trees nearby. Noss straightened his arm and fired a shot, knowing all too well that it was wide. In the short time it took for him to thumb his hammer back again, the shadow in his sights stopped and turned to face him.

Starlight glinted off the long barrel of a rifle at the shadowy figure's shoulder. When a shot popped in the distance, Noss thought he was a dead man. The fact that the sound of the shot was from another direction and quite a ways off didn't register until the bullet cut a hissing path through the air in front of him. The shadow man in Noss's sights cursed and dropped down so he could resume his flight toward the waiting horses.

"Stop where you are!" Noss shouted. "You're surrounded!"

But the rifleman in the shadows wasn't about to give up as easily as his partner with the wounded hand. He wheeled around and kept moving backward toward the horses while firing at Noss. His rifle was held in a looser grip now. The rounds he fired came within a yard or so of the lawman and might have been enough to make anyone with a gentler disposition think twice about going any farther. Although he dropped to one knee to present a smaller target, Noss returned fire.

His next shot was taken more as a way to gauge the following one. Before he could send that next piece of lead through the air, the rifle in the distance popped one more time.

Noss recognized the report as coming from the model of the rifle he'd seen in Father Lester's hands. Surprisingly enough, the preacher proved to be a good source of backup fire. The sheriff was surprised even more when the next shot whipped through the air less

than a few feet in front of him. So it seemed the good
father had his heart in the right place but less than perfect aim.

The rifleman in the shadows had reached the tethered horses and was pulling himself up into his saddle
when Noss shifted his aim a bit higher to compensate.
Before the sheriff could squeeze his trigger, Paul's
hunting rifle spat another round at him that was even
closer than the previous one. It was too late for Noss to
keep from pulling his trigger, and when his body reflexively twitched as the rifle round sped past him, his
.45 sent a bullet into empty air well above the rifleman
who now sat in his saddle.

Even though Wes had seemed all too anxious to toss his
weapon, the wounded fugitive was putting up a
mighty big fight now. Sprole had approached him to
either knock him out or cuff his wrists, but was now
having a difficult time just keeping from being pulled
to the ground. Wes had popped up to his knees and
reached out with both hands to make a desperate grab
for Sprole's gun. The bounty hunter's only response
had been to pull away, which gave the other man a
chance to climb to his feet.

The bounty hunter didn't want to waste a shot on
trying to hit a moving target at point-blank range. Unless a man had a shotgun in his hands, hitting something when it was too close could be almost as dicey as
trying to hit something that was too far away. One
move in the wrong direction would ruin his aim, and
at the moment, Sprole's target was doing plenty of
moving. No matter how good his odds were, Sprole

decided to go with the shot that couldn't miss and swung his pistol around in a vicious arc that was bound to knock into some part of the other man.

The fugitive caught the side of the pistol on his shoulder, sending him reeling backward as he instinctually lifted his right arm to cover his face.

Now that Wes had stopped bouncing like a frightened jackrabbit, Sprole held his gun properly and took aim. As tough as it was to hit something at close range when it was moving, it was twice as tough to miss when that same thing came to a stop. The moment he realized he was about to be perforated by the weapon in Sprole's hand, the fugitive lashed out to bat the pistol away. He succeeded in making contact before the shot was fired, but with his right hand.

Even Sprole winced when he saw the fugitive use his bandaged hand to smack away the pistol. For a moment, Wes didn't seem to notice. Instead, he grinned crazily and jumped at the bounty hunter. Sprole wrapped his arms around Wes's torso, twisting his body so he could divert the fugitive's momentum to a different angle. After that, it was a simple matter of applying some leverage to bring the other man down.

Having been caught like a fish in midair, the fugitive hit the ground flat enough to force the air from his lungs. When he tried to draw another breath, he found he simply didn't have the strength.

Sprole grabbed the fugitive by the back of his collar as if he were holding a dog by the scruff of its neck. He raised his pistol over his head for a clubbing blow, but realized it wouldn't be necessary.

"Son of a . . . my *hand*!" the fugitive hollered as he

cradled his right arm and held it tight against his chest.

In what little light made it over to him from the campfire, Sprole could see the dark bloodstain seeping through Wes's bandages. He kept his pistol tucked in so it could be pointed at the fugitive and kept out of reach while patting the wailing man down. The quick search didn't turn up anything more than a few shotgun shells.

The hunting rifle was still being fired, and Sprole glanced back toward the rocks where he'd last seen the preacher. Sure enough, Paul's silhouette could be discerned among the rocks. A brief flash of sparks announced another shot, and Sprole snapped his head around as if he could follow the path of the bullet sailing through the air.

"Hold your fire!" Noss shouted.

It was difficult enough for him to watch something that was just another shadow amid a mess of more shadows, and the steady rain of lead from on high wasn't making it any easier. Noss fired a hasty shot, which only forced the fleeing rifleman to hunker down over his horse's neck as he rode away. There was only enough time for one more shot, so the lawman steadied himself before taking it.

As if reading the deadly thoughts running through Noss's mind, the rifleman twisted around in his saddle and fired a shot of his own from what sounded like a .38-caliber pistol.

Noss swore under his breath while pulling his trigger as quickly as he could. The time for accurate shots was through. All that remained was to take his chances with Lady Luck. Considering the way things had been going for him lately, Noss wasn't surprised when that particular lady chose to warm up to someone else.

The fleeing rifleman fired wildly over his shoulder. One of those rounds clipped Noss in the right rib. It stung like a wasp that had been doused in whiskey and set on fire, but the impact of the bullet was even worse. It hit him like a swing from an axe handle to knock one leg out from under him and send the lawman face-first toward the dirt. Noss was just quick enough to reach out with one hand to stop himself before getting a mouthful of gravel. Even before he looked up again, he was firing his pistol at the rifleman.

The sound of his pistol's hammer slapping against the backs of spent rounds only made the lawman angrier. He was so angry, in fact, that he was able to push aside the pain in his side when he climbed back to his feet and wheeled around toward Sprole.

The bounty hunter was right where the lawman had last seen him. Since the shooting had come to a stop, Sprole stood up and pulled his prisoner to his feet. More shapes were approaching the campsite. These were large and kicked up plenty of dust, which showed up like inky clouds behind them.

"It's all right," Sprole said as Noss swept up his shotgun and started hastily reloading it. "That's the preacher bringing us our horses."

"I know it's him."

There was a fire in Noss's eyes that would have shone through no matter how dark his surroundings were. Flickering shadows from the campfire washed over his features as he stormed past the little clearing, making his face look even more like a terrible visage scrawled in wet charcoal on the wall of a cave.

The gunman with the bandaged hand was able to stand beside Sprole and stagger along as he was shoved, but the pain from his newly reopened wound was making him dizzy and his head lolled from side to side like something crudely attached to an old doll. Sprole didn't show him the first bit of leeway as he continued to pull him along. "There's another horse out there," Sprole said. "I've got my hands full, so why don't you take it?"

The sheriff's mind had been so set on its course that he'd almost overlooked something so obvious.

"That's . . . *my* horse," the wounded fugitive said.

Sprole gave him a rough shake and growled, "Shut up!" To Noss, he asked, "What are you waiting for?"

"Nothing. I'll see if I can catch up to that one who skinned out of here. Soon as you can, you'd best come after me."

The sheriff ran to the other horse that had been tethered just outside the ring of light cast by the outlaws' fire. As he ran, he watched the ground in front of him to keep from being tripped up by anything that could have been hidden in the shadows. His hands were busy reloading the .45 with fresh ammunition pulled from his belt. By the time he reached the horse, Noss had to pause for only a few seconds to finish preparing his pistol. He holstered the weapon, grabbed the horse's reins, and climbed into the saddle.

Once he'd snapped his reins, Noss quickly acclimated himself to the animal he'd commandeered. No matter how anxious he was to close the gap between himself and the fleeing rifleman, Noss wasn't about to force the horse to go any faster than it was willing to go. With the shadows thicker than mud on all sides, he had to rely on the horse's instincts as much as his own two eyes when it came to avoiding half-buried rocks, narrow ditches, or any number of other hazards that could break legs and send even the best rider to the ground in a heap of broken bones and twisted joints.

Noss squinted into onrushing wind that scraped against his face like nails that had been pulled from a bucket of ice water. After riding a short distance after his quarry, Noss spotted the other horse and rider. They were making pretty good progress, but he was pleased to see that they seemed to be going even slower than him. The lawman fought back the urge to snap his reins, knowing he wouldn't do any good whatsoever if he or his horse wound up breaking his neck.

Just then a thick row of clouds drifted close to the moon, glowing with the pale light reflected off the luminescent sliver to cast a faded glow onto the desert. Because of that subtle shift, Noss was able to see the upward slope of the ground ahead of the fleeing rifleman. It seemed the other man was making a run for the opposite side of the basin.

Noss leaned forward in the saddle that had been left on the horse's back by outlaws who had been prepared to ride at a moment's notice. He did his best to soak up as many details as he could while he still had some paltry bit of light to work with. Although he was able to pick out a few more details, he wasn't at all happy with what he saw.

The rising slope of the basin was closer than he'd first thought. So close, in fact, that the man ahead of him was already beginning to ascend. Casting aside better judgment in favor of getting his job done, Noss snapped his reins to push his horse to go even faster. The animal responded, but only a little. Every one of its steps was cautious as if to make up for the dangerous whims of the man on its back.

Ahead of the sheriff, the rifleman rode up the steep slope toward a ridge of low rocks. Noss thought back to what he'd heard not too long ago to come up with a name.

Theo.

The wounded gunman had called this one Theo. That name didn't ring any bells with Noss, which wasn't saying much. There were too many outlaws seeking refuge in the desert at any given time for one man to keep track of them all. If anything, a bounty hunter might have a better idea of who was about to ride out of the basin. All Noss cared about was catching Theo before he got away.

Doing its best to navigate the mostly flat ground, Noss's horse clipped the top of something that had been hidden in the shadows. For a split second, Noss's gut clenched into a tight ball. He'd known a few men who'd broken limbs or worse when falling from a horse. When he'd heard tell of others who'd met their fate when riding in the dead of night, the lawman had written them off as fools who'd gotten what they'd asked for. Now that he was one of those fools, he could only hang on and hope his horse found its balance before both of them were pitched to an unforgiving earth.

The horse did just that. Its body skidded to one side, but recovered amid a series of frantically scraping steps, ending abruptly when a hoof found a deep groove that had been cut into the desert floor. It didn't matter much to Noss how the groove had gotten there. His horse had found it, and his worst fear was playing itself out. Before he could think about what to do next, he was thrown from the saddle.

A second ago, Noss's ears had been filled with the rush of wind and the thunder of the horse beneath him. Now there was only his own heartbeat as he sailed through the air.

For the next few moments, it seemed he would never come down.

When he finally did, Noss felt as if an entire mountain came crashing down on top of him.

At first, he thought the horse had clubbed his left side with one of its hooves. His mouth was filled with dusty grit, and his feet scraped noisily against the ground. When he tried to prop himself up again, another impact swept his arm out from beneath the rest of his body. As he lay on his side, it was all he could do to remember where he was or what he'd been doing a minute ago.

Finally he lifted his head and got a look at the sloping ground ahead.

The camp.

The outlaws.

The shots that had been fired.

The one who tried to get away.

Theo.

His name was Theo.

All of those thoughts rushed through Noss's mind as his eyes locked upon a silhouette at the top of the basin's lip. In that instant, he could see everything as if it were bathed in the light of a harvest moon. He could see Theo atop his horse, bringing a rifle to his shoulder.

His ears might have been ringing still, but Noss had no trouble hearing the shot that followed.

Chapter 14

Paul sat in his saddle with his back ramrod straight. He stared down the top of the hunting rifle's barrel, watching his target through smoke from the shot he'd just fired. "Go on," he whispered.

The other two horses were nothing more than blobs in the distance. They hadn't gotten too far from the campsite, but the night had swallowed them up whole. Even though Paul couldn't see exactly what the farthest rider was doing, he could tell by the way Theo stood his ground that he was fixed upon his target.

"What's happening?" Sprole asked from where he waited with his wounded prisoner.

"The sheriff's hurt," Paul replied. "Thrown from his horse."

"What about the other one?"

"He wants to finish him off, but I'm keeping him back."

"You think you can hit him from here?" Sprole asked.

Paul remained steady behind his rifle. His finger brushed the edge of its trigger as if he were stroking a woman's ear. "That's what he's trying to figure out right now."

There wasn't much to see where that distant rider was concerned. It had been tough enough to line up a shot, so Paul wasn't about to risk losing his target by lowering his rifle to ride any closer. The most recent shot he'd fired hadn't hit the outlaw, but must have gotten close enough to make the man think twice about putting Sheriff Noss out of his misery.

Sprole was approaching Paul's horse, but his insistence on dragging the wounded gunman along slowed him down considerably. "I think I see them," the bounty hunter said.

But Paul wasn't listening. As he watched and waited, he could feel the gaze of the distant outlaw stabbing through him. When he saw Theo move, Paul levered another round into his rifle. He thought Theo began riding back down the slope toward Noss, so Paul sent another round through the air. Almost immediately, he regretted the shot. Because of the shadows and distance between the two men, it was impossible to tell which way the other rider was going until he disappeared from sight altogether. Since Paul could no longer see him, he knew Theo had crested the ridge and was now making his way down the other side to put the basin behind him.

"Damn!" Sprole said. "He's bolting! Keep an eye on this one here and I'll see what I can find."

Before Paul could say anything for or against Sprole's idea, the bounty hunter took the reins of one of the horses that had been brought down from the other side of the basin and climbed into the saddle. "He's already about to fall over," Sprole said. "Shouldn't be any trou-

ble. He gives you any lip, just crack him in the head."
With that, Sprole snapped his reins and rode into the
shadows.

Paul wanted to follow him. The only thing keeping
him from doing so was the man who swayed on his
feet like a bobber floating on top of a lake.

"You . . . won't hurt me," Wes said.

Paul climbed down from his saddle and worked the
lever on his rifle. The empty bullet casing popped from
the breech, leaving it empty. He wasn't worried about
the outlaw taking notice of such a thing since he barely
seemed to know where he was.

"Who was that with you?" Paul asked.

Without hesitation, the outlaw replied, "Theo."

"Theo who?"

Wes grinned and somehow managed to steady himself. "I don't have to tell you a thing . . . and you ain't
about to shoot nobody."

"You sure about that?" Paul asked, wondering if the
outlaw had noticed that the rifle was empty after all.

"I know who you are. You're a preacher. I don't
know why you're out here, but I sure know you ain't
about to kill me."

"You should sit down before you fall over."

"I'll do what I want!" Wes snarled.

Paul's rifle hit the ground with a loud clatter. When
Wes turned around, he saw Paul come at him like
something from a bad dream. The outlaw lifted his
hands to protect himself, but that only gave Paul something to grab. Once he had a firm grip on one of the
outlaw's arms, Paul twisted his body around to take
Wes down in a single motion.

"What are you doing?" Wes moaned after his back hit the dirt. "I thought you—"

"Who was that man with you?" Paul asked.

"His name's Theo Price. He's been riding with Jack Terrigan longer than any of the others."

"How many more are there?"

Wes's face twisted to reflect every bit of desperation that had seeped all the way down to his core like cold rainwater. "Last I checked, there was six of us. We're supposed to be meeting in East Raynor. I already told you all of that. What more do you want from me?"

"I helped you once and I can help you again. You just need to do what you're told and I can protect you."

"Then why do you keep knocking me around?" Wes moaned. "I been knocked around so much that I can barely see straight. Right when I think I'm better, I get dizzy spells. And when them spells pass, I get knocked around some more. I just wanna go home!"

Paul looked down at the outlaw as if he were a wounded animal. All he'd done to the man was toss him to the dirt before he could get away. Even now, he knew that had been the proper thing to do. If either Sprole or Sheriff Noss saw the outlaw escaping from the camp, a much worse fate would surely befall him. Seeing the dirty bandages wrapped around Wes's hand, Paul felt bad all over again. Even knowing that Wes had been prepared to shoot an innocent woman before killing him back at that hotel didn't make him feel any better.

"Look," Paul said. "I know you don't want to be thrown into another jail, but that's the best place for you."

"You wouldn't say that if you ever been to jail."

"I been to plenty of places worse than that, boy. Right now jail is the best place you can be. It's the only place you can get to with what's left of your hide intact."

"But . . . after what you done for me back in Pueblito Verde . . ."

"That was the best thing at the time," Paul quickly replied. "Right now I'm telling you the best thing would be to stop putting up such a fuss and go along to accept the consequences for your actions."

"Go along? Go along with who?" Wes sputtered as he struggled to sit up. Even after Paul shoved him back down again, he floundered like a windup toy that was still trying to march after being turned over. "Go along with that bounty hunter who wants me dead? Or that law dog who wants me to rot in a cage? Or with some crazy preacher who blows off my hand and then says he wants to help me and then knocks me down? I'd rather take my chances on my own, if it's all the same to you!"

"It's *not* all the same to me," Paul told him. After drawing a deep breath, he took hold of Wes's arms and was careful not to aggravate his injury while helping the outlaw to his feet. He even dusted Wes off a bit once he was standing on his own. "A man's always got choices," Paul said. "Even when it seems like there ain't nowhere else to go, he's got choices."

Wes sneered. "You mean like thumping a Bible and falling to my knees for forgiveness?"

"Well . . . that is an option," Paul said. "Although I don't see how that would do you much good in this particular instance."

Wes seemed flummoxed by that. Then again, after being knocked around so many times, he seemed flummoxed by pretty much everything.

"Here and now," Paul continued, "your choices are simple. You could run and take your chances in the desert without a horse, water, or supplies. You'd also be taking a mighty big gamble in trying to escape the two men out there intent on capturing you after storming this camp. I can tell by the look on your face that you don't much care for that choice."

"No. I suppose I don't."

"Smart man," Paul said with a tired smile. "Another choice is to pretend to come along peacefully until you think you've found a moment when you can slip away. I can tell you right now, after spending time with these men, that any chance you think you have to escape will be short-lived. My partners are already fed up with Terrigan and anyone who ever rode with him, so they'll be more apt to choose shooting you before wasting another moment in trying to bring you back alive."

"What else is there, then?"

"You can go along with us like a man," Paul said in a somber tone. "You can do what you're told, keep your head down and your mouth shut. Behaving that way can only help you."

"Yeah," Wes sighed. "Help me right into a cage."

"Better that than a grave."

Those words hung in the air like thick black smoke. As they settled in, the outlaw nodded and lowered himself to a seated position on the ground. His wounded arm curled inward to be clutched against his chest and he shrugged around it as though he'd lost every bit of the steam that had been in his strides not too long ago. "What brought all this on?" he asked.

Paul bent at the knees and clasped his hands between them. Now that he was mostly at the other man's level, he replied, "You're no different than me, and we're no different than any other man. Sometimes what happens to us is bad timing. Sometimes it's the Lord's plan. Most of the time, though, it's just a simple matter of reaping what we sow."

"No, I get all that. You mentioned that sort of thing plenty of times when you were at my bedside back at that doctor's office."

Paul chuckled. "I thought you were out of sorts for most of that."

"I was for some. I was ignoring you for the rest, but you just kept talking."

"That's my job. Keep talking in the hopes that I get through to someone eventually."

"But that ain't what I meant," Wes said. "I meant . . . what brought all of this on after what you did back in town? Why—"

Heavy steps announced the arrival of Sprole's horse. When Paul looked in that direction, he found the bounty hunter already riding into the dwindling glow of the campfire. Sprole looked down at the other two with wary eyes as he asked, "Everything all right here?"

Wes was either too frightened or too tired to speak, so Paul said, "We're fine. I don't think you'll get any more trouble from this one. Am I right?"

"Yeah," Wes said in a voice that seemed to sap every last bit of strength he had.

Sprole eased down from his saddle. Sheriff Noss had been sitting behind him, and he bared his teeth grumpily while slapping away Sprole's attempt to help him down. "Bad enough I had to ride back like a damn child," the lawman said. "You ain't about to help me down like a woman."

Sprole stepped back and allowed the lawman to climb down from the horse on his own. It wasn't an easy task for Noss, and it was even tougher for Paul to watch once he saw the difficulty the lawman was having. Noss's left arm hung from his shoulder like a thick mess of knotted rope. Every time it swung, Noss winced. Considering the red hue to his skin and the rivulets of sweat rolling down his face, he'd been wincing quite a bit. Finally Noss swung a leg over the horse's back and slid from the saddle. He cussed loudly when his boots hit the dirt with a solid thump.

"What happened, Sheriff?" Paul asked.

Glaring at Wes as if to focus all of his pain and anger into a single fiery stare, Noss replied, "That one's friend got away. No thanks to you, I might add."

"What's that supposed to mean?" Paul said.

"You *know* what I mean! What in the hell were you thinking in shooting at me instead of that killer out there?"

"I was providing cover fire, just like you asked. Once everyone got into the shadows, I couldn't see much. When the shooting started and I couldn't see who was who, I thought it best if I just try to create some confusion so you could get to cover."

"You were watching the whole time," Noss snarled

as he grabbed his shoulder and shuffled away from the horse. "You could've figured out who was who."

Not liking where the conversation was headed, Paul asked, "What's wrong with your arm?"

Noss was more content to snarl to himself, so Sprole walked over to him and said, "His shoulder was knocked out of joint when he fell from his horse." To the lawman, he said, "Maybe now he knows why it ain't wise to ride in the middle of the night when you can't see where you're going."

"Better that than let a killer get away," the lawman said.

"And where is that killer?"

Though Noss's glare was intense before, the one he pointed in Sprole's direction had enough heat to melt iron.

The bounty hunter shook his head and grabbed the sheriff's left wrist in one hand before placing his other hand gingerly on Noss's left shoulder. "We're headed deeper into the desert from here," he said. "It'll be easier tracking him."

"You sure about that?" the lawman wheezed.

"We know where he's headed, right? Besides, all we'll need is high ground every now and then and we'll be able to spot dust being kicked up or any number of signs to let us know we're on the right track. One thing I can tell you for certain is that we won't be able to cover much ground at all with you coddling that arm like a baby bird with a broken wing."

Noss bared his teeth in an angry grimace. "*What* did you just call me?"

Toward the end of that question, Sprole tightened his grip on the lawman's wrist and clamped his hand down harder on his shoulder. With one powerful tug, he pulled the sheriff's arm to form a straight line. The wet crunch that followed might have been muffled since it had come from within the lawman's body, but it was loud enough to make every man in the vicinity cringe.

Wheeling around to face the bounty hunter, Noss reached out for him with both hands. He grabbed the front of Sprole's shirt with his right hand, but his left hand wasn't quite up to the task.

"Looks like your wing is back in place, little bird," Sprole said through a snide grin. "You might want to go easy on it for a while, though."

Eventually the sheriff let go of Sprole and took a step back. "I suppose it does feel a little better now. Much obliged."

"I know that was a difficult thing to say to a filthy bounty hunter," Sprole replied, "but you're welcome."

When he turned back around to face Paul and Wes, he blinked as if he'd only just taken notice of them. "Tell me about that man you were riding with."

Without the slightest bit of hesitation, Wes said, "His name's Theo Price. He's a sharpshooter that's been riding with Jack Terrigan's bunch for a while now." He went on to describe everything short of Price's favorite dessert while Noss watched and listened.

When the outlaw was finished, Noss asked, "You men are supposed to meet in Raynor?"

Wes nodded. "Jack's already there and waiting for us, so Price will want to get there as quick as he can."

While those two had been having their discussion, Paul had fashioned a crude sling from one of his old shirts. He approached the sheriff to tie the sling in place so the lawman's left arm was held snugly against his chest instead of swinging painfully from its shoulder joint.

"And I suppose you'll just come along quietly with us from here in?" the sheriff asked.

Once again, Wes nodded. "I'm through running."

"I bet that's just what you told Father Lester here before you decided to climb out of Doc Chandler's window."

Reluctantly, Wes admitted, "It is. This time I mean it, though."

"And I believe him," Paul declared.

"That's all well and good," Sprole said. "But I think we'll tie you up better than a calf at a rodeo anyways."

"I understand," Wes sighed.

The bounty hunter almost seemed empathetic as he shackled the outlaw's wrists and ankles before making good on his promise by wrapping several loops of rope around Wes's arms and legs. When he was finished, the fugitive could barely take a breath without straining some sort of binding.

"I'll want to have some more words with you," the sheriff said to his prisoner. "About Jack Terrigan and what you've seen or heard since you've been riding with him."

Wes kept nodding. "Whatever you say, sir."

Chapter 15

For the next hour or two, Sheriff Noss asked his questions and Wes answered them. Paul stoked the struggling fire and brewed some coffee while Sprole kept watch for any hint of Price's return. The lawman was still talking to his prisoner when Paul decided to step away from the camp and finish his cup of coffee in the darkness.

"That man's got a lot to say," Sprole said as he approached Paul in steps that could barely be heard. "Were his lips so loose when he was confessing to you back in town?"

Paul lifted his dented tin cup to his mouth and sipped the bitter concoction that still tasted like the metallic innards of a canteen. "I already told you what was said back then. I probably shouldn't have told you that much."

"Right. On account of them confessions you don't normally take."

Meeting the bounty hunter's watchful gaze, Paul said, "That's right."

"And what about what was said a little earlier? Care

to tell me a bit more about that or is that something else you'll be keeping between yourself and a known killer?"

"I doubt Wes has killed anyone."

"Did you look into his soul to figure out that much?" Sprole asked. "Is that some divine ability bestowed upon you when you decide to put on them preacher's clothes and carry a Bible in your pocket?"

"No," Paul said sharply. "I looked into his eyes. He's a thief, I know that much for certain. I don't doubt he's fired a gun at another person. He's hurt folks, I'm sure. But a killer is something else entirely."

"And what if I knew you were wrong?"

"Is that what this is about? You want to prove me wrong? I'm more than willing to admit I've been wrong about a few things."

Sprole stepped up closer so he could lower his voice to a rasping rumble and still be heard. "You sure know how to talk, preacher. But I ain't forgotten about what I asked before you went off on that little sermon just now."

Since pretending he'd forgotten Sprole's question would be an insult to the man's intelligence, Paul said, "Of course I was going to talk to that man instead of knocking him unconscious. What else would you expect?"

"What I would expect would be for a man of the cloth to help where he could but stay in town when the posse rode out to hunt some killers down. At the most, I'd expect you to talk us into forgiving Jack Terrigan or some such nonsense, but you've made a habit out of exceeding my expectations." Cocking his head like a

dog curiously watching a bird before pouncing on it,
Sprole said, "But you're here now and you've told us
plenty of times why that is. Since you are, I'd expect
you to hang back, but you surprised me again by bringing along that hunting rifle of yours and offering to be
of some real use."

"I'd always like to think I'm useful. Men in my profession strive to serve a good purpose."

"Serving on a posse ain't close to anything I've ever
heard about men in your profession. Of course," Sprole
continued, "this ain't exactly a proper posse and these
ain't exactly normal circumstances. You strike me as a
capable fellow, so I went along with it. Then tonight
you surprise me by proving to be someone we can
count on out here in the middle of nowhere."

Knowing there was plenty more to follow, Paul accepted that little compliment with a silent nod.

"I was surprised again when you started shooting
like some kind of blind fool who's never pulled a trigger before." Holding his hand up when he saw Paul
start to say something, Sprole quickly added, "And
spare me the talk about being a simple, godly man who
never hurts a fly. I make my living off sizing other folks
up in as little time as possible. Being accurate in that
regard can make the difference between living and dying. While I may not agree when you say you want to
catch up to Terrigan to talk some sense into him, I still
believe you. I also believe that there's a lot more to you
than what you say or what you wear when you put on
that white collar or them strings around your neck."

Paul reflexively reached for the spot where his
preaching tabs would hang from either side of his col-

lar on special occasions or when he was leading his congregation.

"Just about anyone would have gotten rattled when all the shooting started back at that hotel," Sprole continued. "But you . . . you kept from tearing out of there in a panic. You even managed to step in and capture one of them killers alive. I only wish I could have been there to see how you brought that poor devil down."

"It wasn't pretty."

"Oh, I'll have to disagree with that. So you wound up here tonight and when another moment came for you to step up, you froze. After standing toe-to-toe with a man who wants to put a bullet into you, firing a rifle from a distance should have been simple."

"Neither was simple," Paul said.

"What about firing on one of your own men?" Sprole asked. "How simple was that?"

"That . . . was a mistake. Like I told you, I couldn't see much in the shadows once Sheriff Noss and that other fellow rode off."

Sprole's eyes narrowed again and he shook his head. "Nah. I doubt a man like you makes mistakes. At least, none that are so downright stupid."

"I'm only human."

"And . . . like most humans . . . you got a plan in mind." Backing up a step, Sprole said, "It's nothing to be ashamed of. Everyone from an outlaw to a lawman to an old man on his deathbed all the way down to a kid that hasn't grown into his britches has got some sort of plan running through their head. When I see you fire against the wrong man not once but twice, it makes me wonder what sort of plan you got in mind."

"It was dark. It still *is* dark. How was I supposed to make out who was who?"

"Then you should have held your fire," Sprole said. "But you didn't. That means you're either stupid, sympathizing with them outlaws, or you had something else in mind."

Paul let out a heavy sigh. "Are you going to make me say it?"

"Yes."

"It wouldn't do anyone any good if both of those outlaws were captured here tonight. One had to get away so he could lead us the rest of the way."

"And there it is," Sprole said with a victorious grin. "Every man's got a plan rattling around in his head."

"And what would you have rather done?" Paul asked, trying his best to keep from being heard all the way back at the camp. Sheriff Noss seemed to be finishing up with his prisoner, and both men had to have been exhausted, but Paul didn't want to gamble that they weren't paying attention to what was going on. He turned his back to the camp and dropped his voice to a fierce whisper. "If none of those men made it to meet up with the rest of the gang, Terrigan and any of the others in Raynor would probably have just moved along."

"You don't know that for certain."

"Maybe not, but it makes sense. And even if they did stay around for a while, what do you think they'd do once these two turn up missing and then a lawman comes riding into town asking a bunch of questions?"

"You're assuming the good sheriff would be noticed at all," Sprole pointed out.

"Raynor isn't a big place. He'll be noticed. And when he is, those outlaws will either slip away or wait for the best moment to face him head-on. You're the one who's been tracking Terrigan this far. You tell me which you think would happen."

Sprole closed his eyes. When he opened them again, many of the miles he'd ridden over the last day seemed to catch up with him all at once. "It's hard to say how well he'll fare even if he gets the drop on Terrigan."

"So our best bet is to at least let one of those men loose so they can show us the way to Terrigan. Raynor may be a small place, but we don't know where to go once we get there."

Drawing a slim knife from his boot and flipping it from one hand to another, Sprole said, "Oh, I believe I could have convinced one of them to let us know where they were supposed to meet up with Terrigan."

"I don't want any part of torture."

"You'd rather have a hand in whatever damage that Price fellow may do between here and Raynor? He's a desperate man now, on the run with the hounds nipping at his heels. Could be he's twice as dangerous as he was before."

"And it could also be that he's sloppy and panicked enough to play right into our hands," Paul said.

"You're making it sound like you're really going to be out there in front when the lead starts to fly."

"I've made it this far, haven't I?"

"Sure," Sprole replied. "But that's only because you've slithered along like some lizard stuck to our boots. And that brings me to what I've really wanted to ask you about."

"You mean there's more?" Paul sighed. "Aren't you getting tired of raking me over the coals?"

"Not until you answer for the things that outlaw was saying to you when I brought the sheriff back to camp."

"What are you talking about now? If you've got a point to make, I'd like you to just make it so I can get some sleep."

"The way he was talking, it sounded as if he truly owed you for something."

"Some folks are grateful for the comfort I can provide," Paul said.

"No, that one was talking like you truly did something for him. Something you didn't want to talk about." Sprole glanced back at the camp, where the sheriff was securing one end of a rope to the trunk of a tree before looping the other end around the chain between Wes's ankles. "Now, I didn't hear everything you two were saying, but it sure didn't sound like the kind of talk I might expect after he thought highly enough of you to confess his sins."

"You'd be amazed how quickly and frequently folks will change their attitudes when it comes down to practicing what I preach."

"You're a real fast talker, Padre. It's no wonder you managed to talk your way onto this posse when you've got no good reason for being out here. Come to think of it, you're so talented that I don't even feel bad for going along with such a harebrained plan either. After all, there's no shame in losing to a better man. I just want to tell you that I know what you're up to."

"Really?" Paul mused. "And what might that be?"

"You're not just some preacher trying to do right by

your God. And you're most definitely not some concerned man with good intentions. You want to know what I see when I look at you?"

"If you tell me, does that mean I can get some sleep?"

Continuing as if he hadn't even heard Paul's snide remark, Sprole said, "I see a man who's almost as desperate as the ones we've been tracking. You're desperate enough to fire on Sheriff Noss just to see your plan through, which I can only assume means you'd be desperate enough to shoot at me if the need arose. You're desperate enough to put the fear into that poor idiot that's trussed up like a prize calf, and you were desperate enough to do something good enough to earn his trust back in Pueblito Verde. Would you mind telling me what that was?"

"Do I have a choice?"

"Course you do," Sprole said. "Every man has a choice. Ain't that what you were talking about not too long ago?"

"It is," Paul replied with a weary smile. "And it's nice to know that someone was listening."

"I've been listening to you, preacher. I also been watching. And I won't let up on either until I find out for certain what you're up to."

Paul's voice was stronger than a post sunk twenty feet into solid ground when he said, "I already told you and the sheriff why I wanted to come along on this venture, and I won't be turned back by anyone. Not you. Not anyone, you hear?"

"I sure do. What did you do for our friend with the wounded hand back there when you two were in the doctor's office?"

"I—I was the one who set him free."

No matter how much he'd been fishing for some juicy tidbit, Sprole didn't seem prepared for the one he'd caught. Paul watched to see if the bounty hunter would make a move or even reflexively ball a fist. He was especially careful to watch the knife that was still in Sprole's hand, but he only got to watch as that knife was flicked into the ground by a snap of the bounty hunter's wrist.

"You . . . what?" Sprole growled.

Paul nodded as if to himself or some other presence that nobody could see. "It seemed the right thing to do at the time, and I stand by it now."

"I know a preacher don't exactly see things the way us normal folks do, but you thought cutting a prisoner loose was the *proper thing to do*?"

"I said right," Paul corrected. "As in correct. I'll be the first to admit it was far from proper."

"Good," Sprole said. "At least that shows you ain't gone completely out of your mind. So, forget about proper. What made you think it was right?"

"There was talk about Terrigan and the rest of the gang coming into Pueblito Verde to look for him. If Wes wasn't in town anymore, those men wouldn't bother coming and putting so many innocents in harm's way. Also, I knew you were going to have a difficult enough time tracking that sharpshooter who fired at you and Sheriff Noss when you went out looking for that first camp. I guessed it would be easier if you could just follow Wes when he went to meet up with the rest of his gang. At the very least, you'd have a fresh set of tracks to follow."

"And what about that confession you supposedly heard?" Sprole asked. "Was there anything to that or was that just something to make the rest of your story hold water?"

Paul locked eyes with the bounty hunter and said, "I wouldn't lie about something as sacred as that."

"But you told me you didn't normally hear confessions. Maybe it ain't as sacred to you as it is to someone who makes more of a habit of it."

"You don't go to church very much at all, do you?"

Snapping his head back as if he'd been flicked on the nose, Sprole said, "What's that got to do with anything?"

"You obviously don't know the meaning of the word *sacred*. It was a difficult decision to tell you what Wes had told me."

"And if you were any kind of real, genuine preacher, you would've died before parting with something like that," Sprole said while punctuating his last word with a poke to the other man's chest. "I've gone to church enough times to know that much."

"You're trying to goad me into a confrontation," Paul stated.

"And, by the look in your eyes, I've almost got one."

In the camp behind them, Sheriff Noss was fixing up a bedroll for Wes. Even though the prisoner could only flop onto the blanket like a large worm in a bird's nest, the outlaw was too tired to complain. Every so often, Noss looked over at Sprole and Paul.

"Wanna know what I think?" Sprole asked.

Matching the bounty hunter's hushed tone, Paul replied, "I'm sure you'll tell me either way."

"I don't think you're any sort of preacher at all. I think you're a liar who was hiding in a pitiful excuse for a town and the only thing you were praying for was that nobody else would notice. Your heart may be in the right place most of the time, which is what threw me off the scent for a spell, but you just keep going back to the plan you got rattling around inside your head."

"And what plan is that?"

"I don't know every part of it, but it's got something to do with Jack Terrigan, and I'd wager there's more to it than you saving another wretched soul. And before you answer back with some hogwash, you should know how close I am to handing out some righteous anger of my own, and I doubt anyone else would disagree once they find out what's really been going on."

Sheriff Noss was almost finished with making certain Wes wouldn't be going anywhere until morning. It was plain to see the lawman was anxious to find out what had occupied the other two for so long.

"If you're threatening to tell the sheriff what I've done, then go ahead," Paul said. "It's bad enough that I felt it necessary to deceive you men, but I never planned on hiding it for any longer than what was necessary."

"Why hide it at all?"

"For the same reason I set Wes loose. Because it had to be done. You were intent on capturing Jack Terrigan, even if it meant sitting in the Red Coyote and waiting until he came storming into Pueblito Verde. It didn't matter to you how many folks were caught in the cross fire, just so long as you got your man and collected the reward."

"I wouldn't have stood by to let anyone get hurt!"

"But it would have happened anyway," Paul shot back. "Just like it happened at that hotel. Only things would have been worse. A single stray round through a window can end an innocent life."

"And what do you think will happen in Raynor?" Sprole asked. "You think Terrigan will just throw his hands in the air and come along peacefully? He's a killer, and men like that don't do anything the easy way."

"Things are bound to be a lot less bloody if Terrigan is caught off his guard. You and Sheriff Noss might just take him by surprise."

"The hell we will! Any surprise we could have gained was ruined when you allowed that man to get away tonight! But it seemed you had your reasons for that."

When Paul stared at the bounty hunter, he didn't care who else was nearby or what could be heard. "I'm doing the best I can with what little there is to work with. If I left it up to either of you, we never would have left town and there would have been a bloodbath where good folks paid the price for one man's laziness and another one's pride.

"Sheriff Noss is a good man," Paul continued, "but he's more concerned with proving himself than thinking things through. From what I've seen, you seem to be a good man as well, but you don't think much past what will get you what you want in as short a ride as possible. I have my faults. I've never claimed otherwise, but I'm trying to get the same job done. The only difference is that I'm able to see the larger picture. Yes,

I have a plan in mind and it changes nearly every second. All I can do is try to change with it."

Sheriff Noss stormed over to where Paul and Sprole were having their discussion, but had to shove in between the other two so he could be noticed. "What is the meaning of all this commotion?"

"Go ahead and tell him, preacher," Sprole said with a self-satisfied grin.

"You want to be the one to decide every man's fate? Then *you* go ahead and say whatever you need to say," Paul said angrily.

"Can it wait until morning?" Noss asked.

Paul remained silent, so Sprole told him, "Yeah. I suppose it can."

"Good," the lawman said. "Since you two decided to let me tend to the prisoner on my own, you two can take first and second watch to make sure nobody slips away or sneaks up on the camp. Hopefully that murderous coward with the rifle will come sniffing back around here for his belongings or just to take another shot at us. I'd hate to miss an opportunity to catch him. That would save us some time and effort in tracking him down."

"Making it awfully easy for him to pick us off, aren't you, Sheriff?" Sprole asked.

"That's why I'm putting the fire out. I've already set up some decoys that will give that man something else to shoot at, which you would have noticed already if either of you two had bothered lending a hand to help."

Paul took a more careful look at the camp. Sure enough, the sheriff had been doing more than building a nest for Wes. Everything from rocks and saddles had been covered by blankets to give the appearance of bodies stretched out on the ground. Noss stomped over to kick dirt onto the sputtering campfire and then lowered himself to a spot against a log. From a distance, it would be difficult to distinguish him from the decoys or any number of other shapes in the shadows. Paul felt a bit more at ease once he reminded himself that those shadows alone would have been enough to provide nearly all the cover they would need. That comfort was strained, however, when he thought of all the different threats the desert could offer that might slither or crawl into the camp without a fire to ward them off.

When Sprole slapped a hand onto Paul's shoulder, odds seemed just as likely for the gesture to be friendly as for it to be hostile. Turned out it was a mixture of both.

"Just tell me one thing, preacher," he said. "How did you manage to set that prisoner loose? When I checked on him last, he was chained to his bed by two different sets of shackles."

"Doc Chandler had the key to both sets," Paul said. "The sheriff gave them to him in the event that he needed to be moved. You know . . . fires or the like. I got my hands on the keys, and when the doctor had to step outside to answer nature's call, I unlocked the shackles."

"And you did that strictly in the name of lighting a fire under me and the law dog while doing your best to prevent Terrigan from raiding Pueblito Verde?"

"That . . . and to give you two a reason for bringing me along."

Sprole nodded. "You never told me why Jack Terrigan is so important to you."

"I already told you as well as the sheriff. Terrigan is making a mistake and I need to have a word with him."

"It's got to be you who speaks sense to him?"

Paul's answer to that was a simple "Yes."

"Why?"

"Because it's the path I've chosen. Now, why don't you get some rest? I'll take first watch." Once that was said, Paul walked over to his saddlebags so he could put his empty tin cup away and then dig out some fresh ammunition for his hunting rifle.

For a moment or two, Sprole watched every move Paul made as if he didn't trust him enough to leave him unattended. His face shifted through several different expressions, all of which were difficult to discern in the inky desert night. He stood there until Paul found a spot where he could sit with his rifle lying across his lap. Finally the bounty hunter gathered his own weapons and chose a patch of ground that provided him the same amount of protection as the sheriff's resting place.

Within minutes, Sprole was asleep and Paul was alone.

In fact, Paul hadn't felt so alone for quite some time.

Chapter 16

Sprole had been right. It would have been easy enough for Theo Price or just about anyone else to sneak to within a hundred yards or so and start firing at the camp, picking the men off one by one. But if Price was the sort of killer who preferred to work from a distance, Paul guessed that danger was always there. It had been some time since he'd had to concern himself with such things, and doing so now brought back plenty of unwelcome memories. Those memories, like the rifleman who shared the darkness of that night with him, would always be out there until something was done to clean them out. When this ride was finished, one way or another, plenty of filth would be swept away.

Dawn was swiftly approaching when Noss kicked off his coarse wool blanket, rubbed his eyes, and dragged himself to his feet. He looked around and eventually spotted Paul sitting with his back against a rock and his feet splayed out away from the campsite.

"I thought you took first watch," the lawman said.

Paul rubbed his eyes. "I did . . . along with second watch. There wasn't enough time for a third."

"When will you get your sleep?"

"When I can. You and Dave are the ones that need your rest. The least I can do is see that you get it."

"Won't do us any good to have you falling from your saddle after dozing off." Rubbing the arm that was held by the crudely fashioned sling, he added, "I know what I'm talking about in that regard."

"How is your arm, by the way?"

"It's fine. Shoulder feels like it's still being twisted about by a team of wild horses, but I'll make it through."

"Good," Paul said.

Just then the uppermost portion of the sun crested the horizon. Rays of light sliced through the few clouds that would burn off in the next few hours, turning the entire sky a deep, rich shade of orange. "Always did love this time of day," Paul mused.

The lawman smiled. "Makes you feel closer to heaven, don't it?"

"There's that . . . but I just like the quiet."

"Quiet ain't never a bad thing, Father." With that, Noss closed his eyes to soak in what the morning had to offer. One eye came open to watch Paul's face when he asked, "So, what was all that commotion between you and Dave last night? Sounded like you two were about to come to blows."

"What did you hear?"

"Something about you cutting my prisoner loose and letting him escape from Doc Chandler's office."

Paul studied the lawman's face carefully. There was no anger to be found amid the creases engraved by so many years spent in a hard, cruel world. He didn't even find any accusations in Noss's eyes. What he did find was the tired resignation of a man who'd already thought the worst of his fellow man and had once again been proven correct.

"You hear a lot, Sheriff."

"I make it a habit to keep my ears open. You'd be amazed how much I've learned just listening to prisoners talking in their cell when they assumed I was too dumb, deaf, or lazy to hear them."

Those words stung Paul's heart. It had felt bad enough calling the lawman lazy the night before, but knowing he'd been heard made it even worse. Then again, it only seemed fitting for him to have to pay the price for such actions taken in anger. "Then you must have also heard my explanation for what I did," Paul said.

"I did. After sleeping on it, I gotta admit you were right about a few things. Me and Dave really would have been content to sit back in town and wait for them outlaws to come a-knocking. Riding out after them has done me a world of good. I feel like a real lawman again, even if I could be riding to meet my end at the hands of a cold-blooded killer."

When Paul started to protest, he was stopped by a simple gesture from Noss.

"Don't worry," the lawman said. "I don't honestly think this is a death sentence. Actually, between the three of us workin' together, I'd say we stand a better than average chance of riding back to Pueblito Verde sitting upright instead of being dragged there in a pine box. As for the business with you shooting all over creation with that hunting rifle, I wouldn't have expected any less."

"I beg your pardon?"

"You've always been a man who marches to his own drummer. Back when Martha and I used to go to Sunday services, we could tell you weren't like any other preacher we ever heard. Sometimes you're just like every other minister who talks about forgiveness and all that, but other times you say things that make the usual fire-and-brimstone speeches seem like a bunch of hot air."

"I . . . don't know what to make of that," Paul admitted.

The lawman shrugged and rubbed his aching shoulder. "While you may not be the sort of preacher I was used to, you've never proven yourself to be anything less than a good man. That ain't no excuse for you sneaking about to set a prisoner loose and then lie about it. It's too late for anyone to change that, and you did come to me before taking such drastic action to see about riding with us to find Terrigan. I suppose there are parables you could read to me or scripture you could recite where a good man has to do something the wrong way for the right reasons, but I don't need to hear any of that. What's done is done."

"That still doesn't make it right," Paul said. "Please forgive me."

"I ain't qualified to forgive anyone," the lawman was quick to reply. "Especially considering all the wrong I've done. We're here now and we're doing the right thing. I've been letting too many of my duties slip since losing Martha and the boys for me to pass this one to someone else. As long as I wear a badge, I'm the one that has to stand up to the likes of Terrigan and his men."

"What about him firing on everything but the one man who needed to be shot?" Sprole asked from where he'd been lying the entire night. The bounty hunter propped himself up on his elbow so he could look at the other two through tired, bloodshot eyes. "I still haven't heard a good enough explanation for that."

First, Noss looked at Paul. Then he looked to Sprole and said, "He's a preacher, Dave. Truth be told, I would have been more upset if he had shot anyone. You and me were the ones out there in the thick of it. If we wanted them outlaws shot, we should have shot them ourselves. Expectin' a preacher to pick up a gun and do your shooting for you just don't make much sense."

That brought the bounty hunter straight to his feet. "But . . . he *lied* to us!"

"Didn't he come to you askin' to have a word with Jack Terrigan?" Noss asked. "Because he sure stated his case to me and I didn't take him seriously. I sure am taking him seriously now. I may not agree with his methods or reasons, but I gotta respect any man who goes through such lengths on account of what he believes."

"We can't just let this pass," Sprole said.

"And we won't." Noss turned to level every bit of his stare at Paul when he said, "Trust me on that. If there's something else you feel we should know, now's the time to tell it to us, Father."

Plenty of words rushed through Paul's head. Some had already been spoken. Some were excuses for actions that had already been taken as well as acts that had yet to be committed. The rest were not fit for the ears of anyone within earshot at the moment, so he shook his head and said, "It seems you already know what brought us this far. I just hope we can move on from here."

"You're with us now and I ain't about to turn you away," Noss said. "It seems like you can do us more good than harm, so we should be able to work together just fine."

"And what happens when we get to Raynor?" Sprole asked. He looked over to Wes, possibly expecting a threat or an insult from the prisoner, but there was no such thing to be had. Wes seemed more than content to keep his head down and let the others have it out.

Noss started gathering his bedroll. "When we find Terrigan, Father Lester can have his words with him. That is, if there are any words to be had once the smoke clears."

"And you don't think he'll make sure he gets to him first?" the bounty hunter said, sneering. "He's already stepped in to muck things up for us just so he could have his way. Who's to say he won't do it again?"

"Someone had to go after these killers," Noss replied. "Terrigan and his gang have had free rein long enough. That's because folks are either too scared to run him down or too willing to let those wild dogs scurry off into someone else's jurisdiction. They came to my town when a bounty hunter was there waiting to hunt them down. On top of that, there's another fellow who'll do just about anything to ride along. Some might call those sorts of things signs from above. Whatever you want to call 'em, the father here showed more gumption than my own deputies, so I'm inclined to let him help. We all got our cards on the table now, though." Looking at Paul as if he were staring into his soul, Noss said, "I'm normally not a forgiving sort, but you've shown me through plenty of hard times. Now's my chance to return the favor."

"Thank you," Paul said. "I truly appreciate it."

"Just don't make a fool outta me. That . . . I won't forgive." Turning his attention back to the task of preparing for the morning's ride, he added, "And don't take offense if you're watched even closer than that idiot wrapped up like an inchworm. That's the price you pay for leading me and Dave around by the nose."

Paul nodded. At the moment, he simply didn't want to take a chance on saying anything to ruin the blessing he'd been given.

"You can bet your last cent I'll be watching you," Sprole growled. "And if I don't like what I see, you better hope you're a good enough preacher to call down God himself to save you."

Paul remained silent.

The camp was broken down.

Horses were loaded and the four of them rode on.

In a strange way, Paul hoped that Price would make another appearance soon. At least that would give everyone someone else to scowl at for a while.

The first few hours of that day's ride passed slowly. Noss's cobbled-together posse headed southwest toward the town of Raynor before stopping to eat a breakfast of jerked beef and some oatcakes that tasted as if they'd been at the bottom of Sprole's saddlebag for the better part of a year. They washed it down with a few sips of water from canteens filled at a small puddle of water. The horses were watered and the group ventured on.

As the sun climbed higher in the sky, its heat became unrelenting. Smoldering waves beat down on Paul's shoulders, soaking through his waistcoat until every stitch of clothing felt as though it had been glued to his skin. And, to make things even less comfortable, all of them spent every second looking for a glint of light off a rifle barrel in the distance or listening for a shot that might claim one of them from afar. Price was still out there. Whether he'd decided to turn the tables on the posse or race them to Raynor was anyone's guess.

"Hey!" Noss barked as he shifted to turn toward the horse beside him. "What do you think your friends are up to?"

Wes was still tied and shackled from head to toe. He lay across his horse's back with a few strands of rope connecting his torso to his saddle horn. He was kept occupied by constantly shifting his weight so as not to fall to the rocky desert floor. He tried to answer the lawman's question, but his words were muffled beyond recognition by the red bandanna that had been stuffed into his mouth. Noss removed the bandanna just long enough to hear the first portion of a string of profanities before promptly sticking the dirty rag back into place.

"I thought you talked some sense into that one, Father," Noss said while hooking a thumb back toward the outlaw.

Paul shrugged. "I can only do so much. At least he's not trying to get away."

"That's just because there ain't nowhere to go." Looking around at the bare rocks and prickly bushes scattered for miles on all sides, the lawman grabbed his canteen and opened it to take a drink. "Looks like Dave's on his way back."

One advantage of the barren terrain was that just about anything within a quarter of a mile that was larger than a jackrabbit could be seen the instant it moved. Sprole's horse galloped toward them after having been absent for the last few hours. The three of them met up and slowed to a walk as they continued riding to the southwest.

"Did you find our elusive Mr. Price?" Noss asked.

Ever since the sun had come up, Sprole's face had been etched into a deep scowl. Removing his hat with one hand, he used the other to swipe a rag across his glistening forehead. "Well, aren't you just the chipper one?"

"I'll feel even better when I hear some good news."

"Hate to disappoint you, Sheriff," Sprole said, "but I don't got any of that for you. Found a couple of tracks that must have been put there in the last day or so, but that's pretty much it."

"Were the tracks pointed toward Raynor?"

"More or less. As far as I know that town's the closest bit of civilization within three days' riding."

"Then all's well," Noss said.

The bounty hunter circled around the group until he was riding alongside Wes's horse. "Sure it is. Just so long as we ain't headed into an ambush or there's not some other spot Price is supposed to meet up with Terrigan. What do you say, mister?" he asked Wes. "Got anything more to tell us?"

Wes craned his neck to look up at him. His entire face screwed into a hateful glare around the bandanna that dangled like a dog's tail from his mouth.

"You sure about that?" Sprole asked.

Even though nobody could make out what the outlaw said, the muffled syllables did not sound friendly.

The bounty hunter muttered a few unintelligible words to himself as well as he looked around at the miles of desert to his right. When he snapped his head back around to look at Wes, he drew the big .44 pistol from its holster and yanked the bandanna from Wes's mouth. "What about now?" he snarled while thumbing the pistol's hammer back and pressing its barrel against Wes's forehead. "You recall anything more you'd like to say?"

Wes's eyes widened and he shook his head in trembling motions so as not to rattle the gun in Sprole's hand.

"That's enough of that!" Paul said.

"Keep out of this, preacher! You've done enough damage!"

Noss snapped his reins so he could ride around to get on the other side of Sprole's horse. "We put that behind us, Dave," he said.

"Maybe you did, but I don't forget so easily. And even if this preacher has come clean, having him around just makes this one here think we've gone soft. Ain't that right?" Sprole said as he leaned over to press the barrel even harder against Wes's head as if he meant to bore all the way through to the other side. "You think we're soft on account of the company we keep, don't you?"

"N-no! I—I—I never thought that!" Wes said.

"Then maybe we been too easy on you, because I think you still got more to say!"

"No! I swear it!" Wes hollered.

"Where's Jack Terrigan?" Noss asked. "Best be honest with us now."

Unwilling to move in the event that he might cause the pistol to bump against Sprole's trigger finger, Wes only moved his eyes. They rattled in their sockets, bouncing back and forth between Sprole and Noss, as he said, "East Raynor! I already told you! East Raynor!"

"Would that partner of yours head straight there or would he try to pick us off along the way?" Sprole asked.

"How should I know?"

The bounty hunter cracked the barrel of his gun against one of the darker bruises near Wes's temple, which covered a large welt that had been put there after one of the many other cracks he'd taken to that part of his skull. "Make an educated guess!"

"We were all supposed to meet in East Raynor!"

"Where were you supposed to go once you got there?"

"Some cathouse named the Wayfaire."

"The what?" Sprole asked.

Sensing the bounty hunter's fuse was burning quicker with every question he asked, Wes said, "The Wayfaire! That's all I know! I never even been there before!"

Once the outlaw ran out of breath, the only sounds left were the rustle of a hot, dry wind and the steady clomp of hooves upon baked earth. Suddenly Sprole retracted his pistol and eased its hammer back to a resting position. "I suppose I believe you. What do you say, preacher?"

Paul didn't answer right away, and before either of the other men could check on him, the crack of a distant shot rippled through the air.

"I knew it!" Sprole said as he pointed the .44 once more at Wes.

The outlaw blubbered to himself and turned his head so he didn't have to look down the wrong end of that gun barrel one more time.

"Stop it, both of you," Paul said.

Sprole had his eyes fixed on Wes. "This one's leading us into a trap."

Noss had already drawn his .45 and was searching the horizon for a target. "I heard that shot."

"So did I," Paul told him. "But it wasn't fired at us. Hand over those field glasses."

"What do you see, Father?"

When Paul twisted back around in his saddle to look at the sheriff, his face was that of a man who wasn't about to be refused. "I don't know yet. Just hand me those field glasses!"

Keeping his pistol in hand, Noss leaned over to dig into his saddlebag for the glasses. He found them and tossed them over to Paul. To Sprole, he said, "Stuff that scarf back into his mouth and pay attention. Whatever threat is out there, it sure ain't him."

Wes's labored breaths were once again muffled by

the bandanna, making it easier for the rest of the men to hear not only another shot but some shouting as well.

Paul had the field glasses up to his eyes and was pointing them toward the east.

Now that Noss was looking in that same direction, he could see the small group of people huddled around a covered wagon parked about a quarter of a mile away. "Is that our man?" he asked.

"No."

"Then what's the commotion about?"

"It's . . . hard to say."

"Don't bother saying anything else," Sprole snapped. "If it's not Price or Terrigan or anyone else with a bounty on their head, it ain't our concern."

"Maybe it's not your concern," Paul said as he handed the glasses back to Noss, "but it's mine." With that, he snapped his reins to ride away from the trail, across the rocky plain toward the wagon.

"Let him go," Sprole said with a dismissive wave. "We're better off without him." Wes started to protest with a chorus of muffled cries, which Sprole ended with a backhanded swat across the outlaw's head. "You just want him around because he's the soft touch among the three of us. I got news for you, friend. He ain't enough to save you anymore."

"And I've got some news for you," Noss announced. "We're following Father Lester."

"Why?"

"Because it looks like the family in that wagon is in trouble and I ain't about to let 'em die out here."

"Family?" Sprole grunted. "What are they doing out in the middle of a desert?"

Taking a quick glance through the field glasses, Noss replied, "Looks like they're being robbed. I can see a few young'uns and what looks to be a woman." He dropped the glasses back into his saddlebag. "If this man's an outlaw, he may know something more about Terrigan's gang."

"Or he may just be some robber that ain't worth our time."

"I'm wasting time talking to a man that's been cross ever since the sun came up this morning. I'm not about to waste any more."

"Suit yourself."

"You stay here with the prisoner," Noss said. "If you're not here when me and Father Paul come back, then don't expect my help once the lead starts to fly in Raynor." With that, the lawman snapped his reins and rode in Paul's wake.

For a few seconds, Sprole watched the other two. Then he cursed under his breath and snatched the reins to Wes's horse. "Try to hang on," he said. "We're going somewhere to keep an eye on them, and I won't waste the time to collect you if you slide off along the way."

Thanks to the bandanna stuffed in his mouth and the rumble of hooves against dry rock, Wes's muffled screams went mostly unheard.

Chapter 17

Paul rode toward the covered wagon as if it were his own kin in the midst of the shots that had been fired. Sheriff Noss wasn't far behind and he tapped his heels against his horse's sides in an attempt to catch up a little faster. Since Paul didn't have a weapon in hand, the lawman didn't like the notion of letting him lead the charge. As far as that was concerned, he didn't like the idea of there being a charge at all. He'd heard the shots that had been fired and could now see four people standing near the wagon, but he had yet to discover who was doing the shooting.

"Hold up!" Noss shouted once he'd closed a bit more of the distance between himself and Paul. One of the tricks the desert could play on a man's eyes was to fool him into thinking something was a lot closer than it truly was. With so much open space that was heated to the point of giving off shimmering waves, it seemed as if they were galloping in place instead of getting any closer to the people gathered around the wagon.

When another shot was fired, it was followed by a shrieking cry. Those things caused Paul to grip his reins tighter, lean over his horse's neck, and coax even more speed from the animal's powerful strides.

Noss hung back until he was certain the ground in front of him was nice and flat. Although he was able to hold his reins and use his left hand for some basic tasks, that shoulder still hurt like a bear and he wasn't about to race ahead if there was a chance he might fall off again. Despite his reservations, his horse had soon built up a good head of steam to race alongside Paul's.

"Ease up, Father," he shouted. "You don't know what you're getting yourself into."

"I see at least two small children," he replied. "Whoever is there must have noticed us because the shooting's stopped."

As if waiting for that particular moment, another shot was fired.

Before Paul could answer that shot with some sort of foolish display, Noss gave his reins another powerful snap and surged past the other horse. He could tell Paul was close by, but as long as he was behind him, Noss was fine with it.

The wagon in front of him looked as if it had been in the desert for months. The tarp was covered in layer upon layer of gritty dirt, and the two horses pulling it hung their heads in fatigue. The children Paul had spotted stood near the back end of the wagon. One was a short girl with dark red hair pulled into a messy braid who had her arms wrapped around a skinny reed of a boy with a mop of messy black hair hanging down to nearly cover his eyes. A woman stood between them and a man wearing baggy brown trousers held up by suspenders that had probably been taken from a more formal suit of clothes. His simple white cotton shirt covered a thick chest, and both sleeves were rolled up to expose muscular forearms. Solid pawlike hands were wrapped around a shotgun, which he pointed at the woman.

"Stay away from me!" the man shouted as Noss and Paul came to a halt amid the rumble of hooves.

Noss eased back a few steps and motioned for Paul to do the same. "Put the gun down, mister," he said. "I'm a sheriff. You hurt these people and there ain't no going back, you hear me?"

"He's right," Paul said. "You don't want to do this."

The man's face was twisted into a desperate grimace. Sweat rolled down both cheeks to drip off a stubble-covered chin. "You don't know who I am or what I want!"

Easing himself down from his saddle, Paul held his hands up and out with his fingers splayed wide. "You're right. We don't know each other. I'm Paul Lester."

The man's eyes were drawn to the white collar Paul wore beneath his morning coat. "Are you a preacher?"

"Yes, sir. I am. What's your name?"

"Chesterfield. Gabe Chesterfield."

Still looking along the barrel of his pistol, Noss said, "It don't look like these good people have anything worth stealing, Gabe. Throw that weapon aside and step away before someone gets hurt."

"I ain't stealing from them," Gabe said.

"Then why are you holding a gun on them?"

The next several moments were as heavy as they were quiet. When Paul stepped closer to the wagon, each of his steps crunched loudly enough to echo in everyone's ears. "He's not a robber," he said. "He's riding with them. Gabe, these people are your kin, aren't they?"

Several more quiet seconds passed.

Gabe's face twisted into an expression that was almost as confused as the sheriff's.

Finally Gabe nodded. "Yeah. They're my kin."

"Do you know these folks?" Noss asked.

Paul shook his head slowly and took another cautious step forward. "We've never met, but I can see for myself. That boy looks like Gabe and that pretty lady standing right there. And the little girl . . . she's got her daddy's eyes and hair."

Gabe twitched as if the wind rustling his own dark red hair scraped against his skin like an unwanted touch.

Having dismounted, Noss started to move forward, but was stopped by one of Paul's quickly extended arms. "You're pointing a gun at your own family?" the lawman snarled. "What in blazes is *wrong* with you?"

"Something happened here," Paul said. "Isn't that right?"

"Happened several miles back," Gabe said.

"Back along the trail?"

Gabe nodded.

"What was it?" Paul asked.

Slapping away Paul's arm, Noss took one more step and planted his feet when he saw Gabe lift his gun to take aim. "We can continue this conversation after you put that gun down, mister."

Gabe's expression was that of someone who was drifting far away from everything he knew. "No . . . I—I can't."

"Do it!" Noss said. "Or . . ." He stopped when he saw Paul walk forward to stand directly in front of Gabe's shotgun. Once the preacher was standing almost close enough to bump his chest against the shotgun's barrels, Gabe didn't quite know what to do.

Something rustled behind the wagon, causing Gabe to turn in that direction. "No, you don't, boy!" he shouted.

"Forget about them," Paul urged.

"No! Come out where I can see you!"

The rustling stopped for a moment or two before the sounds became heavy, determined steps. Soon a young man in his early teens stepped around the team of horses hitched to the wagon with both hands held high above his head.

"Get back, Mason!" the woman cried.

But the young man stood his ground. Although he tried to look defiantly at Gabe, he couldn't prevent the tears from trickling down his cheeks. "I won't go nowhere, Ma," he said. "Not until I put a stop to this."

"Ain't no stopping this," Gabe said. "Not no more."

"What are you talking about?" Noss asked. "Tell me before I—"

"Yes," Paul cut in. "Tell us what happened."

"You ain't nobody to me," Gabe said. "And they already know what happened. Don't you, Nora?"

This time, Paul did bump the shotgun's barrel as he inched forward. The jostle snapped Gabe's attention away from the sobbing woman and drew it straight to him. "Forget about them for now," he said. "I want to hear what happened."

"Why?"

"Because it's troubling you."

"This ain't got a damn thing to do with you," Gabe snarled.

Although he didn't move much, Noss tensed every muscle in his body like a coiled snake that was about to strike. "It involves me now," he said. "You either explain yourself or deal with me. Your choice, but I promise you don't wanna deal with me right now."

"He's right," Paul said. "On all counts. We're here, and from where I'm standing it seems I am very much involved. Tell me what happened, Gabe. It will do you some good to get it off your chest."

Sweat poured down Gabe's face and he shook his head as if he was refusing the insistent advances of demons only he could see.

"You lost someone," Paul said. Then he nodded, convinced as if he'd listened to what those same demons were whispering into Gabe's ear. "That's it, isn't it? I can tell."

"H-how?"

"Because I've seen that look on plenty of men's faces."

Almost immediately, Gabe's expression shifted from tired confusion to rage. "You don't know me!"

"Maybe not, but I know sorrow when I see it. A preacher's job is to shepherd folks through sorrow brought about from loss, strife, or just having to find your way through this terrible world."

A single laugh gurgled from the back of Gabe's throat, sounding more like a cough than anything else. "Mighty dark words coming from a preacher. I thought you men were about joy and light and God's grace and all of that."

"We are," Paul assured him. "But this world has just as much shadow as it does light. Can't have one without the other, you know. They balance each other out."

As Paul went on in that vein, Noss slipped back and circled around toward the woman and children huddled near the back end of the wagon. Keeping his pistol aimed in Gabe's general direction, he motioned to them with his free hand. The young boy was the first to start running toward him, and with some insistence from her mother, the little redheaded girl was next.

Paul stepped closer to Gabe and inched to one side to block his line of sight while also making sure to keep the shotgun's barrel pressed against his own chest. "Sometimes it doesn't seem like much of a balance, though, does it?" he said as a way to hold Gabe's eye.

"No, sir."

"Sometimes the dark just doesn't seem to end. When enough of it piles up on a man's shoulders, it makes him think things he might not normally consider. Maybe he'd do things that would never seem right otherwise."

Gabe's fingers clenched tighter around the shotgun's grip. Holding the weapon was enough of a strain, but Paul doubted that was what made his hand tremble now.

"You lost someone," Paul said. "Who was it?"

"Mae," Gabe sighed. "My sweet little Mae."

Nora and the two small children were now gathered around Noss. The lawman stood vigilant while she wrapped her arms around her children. "*Our* sweet Mae," she said.

Gabe barely seemed to hear her words, but nodded absently. "She was just a baby. Born a few months before we all struck out across the territory. We was bound for California and it seemed that sweet, dear little one was a sign from above that we was gonna make it just fine. She picked up a little cough after a bad storm, but we kept going. I insisted we keep going."

"Of course you did," Paul said.

Gabe's eyes flared wide and for a moment it seemed he might pull the shotgun's trigger. "I should've turned back," he snarled while glaring at Paul over both barrels. "I should've stayed put. I should've insisted that Nora and Mae stay behind until they was better."

"You should have split apart your family?" Paul asked. "Abandon your hopes?"

"We kept moving," Gabe continued. "Kept rolling along as Mae coughed and I complained about the noise when she would keep us awake at night. We saw a doctor a few towns back, but all he did was give us some elixir in a dropper to drip onto her tongue. That didn't keep her from crying! Didn't keep her from fussing every hour of every day! Didn't . . . didn't . . ."

In a steady voice, Paul said, "Didn't keep her from dying?"

Gabe's eyes were bloodred around the edges and they narrowed as if they were staring into the heart of the sun. "That's right."

"This world can be a terrible place," Paul told him. "It's harsh and cruel, but things don't happen without good reason. You may not know what the reason is, but it's there."

"You want me to pray?" Gabe asked as if the very words he'd spoken had somehow burned his tongue. "You want me to fall to my knees and thank God for what he's done?"

"No. I can do that for you. All I ask is that you take comfort in knowing that I'll never stop praising your little Mae. You can take care of your family and you all will never forget her. You just think about her face and her laugh. You brought your family this far. You worry about the loved ones you can see and feel. Trust Mae with the higher powers. I promise . . . I won't let her fall."

Gabe was speechless.

"These all seem like fine children," Paul said. "And they seem to love you very much. Otherwise, I'm guessing your son would have picked up that gun by now."

Gabe barely had to turn his head to notice the eldest son standing so close to a discarded pistol that the toe of one boot rested against its handle. He looked down at the weapon before slowly bending at the knees to reach for it.

"It's all right, son," Gabe said. "You're old enough to fend for yourself as well as your ma and the rest."

"No," Paul told him. "That's your job, remember?" Turning to the young man who had yet to pick up the pistol, he asked, "What's your name?"

"Mason," the young man replied.

"You won't need that gun, Mason. Go on and join the others. Your pa and I need to have a word alone."

Despite all that had happened, all that was still happening, Mason still looked to Gabe before making another move.

"Go on," Gabe told him.

That was enough to get Mason to rush over to Nora and the rest of the children, leaving his father's pistol in the dirt behind him.

Gabe had yet to relinquish the shotgun. In fact, he held on to it as though it were the only thing keeping him from falling off the face of the earth. "I know what you're feeling," Paul told him. "I've lost plenty. I've looked into the eyes of more folks who've lost everything dear to them than I care to recall. I've been there when men have lost their wives, parents lost their children, families were blown apart by the cruel wind of fate, and every other horror you can imagine. I'm not about to tell you it'll ever get easy to bear."

"What am I supposed to do, then?" Gabe asked quietly. "If I can't live with myself, I can't stand up for my family. If I can't do that, I don't have much reason for being here."

"You've got your whole life in front of you. So do they."

Hearing those words made Gabe's next breaths heavy as they were dragged into his lungs and laboriously pushed out again.

"What brought you to this?" Paul asked. "Why would you point a gun at your family? You've told me this much, so you might as well tell me the rest."

"Confession is good for my soul?" Gabe asked.

"It can be, but I think you just need to hear the words for yourself."

Reluctantly, Gabe said, "I . . . she . . . Nora . . . Nora wanted to move on after we put little Mae into the ground. She wanted to move on and just leave her behind."

"What were you all supposed to do?"

"I don't know. It just . . . it didn't seem right. We kept going and I wanted to turn back. She said we had to keep going. That we had to forget about Mae like she never even happened."

Paul reached past the shotgun to place a hand on Gabe's shoulder. "Is that really what she told you?"

Gabe's eyes clenched shut.

His finger tightened around the trigger, causing the iron mechanism to creak like a bough in the wind.

Suddenly he let out a breath and relaxed his finger while opening his eyes into tired slits. "No," he breathed. "That ain't what she said."

"What did she want?" Paul asked.

"She wanted to move along. She wanted to put Mae behind us."

Nora had stepped closer now, straining against Noss's attempts to hold her back. "I wanted to put her death behind us," she insisted. "I wanted to put that terrible day and all the tears and all the sadness behind us. Just leave it buried there along with—"

"Along with my little baby girl!" Gabe roared as he swung the shotgun around to point at her.

Paul grabbed hold of the barrel and forced the shotgun upward but toward himself so it couldn't point at anyone else. "You're drowning right now," he said.

"Your head's not right. When you're drowning, things don't sound right. Things don't look right. Nothing's right until you come up and take a clear breath again. This ain't the way back up, Gabe. You know that!"

"I—I don't . . . ," Gabe stammered. Then he strengthened his grip on the shotgun and wailed, "I don't wanna be in this world no more!"

Gabe was a strong man and thick muscles flexed in his arms as he fought to reclaim his shotgun. The weapon went off, roaring like a clap of thunder that blasted through the air and startled the rest of his family into stunned silence. Smoke still rolled from the barrel and churned through air that stank of burned gunpowder, but the shotgun was still aimed at the sky thanks to Paul's unwavering grip.

"No," Paul said tersely. "I won't let you make that decision. No man gets to decide when he or anyone else leaves this world. You'll stay until your time runs out. Just like the rest of us."

Eyes wide and mouth agape, Gabe looked into the face of the man directly in front of him. When Paul pulled on the shotgun's barrel, he relinquished the weapon without another thought. Noss approached to take the shotgun, but wasn't quick to do so before Paul eased his fingers off it.

"Are you all right?" Noss asked.

The skin of Paul's hand was blistered and red from the heat of the barrel. Before either man could see much more than that, Paul hid his hand beneath his coat as if he were reaching for something in an inner pocket. "I'm fine," he said. "We need to finish this."

"I agree," the lawman said. "This man ain't fit to lead a donkey, not to mention a family, anywhere."

"That's not what I meant." Looking over to Gabe, Paul asked, "Can you show me where your little girl is buried?"

It had been the better part of a day since the Chesterfield family put Mae's grave behind them, but the spot marked by a little wooden cross was less than a mile from where Gabe had made his stand. When they all rode back there, Noss insisted that Gabe ride with him away from the rest of the family. Sprole got no explanation apart from instructions that he was to remain behind until the other two returned.

When they arrived at the grave, the family was slow to approach it. Nora was first and she stepped up to the mound of freshly turned dirt to drop to her knees while sinking her hands flat into the earth. The children closed in around her, rubbing her back or staring down silently at the little portion of ground that would hold their baby sister for all time.

Paul reached beneath his shirt to remove a simple silver cross from a chain. Holding the cross in one hand, he walked behind the little grave marker, placed a hand on it, and began to pray out loud.

Some of the prayers, Noss recognized. Others, he didn't. Some were just simple thoughts spoken in Paul's own words reflecting upon the joy of family and the simple peace to be found in shared love. Noss didn't latch on to the words themselves, so much as the meaning behind them.

Somewhere along the line, Gabe approached his family.

His arms hung limply at his sides and when Nora realized her husband was standing directly behind her, she reached out and took his hand. The children looked up at their father and responded joyfully when he encircled one arm around Mason's shoulders. The entire Chesterfield family embraced and cried as one while Paul spoke gentle words to soothe their souls.

When the service was completed, Noss bowed his head and wept for a little girl he'd never met.

Afterward, Paul approached the lawman and led him away from the grave. "I don't think they'll stay long," he said to Noss. "But I think we should be here until they decide to get moving again."

"Yeah. I suppose you're right. What should I do about him?"

Paul looked over to Gabe, who hunkered down to have a few quiet words with his youngest son. "He was a tortured man who had a terrible day. He reacted badly. Do you think there's more to it than that?"

"I don't know. Perhaps I should ask her."

Paul followed the sheriff's line of sight to find Nora walking over to them. She smiled through a mask of tears and extended a hand to Paul. "I don't know how to thank you," she said. Her eyes widened when she saw the hand she was reaching for was reddened by ugly burns that had been put there by the hot shotgun barrel. Paul tucked it away so as not to disturb her any further.

"Your husband," Noss said. "Did he hurt anyone?"

She was quick to shake her head. "He was terribly

upset when I wanted to leave. Truth be told, I know he was taking it hard and thought it best if we move on. I should have let him stay but," she added while smiling at Paul, "he needed this more than anything else."

"Has he ever hurt you or anyone for that matter?" Noss pressed.

"No, sir," she told him.

"What should I do, then? Will you be safe with him?"

"Yes. When Gabriel picked up that shotgun and demanded for me to turn back, I refused. The man who looked at me then . . . I've never seen him before. As frightened as I was and as loud as he shouted, he didn't harm any of us."

"We heard shots," Noss reminded her.

"He fired a pistol into the air a few times while he was screaming, but he tossed it away."

"He had that shotgun pointed at you."

"He was angry, but he wasn't going to shoot," she said. "He never even had his finger on that trigger. Not until you two showed up."

"For all we know," Paul said, "he could have thought we were robbers and he was trying to protect his family."

But Noss still wasn't happy. "Or he could have cracked in the head. Just because this was the first time he went off like this don't mean it'll be the last."

Paul pointed to the children who were gathered around Gabe. "Look at them. Do they look scared for their lives?"

"Let's ask them that the next time their father gets a shotgun in his hands."

"The only person he wanted to hurt was himself," Paul said. "And I believe that's passed."

"Maybe," Noss grunted. "Maybe not. It's your family, ma'am. You should be the one to tell me what to do. Whatever you choose, I'll abide by it."

"Gabriel is one of the gentlest souls I know," she said. "I think that's why he was hurt so badly by Mae's passing. This is the hardest thing I've ever had to bear. I like to think I'm a strong person, but even I felt ready to crack today. Have you ever lost a child?"

"Yes," Noss said tensely. "I have."

"Then you know how badly it hurts. Do you think that might explain some of what drove Gabriel to that?"

"I—I suppose. I just don't want it to happen again."

"If he meant to hurt any of us, he would have," she assured him. "We were standing in that spot for a while before you happened by. He was angry because he was missing something." Turning to Paul, she said, "And you gave it to him. Gave it to us all. Thank you."

"You're welcome," Paul said with a smile.

"We'll be all right now. I'll take care of Gabriel," she said. "We'll all take care of each other. Thanks again." With that, she turned and went back to her family.

Noss wasn't altogether happy about it, but he and Paul left the Chesterfields after they'd taken the time they needed with Mae. They were piling back into the wagon when Gabe came over and asked, "You all right, Reverend?"

"Yes," Paul replied.

"What about your hand?"

"I'll see to it."

"Let us dress it properly. It's the least we can do."

"That would be good of you."

Noss watched Gabe carefully as Nora spread oint-
ment onto some bandages and wrapped them around
Paul's hand. He waited for any sign that Gabe needed
to be restrained or otherwise dealt with in a manner to
which the sheriff was accustomed, but he found no
cause for alarm. If anything, Gabe seemed tired and
embarrassed. His children swarmed around him without pause. More than anything else, that put the lawman's mind at ease.

Excusing himself as soon as the bandages were tied,
Paul made his way back to his horse. "You ready, Sheriff?"

"I am. I just don't know if I'm comfortable leaving
that man with his family."

"He made a mistake and he won't forget it. He's
where he belongs now. After what he's been through,
he deserves that much."

Chapter 18

"So, what took you two so long?" Sprole asked the instant Noss and Paul returned.

"There was business to tend to," Noss told him.

"What kind of business?"

"The important kind. It's tended to so don't worry about it."

They were back on the trail to Raynor, moving along at a steady pace. Wes was still tied up and breathing through the bandanna in his mouth, and the bounty hunter hadn't stopped glaring at the other two. "No need to worry, huh?" Sprole grunted. "We lost the better portion of a day on this nonsense. Time, by the way, that was used by that killer to get ahead of us and warn Terrigan that we're after him."

"Do you honestly think that will frighten Jack Terrigan away?" Paul asked.

Without much thought, Sprole shrugged. "Probably not, but it'll take away any element of surprise we might have had."

"Then we'll just have to think of something else."

"Easy for you to say, preacher!" Sprole snapped.

Suddenly Noss twisted in his saddle as if he was about to draw his pistol and point it at the bounty hunter. "You should watch your mouth!"

"What did I say?"

"When you call him preacher, it sounds like you're spitting the word at him. Learn some respect or I'll teach it to you!"

"All right. Fine. You two grew real close while you were away. That's real sociable. I ain't interested in swapping spit with either of you, so get as close as you want. You know I'm talkin' the truth when I tell you that letting Price get farther ahead of us, whether we know where he's headed or not, ain't such a good idea."

"Did you ever think ahead to the possibility that this sort of thing might happen where we might get delayed somehow?" Paul asked.

"Sure I did, but that ain't—"

"Well, that's what happened. We've gotten a bit behind from where we thought we'd be, so let's make up that time. Can't we still regain some advantage if we arrive without being seen or find a way to get the drop on Terrigan once we're there?"

Sprole scowled at Paul as if he'd just picked something sour from between his teeth. "Listen to you. And here I thought you just wanted to have a nice chat with Terrigan to discuss the error of his ways."

Pointing a finger at the trail directly in front of them, Noss asked, "Is this still the way to Raynor?"

"You know it is," Sprole replied.

"Then let's not waste any more time and just get there before we grow too long in the tooth to do much of anything against Terrigan or his gang." With that, the lawman snapped his reins and galloped ahead.

Shooting one more quick, irritated glance at Paul, Sprole followed and took Wes's horse along with him. The prisoner's hands had just enough wiggle room to grab on to the edge of the saddle so he could hang on for dear life.

Paul brought up the rear of the group. They had enough water to make it to Raynor, and the terrain was flat. Even so, it looked as if he had a long, grueling day in front of him.

Under normal circumstances, they would have made camp before heading the rest of the way into town. Considering what was at stake, however, even Sheriff Noss was willing to press onward awhile longer until they reached the outermost reaches of the little pocket of civilization called Raynor.

Like many settlements in the Arizona Territory, most of Raynor was situated in a clump of narrow streets, dusty buildings, and crooked alleyways surrounded by smaller structures, tents, corrals, and fenced-in vacant lots. Smaller structures extended from the main portion of town like wisps of smoke curling from a larger fire. By the time they arrived at the outermost extension of town, Paul, Noss, Sprole, and Wes were too tired to ride any farther.

The first place they found that suited their needs was an old barn that had been converted into a stable. Judging by the sorry condition of the wooden planks that had been used to cobble the barn together, it might have been standing there long before the rest of the town. A thin ghoul of a stableman greeted the weary group and demanded too much money to rent three stalls for the night.

After a small amount of bargaining, none of the men minded sleeping in the stalls. Actually, one did have a problem with the arrangement, but couldn't say so because of a bandanna stuffed into his mouth. After several flips of a coin, Noss wound up sharing a stall with Wes. All he needed to do was threaten to crack the butt of his pistol against the prisoner's head for the muffled complaints to stop. After that, the barn was filled with nothing more than the shuffle of hooves against old straw, the creak of wind passing between loose boards, and the snoring of three exhausted men.

Paul found it difficult to sleep. Although he had yet to lay eyes on Jack Terrigan, his muscles were tensed as though he were already staring straight into the killer's eyes. Noss insisted that Paul carry his pistol with him at all times. The lawman's reasoning was that, even if Paul never intended to pull the trigger, it would do some good for others to see three armed men on the posse instead of just two. Naturally, Sprole had questioned the value of that armed man being a preacher, but the old Colt remained on Paul's person all the same.

The weapon felt cold and familiar in Paul's hand. Lying in the corner of that stall, curled up on a pile of straw and a bedroll, he checked the weapon to make sure it would be good for anything other than blowing his hand apart if it was eventually fired.

One thought rattled around in the back of his mind like a rock in his boot, annoying him more and more until it developed into one simple question.

If the need arose, would he be able to kill a man?

As much as he wanted to have his talk with Terrigan, he knew it would be plain foolish to do so while unarmed. There was much to be said for going in with empty hands and a comforting smile, but men like Jack Terrigan didn't respect that sort of thing. On the other hand, carrying a gun could be nothing but trouble. It went against everything Paul believed, and despite that, leaving the Colt behind hadn't been an option.

He needed to bring the gun with him, whether anyone else agreed with the decision or not. Sprole would be behind him. In fact, the bounty hunter no doubt found it amusing for Paul to present himself as a walking, talking contradiction. Noss might take comfort from knowing Paul could defend himself, but he still got a twitch in the corner of one eye whenever he'd looked back to check on him and seen the holster beneath his morning coat.

In darkness smelling of horseflesh and rotten wood, Paul put the gun in his hand to feel its weight within his grasp.

The pistol wasn't loaded. His thumb brushed against the cylinder, clicking it from one chamber to the next, while his eyes closed to count them off. The hammer cocked back and was eased back down again. These were motions that Paul had done countless times throughout his life, but were out of character now.

A man of God wasn't supposed to arm himself.

A preacher wasn't supposed to ride on posses.

A man of faith wasn't supposed to be so familiar with what went on inside a killer's head.

Perhaps these were just the way things were supposed to be. Paul had to grin when he considered that. Even a quick glance into history was enough to prove he wasn't the first man of faith to take up a weapon. He surely wasn't the only one with questions in his head or doubt in his heart. In fact, thinking he was alone in those regards seemed downright arrogant. Unfortunately, none of the others who'd traveled that road before were there at the moment to ease his troubled thoughts.

The only thing that gave him any peace at all was the knowledge that, although he might not be going about things in a regular way, the path he rode was a righteous one. If he could have faith in that, then it didn't really matter who rode that path with him.

Paul didn't exactly sleep the sleep of the just, but he did manage to drift off after keeping his eyes closed long enough.

Chapter 19

When Paul awoke, he was alone in the stable. At least, it sure seemed that way when the only other living things he could see were horses and a few rats making a nest in another stall. After peeking over the gate of his stall, he opened it and walked down the middle of the barn to take a closer look at his surroundings. Noss and Sprole were both gone, as were their horses. In Noss's stall, Wes remained. Paul approached him to find the outlaw still dozing in a twitching, fretful slumber.

"Wake up," Paul said while plucking the bandanna from Wes's mouth.

The outlaw awoke with a start, trying to stretch his arms and legs, which only served to reacquaint him with his bindings. "Wha . . . ?" he grunted as he collected himself.

"Where did the others go?"

"How should I know? I ain't nothing but another saddlebag to you three!"

"Don't tell me you didn't notice you were here alone," Paul said.

"Even if I did notice, that don't mean I know where they got off to."

Paul cocked his head and placed his hands on his hips in a stance that he usually used on kids who'd either misbehaved in Sunday school or tried to sneak a sip of wine during a church supper when their parents hadn't been looking. Surprisingly enough, it worked even quicker now than when he'd attempted the same stern glare on young ones. Of course, this time one hand had brushed aside his coat to show the holstered Colt.

"All right!" Wes whined. "The sheriff got up just after sunup, I think. Him and that other one had a few words and then headed out. But like I said before, I don't know where they went."

"Did they say anything to you before they went?"

"Just that I should behave. I'm sick of bein' treated like a dog, you know."

"Yeah," Paul said. "I know."

"After what you did before . . . letting me go and all . . . how about you let me go again? I heard you just wanted me to flush out one of the others. It worked to bring Price into the open. I bet it'd work even better now."

"You promise you'll set your life straight?" Paul asked.

Wes's eyes became wide as saucers and he nodded fiercely. "I do! This whole experience has soured me on ever wanting to break the law again!"

Paul left the stall and closed the gate behind him. "Lying is a sin. And lying to a preacher is even worse."

"Well, I ain't . . . aw, just go," Wes grunted.

When Paul stepped out of the barn, he was greeted by an old man with suspenders keeping a pair of tattered brown trousers hitched up to his chest. What caught Paul's attention even more than the dented stove-top hat the old man wore was the scattergun clutched in the old man's hands.

"Where the hell you think you're goin'?" the old man asked in a grating voice reminiscent of a hoe being dragged across rusted steel.

Reflexively raising his hands, Paul said, "I was just checking after my friends. Have you seen—"

"Where'd you get that gun?" the old man demanded as he brought the scattergun to his shoulder. "How'd you get out of all them ropes?"

"Oh, I see. You have me mistaken for the other fellow in there. My name is Paul Lester."

"I don't care what yer name is. Dressin' up like a preacher ain't gonna change my opinion of you for the better."

"I am a preacher. My congregation is in Pueblito Verde."

"I ain't never seen a preacher wearin' a gun."

Sometimes even Paul was amazed at how swiftly a man could be shown when he'd overstepped his bounds. The first time he wore the Colt around his waist instead of tucked away in a saddlebag, he was forced to pay the price. Keeping his hands raised, he asked, "Didn't the men who left here tell you who I was?"

"That sheriff told me plenty," the old man replied.

"And he paid me to keep watch to make certain that outlaw fella didn't get away."

"He didn't tell you he had a third man riding with him?"

"Yes, but . . . aw, stand still for a second." The old man was still muttering to himself when he waddled over to Paul and squinted at him with cloudy blue eyes. The barrel of the shotgun bumped against Paul's stomach and was pulled away once the old man got a chance to study his face. "That *is* you. Didn't recognize you when you weren't sprawled out in a pile of hay. There's a hotel or two in town, you know. Any one of them beds should beat the stuffin' out of sleeping here. Well . . . most of them beds anyhow. What about that prisoner?"

"He's awake, but not going anywhere. Is there anyone guarding the back door?"

"A wild horse with a burr under its saddle couldn't get that back door open, so no one man could do the job. He'd have to come through me if he's goin anywhere."

Paul looked up at the barn to pick out a few more details than he'd been able to see the night before. Any windows he spotted were boarded up, and the little square opening to the loft was sealed by a door without so much as a strand of rope to help anyone up to it even if they could break the lock and open the door without making a sound.

"If you're lookin' for them others that were sleeping with the horses," the old man said, "they rode into town just after sunup."

Removing the dented watch from his pocket, Paul

saw it was just past eight o'clock in the morning. "Can you direct me to the Wayfaire?"

The old man cocked his head, raised his eyebrows, and took half a step back as if he was about to put his scattergun to use after all. "What's a preacher want at a cathouse?"

Rather than explain his entire situation to the old-timer, Paul clasped his hands in front of him and declared, "I intend to preach to those most in need of the Good Word."

"Lookin' to show the light to a few soiled doves?"

"I do what I can, wherever I can."

"What about the six-shooter?"

Straightening his coat so it fell around the holster, Paul said, "The good Lord gave us the means to protect ourselves in a harsh world."

"Amen to that. I suppose that fella was right about you."

Although the old man had lowered the scattergun and relaxed somewhat, Paul had to ask, "Which fella? The one with his arm in a sling?"

"No. The other one."

"What did he say?"

"Told me you were a strange bird, but a good man."

Compared to some of the other things that had come out of Sprole's mouth in the time he'd known him, being called strange was downright complimentary.

"Besides," the old man added with a sly grin, "there ain't no law sayin' a preacher can't enjoy the company of a good woman. Or a bad one, for that matter. The Wayfaire is over in East Raynor."

There was still some sleep in Paul's eyes, so it took

him a moment to get his bearings enough to point to the east. "So . . . that direction. Do you have a street name to help me narrow down the search?"

"You shouldn't be able to miss it, but you may want to saddle up your horse."

"I don't mind a morning walk," Paul said. "Helps get the blood flowing."

Once again, the old man looked at Paul as if he'd sprouted a tail. "You've got over a mile to walk. Might be quicker to ride a horse."

Paul looked past the barn to see the bulk of the town spread in front of him. From what he could tell, the tents on the periphery became houses and the trail leading into Raynor became a proper street in a fraction of that distance. "Town doesn't look that big," he said. "It's over a mile to the east side?"

"Not if you want to go to the east side of Raynor. The Wayfaire is in East Raynor. It's the settlement outside town where you'll find some of the rowdiest saloons and cheapest whiskey in these parts. I thought you would have known as much."

Now Paul could see why the old man had been so quick to accept the fact that a preacher was heeled to go out for his morning constitutional. "Of course," he said, "it has been a while since I've been to town and I did just wake up."

"Say no more," the old man said as he used his elbow to give Paul a nudge. "The last preacher we had in town had similar troubles. He was pickled most of the time, if you catch my meaning."

"I do indeed. Thanks for the help. How much longer will you be able to watch our friend in there?"

"The sheriff paid me to keep watch until he gets back. Told me that one's tied up tighter than a corset. As long as that's still the case, everything should be well in hand."

Paul went back into the barn and checked on Wes. The prisoner was back to pretending to be asleep, so Paul set about saddling up his horse. "Too bad you drifted off again," Paul said in a conversational tone. "I was thinking about taking you up on that offer to flush out some of those other—"

"I'm up!" Wes said.

"Good. Get to your feet."

After no small amount of struggling, Wes groaned, "I can barely move!"

"Just get up and be quick about it. If you can't leave now, then forget about going at all."

Paul listened to the prisoner struggle some more while saddling his horse. When he was leading the horse from its stall, Paul looked in to find Wes flopping around like a fish that had been dragged from the middle of a lake. The prisoner craned his neck to get a look at him.

"I'm telling you, I can't move!" Wes said.

"Then it seems the sheriff knows how to tie a solid knot. Sorry about that, but I didn't think it prudent to get close enough to check on the ropes firsthand. Worked out better to see if you could get loose if you really needed to."

Wes glared at him. "I thought lying was a sin."

"It is. And what were you planning to do to me once I got within your reach or set you loose again? Was it less of a sin?"

"You got real cold blood for a preacher, you know that?"

"And you got real high expectations for a thief. Consider this a lesson. If you want to be treated like you're worthy of trust, then you should be more trustworthy."

"What is that supposed to mean? Hey!" Wes barked as Paul tipped his hat and led his horse toward the barn's front door. "Come back here! What was that nonsense supposed to mean?"

One of the benefits of being a preacher was that Paul was allowed to talk in parables and riddles. Most of the time, it was to make a point or inspire someone to think a little harder. This time, he truly was too lazy to check all the knots and strands of rope keeping Wes in place before saddling his horse. Certain that the prisoner wasn't getting loose any time soon, Paul climbed into his saddle and gave his reins a flick.

"East Raynor's that way, right?" he asked the old man.

"Last I checked, that was still east."

"Good day to you."

"And to you, my pickled friend."

Paul didn't bother correcting the old man's assumption that he was drunk. There were more important concerns waiting for him less than a mile away.

Raynor was a quiet little town that had done fairly well for itself thanks to a few modest silver and turquoise mines in the surrounding area. Like with most towns found in the desert territories, its rooftops were baked by an unrelenting sun and its streets were worn smooth by the constant flow of gritty sand swept along by arid winds. Folks spent their days huddled beneath awnings for shade or hurrying across the streets so as not to dwell in the harsh elements. Most of the eyes he saw were narrowed and focused, yet friendly enough when they saw Paul's garb and the smile on his face as he tipped his hat to them. He figured he should enjoy such responses while they lasted. From what little he'd been told about where he was going, those neighborly waves would soon be in short supply.

Not wanting to dawdle, Paul rode straight through town until the street opened to a wide stretch of barren terrain. Just as the old man had promised, another smaller settlement lay in the distance about a mile away. Paul probably could have walked, but it would have taken a lot more time and the heat was already approaching unbearable. Snapping his reins, he rode out of the larger town and into what quickly felt like a whole other world.

Where Raynor had been peaceful and quiet, East Raynor set every one of the hairs on Paul's arms on end. No gunshots rang out and there were no fistfights in the streets, but he couldn't help thinking those sorts of things could take place at any moment. The faces peering at him from the shade of doorways were suspicious and guarded. Saloons, gambling houses, and worse flanked him on both sides.

Women called down to him from balconies of garishly painted brothels.

Filthy men slept in gutters.

And everywhere Paul looked, he found guns. Hardly a soul ventured outside without a pistol strapped around a waist or a rifle slung over a shoulder. Paul did his best to match the careful expressions being pointed his way, but nearly went for his Colt out of pure reflex when someone rode up alongside him.

Most of Sprole's face was hidden by the hat drawn down low over his brow and the turn of his collar, but his voice was unmistakable when he whispered, "Trying to draw more attention, Padre?"

"You know why I'm here and I don't appreciate being left behind."

"We wanted to get the lay of the land. Now follow me and don't make a production out of it. This place is filled with them who'd like nothing more than to get on Terrigan's good side."

When Sprole steered his horse around the back of a little building marked by a sign with Chinese lettering, Paul followed him. The main street made him feel as if every poorly constructed building was getting ready to fall on top of him. Behind the Chinese place, there was so much open land that he almost felt as if he were falling through open air.

Sprole climbed down from his horse and tied his reins to a post beside the building's rear door. "You already nearly ruined our chances of getting the drop on Terrigan once, and now you mosey down Billings Street like a one-man parade! I'm beginning to think you truly are working against us."

"If I had been brought along as we agreed, I would have been in on whatever it is you and Sheriff Noss have planned."

The bounty hunter's face took on a brutal edge and he approached Paul's horse as if he meant to drag him from the saddle by whatever part of him he could grab.

"There ain't much of a plan yet, but if it gets around that any of us have anything at all to do with the law, you might as well put a bullet through our heads using that rusty gun of yours. Just because you dragged that pistol from your saddlebag, you think you can hold your own in a sty like this?"

"I've seen worse."

"Sure you have. Why don't you just ride on back to civilization before you get yourself or one of us hurt?"

Paul buttoned his coat, fixed his collar, and straightened up as if he were about to walk to the front of his own church. "I'd say it would be unwise for us to remain back here like this. Seems to me that this place doesn't allow much privacy."

"You'd be amazed at how many hidey-holes there are around here," Sprole said. Drawing a breath, he calmed his nerves enough to say, "We weren't going to leave you behind in that stable. We thought we just had to walk down the street a ways to get where we were going. Turned out we had to leave one town behind for a smaller one. Noss said you could use some sleep."

"Have you found . . ." Reminding himself about the lack of privacy that had already been mentioned, Paul stopped short of saying any names. "Have you found our friend?"

"He's here all right," Sprole said through a grin that had sprouted beneath the stubble covering his face. "And we caught some bit of luck. That gang is on the lookout for three strangers who aim to bring him in. Noss and I came here separately, but you've drawn some attention. I just don't think they're expecting someone in your line of work."

"That should act in our favor," Paul said.

Sprole's eyes shifted back and forth, responding to every rustle or scrape he heard. "Yeah, but that don't change the fact that plenty of folks saw me drag you back here. I've already found someone who's willing to talk about Terrigan, but he's skittish. Fact is, there may be someone watching over us right now."

"You've learned quite a bit in a short amount of time."

"That's how I earn my daily bread," Sprole replied with a mischievous glint in his eye. "Wouldn't do any of us any good to ruin that. I got a thing or two to tell you, but it'll have to be while I'm tending to other business."

"What business is that?"

Cracking his knuckles, the bounty hunter stepped up close to him and spoke in a low, snarling whisper. "Anybody asks, you don't know who I am and you never laid eyes on me until I dragged you back here to rob you. I'm gonna make this look good and it shouldn't hurt too much. You ready?"

Paul was about to ask what he was talking about, but the picture took focus on its own. Tensing his stomach, he nodded.

Sprole grabbed him roughly by the shoulder, balled his fist, and drove it into Paul's midsection. The blow thumped against Paul's stomach, but barely enough to make a bruise. "The Wayfaire is just down the street at the only intersection in this camp."

After being allowed to catch his breath, Paul straightened up so he could be grabbed by both upper arms and slammed against the wall. His back made a lot of noise on impact, but Sprole's knuckles hit the wooden slats harder than anything else.

"Terrigan is holding court in that cathouse," Sprole continued. In a louder voice, he snarled, "I know that ain't all! Hand it over!"

Paul let his head hang forward as the bounty hunter made a show of riffling through his pockets.

Sprole dropped his voice to a raspy growl again and said, "Near as we've been able to tell, Terrigan's only got two other members of his gang with him, and one of 'em is Price. He's recruiting, though." He sent a quick jab into Paul's gut.

That one took a good amount of wind from Paul's sails. "I wasn't ready for that one," he wheezed.

"What'll you do about it, preacher?"

Paul's hands balled into fists. He was very aware of the weight of the old Colt hanging at his side, especially since he couldn't tell if Sprole's threatening tone was still just for show. When he lowered his hands and relaxed his fingers, the bounty hunter grinned.

"That's what I thought," Sprole said. Then he grabbed Paul by both shoulders and pulled him forward while bringing his knee swiftly upward.

If that had connected, it would have doubled Paul over and dropped him to the dirt. Since it barely tapped against him, Paul went through those same motions while grunting in pain.

Sprole leaned down as if to snarl one last insult into his ear. "Men around here look up to Terrigan like he's some kind of hero. To these murderous dogs, that's just what he is. Any one of them . . . maybe all of them . . . could step up on Terrigan's behalf just to prove themselves to him. You'd do well to remember that and find somewhere safe to go so me and Noss can do our work."

Paul's back bumped against the wall behind him and he slid down to sit while wrapping both arms around his midsection. When Sprole hunkered down to leer at him, Paul said, "I can still help. I came to speak with Terrigan, and that's what I'll do."

"That don't help us none."

"It does if it keeps him busy while you tend to the rest."

"And what if Terrigan won't have any of what you got to say to him?" Sprole asked.

"Then he's all yours."

Sprole's eyes narrowed. He stood up and stuffed a hand into his pocket as if he'd claimed a reward. "This fool's errand of yours might just end with you getting killed. Ever think about that?"

"And you must have thought I'd do something once you told me where to find Terrigan. Wouldn't it have been easier if you'd just knocked me over the head so I wouldn't be underfoot any longer?"

"You may be a pain in my backside, but you seem to be a good man," Sprole said through a contradictory sneer that was necessary to maintain his charade. "I told you about the Wayfaire because I knew you'd just go snooping around asking for it anyway, which would only draw more attention."

"Is that the only reason?"

"I also know why you wanted to come along on this ride in the first place. Ain't like you ever let any of us forget. The least you deserve after coming this far is to get your chance to have your talk with Terrigan." After a moment or two, Sprole shrugged. "And yeah. Maybe I did think it could do us some good if you kept Terrigan distracted long enough for me and Noss to round up them others."

Paul had to fight to keep from smiling. "Does he know about that?"

"He ain't happy about it as such, but he knows."

"After all the grief you two have given me throughout the last several days, it's a miracle we can still work together in any capacity."

"You ever, just once, think all the grief me and Noss have been givin' to you was to keep you alive?"

Lifting his chin just enough to look the bounty hunter in the eye, Paul said, "If Terrigan or any of these men kills me, then you can tack my death onto the list of charges when you two bring them in."

"That anxious to be a martyr for your cause, huh?"

"Not at all," Paul replied. "Just planning for any possibility. Promise me one thing."

"What's that?"

"If I don't come back from this, you'll remember what I tried to do."

The grin on Sprole's face somehow managed to be both warm and ugly. "Trust me," he said as he backed away. "I won't soon forget what happened on this venture. Just keep your head down when hell breaks loose."

Paul remained still after the bounty hunter strode off. When he looked up, the blaring sun was hardly kept at bay by the wide brim of his hat. Picking himself up and dusting himself off, Paul took another look around to find no fewer than five faces peering out from various windows or from shadowed doorways. Like with rats in a cellar, there were surely plenty more that couldn't be seen lurking about. He was no actor, but Paul did his best to maintain the performance that had been done for the spectators' benefit and limped away.

Chapter 20

From what Paul could gather, East Raynor was something between a town and a camp. Not quite big
enough to be considered one and just a bit too large to
be the other. It consisted of two real streets and several
smaller paths branching out from them like crooked
veins from the two main arteries. At the heart of the
rowdy settlement was the Wayfaire: three floors of
shouting, drinking, singing, and gambling. The largest
front window was so completely broken that Paul
couldn't see a single shard of glass in a frame covered
by a thick tarp nailed in place to keep some of the elements at bay. Judging by the tattered edge of that
stained canvas, it too had been knocked out of place
more than once.

Paul opened the door and walked inside. Almost
immediately, he was surprised that his senses could be
assaulted any further than they had been on his way
through town. Rowdy laughter, roaring profanities,
and wild notes from a tinny piano filled the inside of
the main room like a storm. Adding to the assault were
odors ranging from overly sweet perfume all the way

to bitter vomit riding on waves of tobacco smoke. It was nearly impossible for Paul to decide whether breathing through his mouth or nose was worse. He quickly decided neither would be any better than the other.

Normally Paul's collar and dark clothes drew some attention. Some folks smiled and tried to make him feel at home, while others turned away as if the man wearing those things could somehow see into their soul and report what he found to the highest of all authorities. The men and women inside the Wayfaire were unusual in that they looked upon him the way some might look at a puppy that had wandered in from the street. He saw smiles that were amused at best, predatory at worst.

The bar was a long structure at least twenty feet from one end to the other. Its top was made from old doors that had been sanded down and nailed into place. Some still bore the bullet holes and boot prints that could very well have knocked them from their hinges in the first place. When Paul stepped up and placed both hands on its stained surface, a tall fellow with a barrel chest behind the bar took notice.

"What'll it be, Reverend?" the bartender asked. His thick brow gave him a primitive appearance that didn't quite match his sharp eyes. The hands he used to clear away a mess of newspapers and beer mugs were at least twice as thick as Paul's and covered with enough calluses to stand up to an open flame. "I heard you've had a bad day."

"You heard that, did you?"

"Yep. Unless there's more than one preacher in East

Raynor, you'd be the one that was dragged behind Chan's opium den and robbed."

"News travels fast around here. I just walked up the street from there."

"East Raynor ain't a large place, Reverend," the barkeep said. "And we don't get many holy sorts around here. Tell you what . . . first drink's on me. Care for some wine?"

"How about a whiskey?"

The barkeep grinned and nodded. "Whiskey it is." Swapping out the mug he'd grabbed for a smaller glass, he took a bottle from the shelf behind him and poured out two fingers of liquor. "So . . . you really did got robbed?"

"I did."

"That's a hard bit of news, even for this place. Heard about it from one of my runners who was bringing in a keg from Raynor Proper. That's what we call the town to the west of us."

"I guessed as much."

Leveling his gaze at one of the dregs who had drifted to within arm's reach of Paul's back, the barkeep raised his voice a bit when he said, "Yeah, I didn't much like hearing that my runner didn't lift a finger to help a man when he was getting robbed of everything he owns, but at least you're in one piece. Barely, that is."

Although Paul wanted to dispute those words just so he wouldn't be made to look so frail, he quickly saw the reason they'd been spoken. He'd only spotted a pair of shabbily dressed men closing in on him, but another pair had come in from his blind side. Now that they'd heard his pockets had already been picked clean, they drifted away in search of a carcass with a bit more meat on its bones.

"I wasn't carrying that much anyway," Paul said. "I honestly don't know what that thief was expecting to find."

"Doesn't take much to entice the scum around here into spilling another man's blood. What brings you into these parts anyway? Wrong turn is my best guess."

"I'm looking for someone."

"Ah. Then you've come to the right place." With that, the barkeep snapped his fingers loudly enough for the crisp sound to slice through the other noise and catch the ear of a short woman dressed in a frilly green dress with matching ribbons in her curly, shoulder-length blond hair. "We're known far and wide for providing company for anyone who walks through our doors. And not just any company, mind you. Only the best at the Wayfaire!"

That last sentence elicited a smattering of drunken cheers from men who seemed barely able to remain in their chairs while wildly waving their glasses over their heads.

The blond woman smelled of rosewater and she placed a gentle hand on Paul's back. When she got a closer look at the clothes he wore, she smiled at him as if he were a long-lost friend. "You poor thing," she said. "I heard what happened and I'm so glad to see you weren't shot up too badly."

When Paul looked across the bar with a confused look on his face, the man standing behind it shrugged amicably and said, "News travels fast, but it ain't always accurate." To the blonde, he said, "I think our reverend friend here was just knocked around a bit. Not shot."

"Still," she cooed, "that must have been terrible."

Not wanting to undo the stage Sprole had set for him, Paul replied, "It was. I'm quite all right, though."

Leaning over the bar, the burly bartender said, "Take yer sympathy when you get it, Reverend. I shouldn't have to tell you it's in short supply around here."

"When I said I was looking for someone, this isn't exactly what I had in mind."

"It's all right," the blonde said. "No need to be shy."

Judging by the shift in the barkeep's demeanor, he'd picked up on the businesslike tone in Paul's voice and responded in kind. "Who might you be looking for?"

"Jack Terrigan."

Even though the music, shouting, and other general commotion were still almost loud enough to cover a gunshot, the bartender reacted as if the name of the Devil himself had been shouted from the highest rooftop in town and was echoing through every room. "Becky, bring him to the back room."

She patted his shoulder and said, "Follow me, sweetie."

As Paul was led down the length of the bar to one of several narrow doors, he was greeted by lewd smiles, a few raised glasses, and several unsavory suggestions as to how he should spend his time with the woman holding on to his arm. The bartender had disappeared in the last few seconds, and the room Paul was taken to was empty apart from a narrow cot and a milking stool in one corner.

"Before you get too far down this road," he said

sternly as the blond woman stepped in and closed the door behind them, "I'm not here for this."

A tall, narrow panel in the wall behind the stool slid away so the bartender could step through. His appearance was sudden enough to make Paul's hand twitch toward the Colt that remained tucked beneath his coat.

"Look here, Reverend," the bartender said. "You ain't got any business in East Raynor. I would have thought you'd learned as much after getting robbed, but since you're still here I'll tell you again. No godly man has any business here. As for the man you were asking about, you'd better pray that he didn't hear you mention his name. He's been on a drunken tear since he's gotten to town, and men have died for doing nothing more than looking at him cross-eyed. If some preacher starts drawing attention to himself, it's hard to say what he might do."

"You think I'm in danger just for mentioning his name?"

"No," the other man snapped. "I think any man who claims to be looking for Jack Terrigan ain't got long to live. Jack's a wild dog on good days, and the last few days ain't been good at all!"

"Does he think someone is looking for him?" Paul asked.

"He knows it!"

"How?"

All of the friendliness that had been on the barkeep's face outside that little room was gone when he said, "Forget it and forget him. Forget you came to this place. Put it behind you. It's too far gone for you to save, so get out. We don't want you here!" The barkeep turned around and left the same way he'd come in. Under different circumstances, watching him squeeze his bulky frame through that opening might have been funny. Now nobody felt much like laughing.

Once the bigger man was gone, only Paul and the blond woman remained. He turned to her and she shrugged. "This is a room where we usually bring men who pay for our company," she explained. "That panel is there so . . ."

"It's there by the stool because that's where a man would put his clothes," Paul said. "Someone opens it and picks his pockets while he's . . . otherwise occupied."

Her eyes widened and she gasped, "You know about that?"

"It's an old trick. Do you know about Jack Terrigan?"

"Only what I've seen since he got to town," she said as a chill seemed to work its way beneath her skin. "Kyle was right in what he said. Jack Terrigan is a cold-blooded killer. He shot three men on account of them trying to say he wasn't who he said he was. Cut up another two with a broken bottle over a game of cards. One fellow came in from Raynor Proper, claiming to be on some sort of committee or something like that. He said he wanted to have a word with Terrigan to try and put an end to the wickedness taking place here." Her eyes reddened and she swiped at them with the back of one hand. "One of Terrigan's men stabbed him so many times I thought the blood would never stop running. It was one of the worst things I ever seen."

Slowly, Paul nodded. "That's why your friend the bartender wants me to leave so badly?"

"Yes, sir, Reverend."

"Please don't call me that. I'm not a reverend."

"But . . . ," she protested while pointing meekly at Paul's collar.

"There are lots of titles for men of faith, but the proper one depends on things like . . ." Seeing he was losing her, Paul simply told her his name.

"Shouldn't I call you Father or something like that?"

Back in Pueblito Verde, and in a few places outside it, plenty of folks called him that. Hearing her call him by that title in his current surroundings, however, didn't even seem close to right. Rather than tell her as much, he said, "Paul is fine. What's your name?"

"Becky."

"I'm looking for Jack Terrigan, Becky, and it's not just to bark scripture at him. I've come a long way to get here, so I'd be much obliged if you could tell me where I should go next in order to find him."

"Why do you want to talk with Jack Terrigan? He's not the sort who listens to reason. He's an animal."

Paul could hear something in her voice that led him to believe she knew more about the matter than just what had been spread by town gossips. "Has he . . . paid for your company?"

"No," she replied while sitting on the edge of the cot and folding her hands on her lap. "But one of his men has taken a shine to me. Theo's his name."

"Theo Price?"

She nodded. "He just got back to town and hasn't

come to pay me a visit yet, but I'm sure he'll get around
to it sooner or later."

"Then you shouldn't be here when he does." Paul
took a seat beside her and removed his hat. "Terrigan
is right in thinking some men are looking for him. And
if these men don't find him, the next bunch will. He's a
wild dog and sooner rather than later, he'll be put
down."

A spark of hope lit in her eyes when she asked, "Is
that why you're here?"

"I'm a man of peace."

"But you carry a gun. I seen it."

Ignoring the Colt that had caught her eye, Paul
placed a hand on her knee and spoke in a voice that
was low enough to force her to pay extra attention.
"I'm not here to kill Terrigan, but it is very important
that I speak to him. Otherwise, things won't just go on
the way they have been. They'll get worse."

"I don't see how they can get worse," she said.

"They can. Trust me. For those outlaws and for anyone in their sights."

Becky shook her head and stood up. "Jack ain't the
sort to listen to anyone, and the men riding with him
only listen to Jack. Whatever you hope to do, it'll only
end with you getting killed. I won't be a part of hurting
a reverend."

Outside in the main room of the rowdy place, something heavy was dropped or cracked. The music
stopped and some of the voices let up, allowing Paul to
better hear the sound when it came again. Nothing had
been dropped, at least not yet, and the only thing that
had cracked were gunshots through the air.

"You hear that?" Paul said as he grabbed hold of Becky's arm to keep her from going anywhere. "I told you things were bound to get worse, and there they go."

Oddly enough, she was less panicked now than ever. "Someone's always shooting at someone else around here. Things can't get any worse than they are every day in East Raynor."

"If you don't tell me where to find Jack Terrigan, I'll just march out and keep asking around until someone tells me. Either that or he'll eventually hear about me and find me on his own. How well will you be able to sleep knowing you could have kept things from getting so messy for a man of the cloth?"

"You're crazy, mister."

"Maybe a little, but this is something that I need to do. From the moment I heard about Jack Terrigan riding through this territory, little signs have cropped up here and there to let me know I was supposed to find him. Just when it seemed that was an impossible task, something happened or some other little opportunity presented itself to bring me a little closer to this very spot. Becky, I think you're the last angel to see me along my trail."

She let out a very quiet, very tired laugh. "I'm no angel, that's for certain."

"Folks prove what they are by what they do. Even if they do things they're not so proud of, what truly matters is that they see how wrong they were and work to fix it."

"Is that really how things work?"

"I'd like to think so. All I know for certain is what I believe, and I believe that with all my heart. That's what faith is."

"What do you hope to do about Jack Terrigan?" she asked.

"That's between me and him. All I'm asking is that I be given the chance I've worked so hard to get. One thing I can promise you, one way or another, this place won't have to worry about Terrigan or the rest of his gang by the time this day is out. How much blood is spilled when it's all said and done could very well come down to how much time is wasted before I do what I came here to do."

She stood up and started to walk to the door. It was a short trip to get there, but she moved as if her feet were stuck in molasses. "Just leave," she said.

Standing up to reach past her so he could hold the door shut, Paul asked, "He's here, isn't he?"

"Why won't you listen? Or don't you have the sense God gave a mule?"

"This doesn't have to do with God anymore."

Hearing those words from anyone else might not have had much impact on a woman who'd seen as much as she. But when Becky heard that statement coming from Paul, it shook her to the bone. "Room Four," she said.

"Thank you."

The moment Paul let her go, Becky reached for the door. Outside, there was more shooting. Some of the voices in the main room had grown more excited, like dust being kicked up by a passing stampede. Heavy footsteps clomped across the floor, sending a ripple through the boards beneath Paul's feet.

Becky's hand lingered on the door handle, and her

head drooped forward. "Not like it matters anyway," she said. "Sounds like it's starting again."

"You can leave town, you know," Paul told her. "Whatever was keeping you here, it can't be strong enough to make you put up with whatever is making you so miserable."

"And what will I do once I leave town? Just walk to the next place?"

"If you have to. Find a way to take a few more steps, and before you know it, you've covered a whole lot of ground."

"It's not that easy," she sighed.

"If you don't even try . . . it's impossible."

She turned to look at him and started to smile. The gesture was cut short when the door was pulled open with so much force that she was dragged a few steps outside by the handle in her grasp.

The man who stood in the doorway had thick hair and a face covered in dark stubble. Two front teeth were chipped and his nose was skewed at an odd angle after having been broken at least twice. His eyes were clear and cruel, fixing on Becky's frightened expression before looking past her to Paul. "I hear someone's been looking for me," he snarled.

Chapter 21

"I *knew* I should have tied that preacher up and left him next to Wes in that stall!" Sprole said as he huddled with his shoulder pressed against the side of a barrel that he guessed was filled with grain. Sheriff Noss was a few paces away from him, leaning against a post that wasn't nearly wide enough to cover him fully. Another shot blasted through the air, punching a hole clean through the upper edge of Sprole's barrel to spill some of its contents across the top of his hat. Yes, it was grain.

Leaning around the post that supported the awning in front of a saloon that advertised the cheapest whiskey in town on a crudely painted sign, Noss fired a shot at one of the rooftops across the street and shouted, "What makes you think this was his fault?"

"Because he marched straight over here and was headed to the Wayfaire when I found him!"

"He was doing *what*?" Even when another shot was fired at him, the lawman barely moved. The anger on his face was more powerful than the urge to clear a path for hot lead. "Why didn't you tell me about that?"

"Because I barely had enough time to tip my hat after meeting up with you just now before we were bushwhacked!"

Noss fired another shot from his .45, which drilled into the roof of the Fan-Tan Parlor across the street. All he could see of the man who had started firing down at them was a rifle barrel and part of a hat poking over the top of the gambling den's sign. That, along with gut instinct and experience, was enough to tell him who he was dealing with. "Price must have been watching the Wayfaire from up yonder," he said.

"Or he could have run up there after seeing the preacher march into that cathouse like he owned the place along with everything else in his sight."

"Enough of your bellyaching!" the lawman snarled. "I'm tired of it!"

"And I'm tired of getting bushwhacked. I'm putting an end to it!" With that, the bounty hunter drew his .38 so he now carried a pistol in each hand. He fired a few quick shots before rushing across the street toward the Chinese gambling den.

Noss swore under his breath and fired at the rooftop. Although his shots were rushed, they provided enough sound and fury to force the rifleman across the way to duck and wait out the storm of incoming lead. By the time Noss's pistol ran dry, Sprole was storming into the Fan-Tan Parlor through the front door.

Placing his back against the post, Noss hurried through the motions of reloading his pistol. He was halfway done when footsteps knocked against the second-floor balcony of the Wayfaire. He looked in that direction and spotted a bare-chested man with a dirty face hitching up his britches with one hand and gripping a Smith & Wesson revolver in the other. It took the man a moment to get a good look at what was happening on the street below, but by the time he spotted Noss, the lawman was already running toward the horse tethered to a nearby post.

After stuffing his .45 back into its holster, Noss grabbed the shotgun kept in one of the saddle's boots and made a mad dash toward the Wayfaire. The half-dressed man on the balcony started firing down at him while shouting, "I found another one, Jack! Price! You seein' this? I got one for ya!"

As bullets screamed down at him before punching into the street below, Noss kept running until he was directly beneath the Wayfaire's balcony. He gripped the shotgun in both hands, raised it as high as he could while aiming at a point over his head, and pulled both triggers. The shotgun roared, both barrels spitting enough fiery destruction to blast a hole through the bottom of the balcony and put an end to the shots coming from above. The bare-chested man's voice went silent as his body hit the balcony with a solid thump.

Since his spare shotgun shells were in his saddlebag, Noss tossed the spent weapon toward his horse and drew his .45 while stepping away from the cathouse's front doors. Another shot cracked from the rooftop of the building across the street, chipping a post in front of the Wayfaire and encouraging Noss to retreat a little faster. "Come on, Dave," he said under his breath while filling the remaining cylinders of his pistol with fresh rounds. "Now ain't the time to dawdle."

*   *   *

Sprole charged through the front door of the Fan-Tan Parlor with a gun in each hand and a vicious snarl on his lips. His surroundings rushed past him in a blur of faded paintings of foreign landscapes, tables covered in felt, and tiles bearing dozens of symbols ranging from Chinese lettering to flowers. Having played more than his share of fan-tan, mahjong, and any other game of chance under the sun, Sprole didn't have to break his stride to know what the people gathered around those tables were doing. The smells in the air also told him what was being smoked in the rooms upstairs. He shoved past a few slender men at the bottom of those steps before charging up to meet one guard, who wasn't about to be moved so easily.

The man was almost as wide as he was tall. A long, stringy mustache hung from his upper lip, and wide arms stretched out to grab hold of Sprole as the bounty hunter attempted to get past him. Those arms snapped shut like the jaws of a bear trap to take Sprole completely off his feet.

Sprole's left arm was pinned against his side, but his right was free. He twisted around to get a look at the man who was now trying to squeeze the life out of him before knocking the side of his .44 against the man's skull. The guard, a stout bear of a man with pockmarked skin and a collection of scars on one side of his face, let out a grunt when he was struck but didn't relax his grip.

Before Sprole could swing the .44 again or bring the pistol around to fire at any of the other guards climbing the stairs to get to him, the arms wrapped around his torso cinched in tighter. His next breath flowed outward in a strained wheeze, yet somehow he found the strength to kick his legs furiously until one of his feet found purchase on the banister. Sprole pushed with all his might, which was barely enough to send the big man stumbling backward a few steps.

The thick guard grunted but showed no other effects from Sprole's efforts.

"Gonna force me . . . to do this . . . the hard way," the bounty hunter said. Then he turned the wrist of his trapped left hand to angle the .38 downward before pulling his trigger.

The gun went off, sending a round through the side of the bigger man's foot as well as the floor beneath it. Cursing in an unfamiliar language, the man let go of Sprole and hopped away to rebound off the closest wall.

As soon as he was free, Sprole rushed down the hallway. He passed several doors along the way, but realized he didn't know exactly where he was supposed to be going. Just then one of the doors opened and a slender woman with smooth, pale skin poked her head out to take a look. Sprole lowered the .38 and rushed at her immediately. He managed to grab the doorknob before she could retreat into her room.

"The roof!" he shouted while holding the .44 so she could clearly see it. "How do I get up to the roof?"

Too panicked to speak, she pointed toward a narrow door at the end of the hall. He raced to the door and pulled it open to reveal an exterior set of stairs that led down to an alley and up to the top of the building. Sprole took the stairs two at a time, hoping none of the rifle shots that had been fired in the meantime had found their mark. When he got to the top, he wasn't thinking about his own well-being. On the contrary, he hoped the rifleman would point his weapon at him instead of taking a shot at anyone in the street below.

Price was on one knee at the edge of the roof. His rifle was at his shoulder and he was steady as a rock while lining up his next shot.

"Hey!" Sprole shouted. It wasn't much, but it did the trick. Price twisted around to look at him, bringing a Winchester around to take aim.

Sprole dashed along the edge of the roof, firing a single round from his .44.

Price's Winchester cracked once, spitting a piece of lead through the space where his target had been less than a second before.

Knowing how long it would take for a man to work the rifle's lever and adjust his aim, Sprole rushed straight at Price while blazing away with his pistol. One of the .44's rounds knocked Price back, and the one that followed sent him toppling over the side of the roof.

Noss's .45 was reloaded and he'd even gotten to the spare shotgun shells in his saddlebag by the time Price's body hit the street. None of that made Noss feel any better when he saw no fewer than a dozen men emerge from various doorways and tents to glare at him like a pack of hungry wolves.

"That'll be enough," the sheriff declared loudly. "This is a private matter. It don't concern none of you!"

Most of the men now stalking down the street had come from the Wayfaire. One of them brandished a

Schofield revolver as he said, "You're a dead man, stranger!"

"Stand down!" Sprole shouted while leaning over the edge of the roof to get a look at the street. "This fight's over!"

The man at the front of the growing mob shook his head. "No, it ain't. Not by a stretch. But it will be soon."

Noss took no comfort from the gun in his hand or the badge pinned to his chest beneath his jacket. Those things could only serve to speed his trip to the grave once the men closing in around him decided to make their move. Since it seemed things couldn't get much worse, he decided to play the one card left in his hand. "I'm a sheriff! I came here for that man right there," he announced while pointing over toward Price. "He's dead, so I'll be on my way. Any man fires one shot at me or my deputy and you'll hang."

"Ain't nobody'll be left to say what happened to you," someone from within the mob pointed out.

In a cold, unwavering voice, Noss said, "The rest of my men know I'm here. If I don't come home, the lot of you will regret it. Whether it's now or later, I guarantee you, there'll be hell to pay."

While that silenced a few of the men, it didn't make a dent on the ones who'd been first through the door to stalk into the street. The man at the front of the pack shook his head as a cruel grin eased across his face. His grip tightened around his gun.

Sheriff Noss prepared for war.

"Stop it!"

Everyone froze at the sound of that voice. It hadn't come from the mob, the lawman, or the rooftop across the street. Instead, it came from the front door of the Wayfaire as a single man stepped outside.

Sprole spotted him immediately and shouted, "Show me your hands, Terrigan!"

Noss could scarcely believe his ears. Although he'd never seen Jack Terrigan's face, there was no mistaking the reverence in the eyes of the scum who looked at the outlaw now.

"What are you doing, Jack?" the man at the front of the mob asked.

The man with the thick, greasy hair and broken nose took two more steps outside and raised his hands high. "Nobody make another move, you hear me?"

"But, Jack—"

"*Nobody!*"

That single bellowing word rolled like thunder through East Raynor, taking the fight from all of the men in the street. Rather than question what happened to swing things his way, the lawman said, "Come along with me, Terrigan. I'm putting you under arrest."

Someone in the mob hollered, "There's only two of 'em! They can't do a thing!"

Terrigan bared his teeth and shouted, "This don't concern any of you! Get out of my sight!"

Slowly, the mob began to disperse. The faces on the men who'd taken a stand against Noss were now twisted into confused grimaces. Soon disparaging remarks drifted through the air as the men who'd spoken them drifted back from whence they came.

Terrigan stepped forward. His face was drenched in sweat, and spittle ran from both corners of his mouth after shouting loud enough to be heard back in Raynor

Proper. Noss moved forward with pistol in hand, but he didn't need the weapon any longer. None of the men in the vicinity were interested in standing against him, and Terrigan was offering both hands to him like a whipped dog baring its neck to a stronger foe. But the sheriff noticed something else as he dug the handcuffs from his saddlebag and locked them around the outlaw's wrists. It was an unmistakable expression etched into Terrigan's face.

He wasn't beaten.

He wasn't drunk.

He was petrified.

Sprole came out of the Fan-Tan Parlor, looking almost as confused as some of the outlaws still lingering in the street. "What happened?" he asked. "Did you get the jump on Terrigan?"

"Not exactly," Noss replied.

"How'd you get a hold of him? What did I miss?"

The bounty hunter continued asking questions as Noss looked at one of the figures standing outside the Wayfaire. Because of the grim expression on Paul's face, Noss almost didn't recognize him. "Father!" he shouted when he saw Paul turn his back to him. "You'd best stay close to us. It's—"

But Paul was already gone, vanished like so many of the others who'd found something better to do once Terrigan had dismissed them.

"Come on, Dave," Noss said to the bounty hunter. "No sense in pushing our luck."

"Go on," Sprole said. "I'll be right back."

Terrigan didn't put up any fight whatsoever as he was shackled and taken into Noss's custody. He even told the lawman where to find his horse so he could be helped into the saddle and taken back to Raynor Proper.

Sprole went inside the Wayfaire, ready to wade through a hailstorm of lead to get the answers he was after. Instead, he was met by a bunch of steely-eyed glares and a single, frantic woman with blond hair carrying Paul's wide-brimmed hat.

"Where did you get that?" Sprole asked.

"H-he left it here," Becky said. "Along with these." After Sprole took the hat from her, she extended her other hand, which was wrapped around the barrel of Paul's old Colt. His preacher tabs hung from that same fist.

"Where did he go?"

"I don't know. I thought Jack was going to kill him when I left the two of them alone, but instead he walked straight outside and surrendered. I checked in my room, and these things were all that was left."

Sprole had plenty of questions to ask the preacher, but it seemed Paul didn't want to be found. Even if that wasn't the case, judging by the fierce expressions worn by the men inside the cathouse, it wasn't wise for the bounty hunter to stay there any longer than what was absolutely necessary.

All that was left was to get back to his horse and help Sheriff Noss deal with his prisoners.

Chapter 22

It was a town very similar to Pueblito Verde in many respects. Quiet, small, and surrounded by miles of open terrain, Whitley differed in one important aspect. The folks who lived there didn't have a preacher to lead Sunday services. Two men rode into town, both unable to look away from the little church that stood empty beside a blacksmith's shop. They rode down the street that cut straight through the middle of town, reining their horses to a stop at a small stable near a square lot marked by a sign that read DOUBLE T COR-RAL.

There was hardly anyone in the streets apart from a few dogs being chased by a small boy and some old folks chatting on the porch of a nearby house. A rustling sound drifted from within the stable, accompanied by the labored breathing of a worker who used a pitchfork to clear a path between the stalls within the drafty structure.

Both men who'd ridden this far dismounted and approached the stable. The wind that blew had acquired the chill of an approaching autumn, which caught in the coats of both men to flap their heavy wool garments against the holsters strapped around their waists.

The rustling within the stable came to a stop and the worker stepped outside with pitchfork in hand. He regarded the other two through eyes reddened from swirling dust and nodded to each of them in turn. "Hello, Sheriff. Mr. Sprole."

Both men tipped their hats to him.

"Good to see you, preacher," Sprole said.

"Only it ain't *sheriff* no more," Noss said as he opened his coat to reveal the shiny new badge pinned to his shirt. "It's *marshal*."

Paul squinted at him and smiled. "U.S. Marshal, no less. I suppose catching the bloodiest gang in the Arizona Territory brought some much-deserved attention your way. Good to hear."

"Brought it both of our ways, actually," Sprole added. He also peeled back his jacket to show a badge matching Noss's.

"From bounty hunter to U.S. Marshal?" Paul mused. "I wouldn't have expected that."

Sprole shrugged and allowed his jacket to fall back in place. "Isn't much of a difference, really. They got us hunting down fugitives and bringing 'em in kicking and screaming. Only difference is less pay."

"I was thinking I might see you again," Paul said as he stuck the pitchfork into the ground. "One of you seemed more likely to show up than the other, to be honest. How did you find me?"

"It's my job to find men on the run," Sprole replied. "Remember?"

"Yeah. I remember."

"There's some questions that need to be answered," Noss said. "And both of us wanted to hear the answers."

"You took your prisoner alive from East Raynor," Paul said. "Didn't he give you your answers?"

"He told us plenty, but we still want to hear it from you."

Paul let his eyes drift to the ground at his feet. When he didn't say anything, something landed heavily in the dirt and skidded several feet before knocking against the pitchfork. He stooped down to collect the old Colt. "Never thought I'd see this again. Never wanted to see it again."

"What did you say to Terrigan back at East Raynor?" Noss asked. "I thought it would be close to impossible to take him alive *or* dead, and yet he marched out and couldn't hand himself over fast enough."

"What did he tell you once you took him back?"

"He said we made a mistake."

"If you were truly after Jack Terrigan," Paul explained, "you did make a mistake." He sighed, drew himself up, and looked the lawman in the eye. "That man isn't Jack Terrigan. I am."

Sprole shook his head. "No matter how many times he told us that, I never believed him."

"Believe it," Paul said. "That man's name is Eddie Pullman. He rode with me and the rest of us back in the last days when I led that gang. We robbed and killed and drank and robbed and killed some more. Then . . .

when I decided to stop . . . I parted ways with the others and hid for the better part of three years. In that time, I decided to change my ways and help others do the same. I thought I could make good on some of the wrongs I did. But the sad fact is there's no way to make up for that much wrong."

"What made you decide to give up the outlaw way of life?" Sprole asked. "What could turn you into a preacher?"

The face that glared up at Sprole at that moment was carved from cold granite. The eyes burning within that cruel visage sent a shiver down the bounty hunter's spine, making him understand much better what Eddie Pullman might have faced in East Raynor that was powerful enough to send him running into the hands of the law.

"I never was a preacher," Terrigan snarled. "My father was a preacher. It's his collar, his Bible, his words I passed on as my own. And as for what happened to make me choose another path, that's between me and the Almighty. If there's any explaining to do, I'll only do it once when my days on this earth are through."

"You may believe that," Noss said. "But the folks back in Pueblito Verde miss the man who stood in front of them every Sunday. They miss the man who guided them through their rough times."

Jack Terrigan took hold of the pitchfork and yanked it from the ground. "They can get along on their own now. Just like me."

Noss reached into a pocket. "They're not alone and neither are you." He removed something from his pocket and tossed it through the air.

When Terrigan saw the little Bible encased in its familiar, dusty cover sailing toward him, he grabbed it with speed that would have been more than enough to beat any would-be gunslinger's draw. Holding the Bible in his hand melted the fire in his eyes. "I went through hell to come to a place where I could put my cruelty behind me. I couldn't bear to see someone else start it all over again by using my name. Eddie always was eager to be at the head of the gang. Once he convinced enough folks he was Jack Terrigan, he got what he wanted. That . . . couldn't be allowed to stand. Sorry I lied to you men, but I had to do what I had to do."

"We understand," Noss told him. "But now we have our own job to do."

Terrigan nodded. Clutching his Bible, he lowered his head. "I'll go with you. If I'm to hang for what I did before, that's how it should be. It was wrong for me to run away."

"Pick up that gun," Noss said.

But Terrigan didn't move. "I won't. Not now and not ever. The only reason I carried any weapons when I rode with you two was to make sure I got to have my talk with Eddie."

"You're not going to hang, preacher," Sprole said.

When Terrigan looked up at him, the former bounty hunter didn't flinch.

"It's true," Noss said. "After what I saw on the ride to East Raynor and what I already knew about the man who preached in Pueblito Verde, there's no way I'd allow you to swing like a common criminal. I didn't know you back when you rode at the head of that gang, but you're no wild-dog killer anymore. If anyone deserves another chance, it's you."

Propping one hand against his saddle horn, Sprole leaned forward and grinned as if he was truly savoring each moment. "But we can't exactly let you go free. Not after all you've done and all you've got to offer."

"All I can offer is the sweat from my brow," Terrigan said. "It's all I have left."

"You ain't about to get off that easy," Sprole chuckled. "You were Jack Terrigan. East Raynor ain't the only place where that name carries some weight. Put that to work as something other than a stable boy."

"What are you talking about?"

Noss straightened in his saddle, looking nothing at all like the wilted creature who'd been too distracted by grief to bother walking the streets of Pueblito Verde. "I'm through sulking," he said. "And so are you. You want to truly help make amends for being an outlaw? Then help us track down the mad-dog killers who haven't found a better path."

"I know plenty about tracking wanted men," Sprole said, "but you must know right where to look for a whole lot of them that would take me years to find. Seeing as how you frightened poor Eddie Pullman into federal custody, I imagine you could make our job a whole lot easier when we track down other men worse than him. It's the least you could do to clean up the mess you made."

"And," Noss added, "it's a way for us to keep an eye on you. Don't give me that look, Paul. It beats being tossed into jail, don't it?"

"Or into a noose," Sprole said.

"So it's Paul again?" Terrigan asked.

Noss nodded. "A couple of upstanding U.S. Marshals couldn't exactly ride with the likes of Jack Terrigan. Especially after those same marshals turned in Jack Terrigan after putting down the rest of his gang. Rumor has it that Terrigan knew some real bloodthirsty cusses who've been seen in the Dakota Territories. They're the ones we're after nowadays."

Paul nodded and slipped the weathered Bible into the pocket of his jacket. "I know where you can look for those men. If we can't find them in the Badlands, I can think of some folks we can ask about their whereabouts."

The man who'd quietly ridden into Whitley three months ago took his pitchfork into the stable, squared everything away, and left with nothing more than the horse and saddle he'd brought to town in the first place. Nobody in town had gotten to know him very well, and they didn't know why he left with two strangers on that chilly afternoon.

They also didn't know what to make of the old Colt lying in the dirt outside the stable. Carved into the gun's handle were the initials JT, surrounded by dozens of deep, neatly arranged notches.

Read on for an excerpt from the rip-roarin'
Ralph Compton classic

The Killing Season

Available from Signet.

Newton, Texas
March 5, 1873

Astride a grulla and leading a packhorse, Nathan Stone rode in a little more than an hour before sundown. His hound, Cotton Blossom, trotted alongside. The procession passed several saloons, and that alone was enough to draw attention. Few men just off a long trail would pass up the first saloon, and it was enough of a curiosity to tempt some of the patrons away from the bar to have a look. Seemingly unaware of the spectators, Nathan reined up before the mercantile. Dismounting, he looped the reins of the grulla and the lead rope of the packhorse around the hitch rail. He then paused, as though allowing the men from the saloons an opportunity to size him up before he entered the store. While he didn't wish to be recognized, he dared not seem fearful.

Just a few weeks past his twenty-sixth birthday, his dark hair was well laced with gray. A dusty gray Stetson was tilted over his cold blue eyes. His polished black boots with pointed toes and undershot heels would have been the envy of any cowboy, but the *buscadero* belt with its pair of tied-down Colts said this hombre didn't earn his bacon and beans wrassling cows. His trousers were black with pinstripes, while his shirt was almost the gray of his Stetson. There was but little to liken him to a man of the range except the red bandanna around his neck and the unmistakable effect of sun and wind on his hands and face. A long sheepskin coat tied behind the cantle of his saddle suggested he might have come from the high country. Stone entered the mercantile, and without command, the dog remained with the horses.

Nathan Stone preferred larger towns where he was less likely to be recognized, stopping only in the villages to replenish his supplies or to buy needed grain for his horses. When he left the mercantile, he purposely carried only a sack of grain under his left arm, for it was a situation he had come to expect. Men from the saloons had congregated across the dusty street, and one of them stepped forward. His right thumb was hooked under the butt of his Colt. He wasn't drunk, but he'd had enough to respond to the taunts of his comrades. He spoke.

"Ain't you Nathan Stone, the killer?"

"I am Nathan Stone," Nathan said coldly.

"Well, I'm Vern Tilton, an' I think I can take you. Draw."

"Tilton," said Nathan, just as he had tried in vain to reason with other foolish challengers. "I have no argument with you and I have no reason to draw. Now back off."

"By God, Vern," one of the onlookers shouted, "he's scairt of you."

"Damn you," Tilton bawled, "you ain't a-gonna cheat me out of provin' I'm faster'n you. Pull your iron."

He emphasized his angry words by jerking out his Colt. He was clumsy, painfully slow, and Nathan waited until the last possible second. He finally drew his right-hand Colt as Tilton was raising his weapon to fire. Tilton's Colt roared, blasting lead into the ground, as Nathan's slug ripped into his right shoulder. Tilton stumbled back and would have fallen, if one of his companions hadn't caught him.

"Take him," Nathan said quietly, "and get the hell out of here. I could have killed him. I had every right, and next time, I will."

They backed away but they didn't leave, for though it was nothing more than a village, there was a sheriff, and he arrived on the run. Taking just one look at the bleeding, swearing Tilton, he turned on Nathan.

"I'm Howard Esty, sheriff of this county. Now you shuck them guns."

"No," said Nathan. "I only defended myself, and any man that disputes me is lying."

"Speak up, damn it," Esty said, turning his attention to the townsmen who had begun edging away. "Who started this?"

"Vern pulled iron first," one of his companions said grudgingly.

"Then take him to the doc and git him patched up," said Esty. "And you," he said, pointing to the injured Vern, "be thankin' your lucky stars you're still alive."

They drifted away, some of them casting sour looks at Nathan and Esty. The sheriff was showing his years, gray hair poking through a hole in the crown of his

Stetson. He was lean, his hands, face, and neck as leathery and weather-beaten as an old saddle. When Vern and his disgruntled friends were well beyond hearing, he spoke.

"There'll be no charges, an' I'm thankin' you for not saltin' Vern down for keeps. You'd of been within your rights. I'd not want you takin' this personal, but I'd be obliged if you'd finish your business at the store and ride on."

"I aim to," Nathan said.

He loaded the sack of grain on the packhorse, and returning to the store, brought out the rest of his purchases. He tied the neck of the sack, divided its weight behind his saddle, mounted, and rode out. Sheriff Esty watched him until he was out of sight, sighing with relief. Nathan rode warily, for he didn't know where the bunch had gone who had prodded Vern Tilton into drawing. It was a town he wished to leave behind, and Cotton Blossom felt the same, for he had forged on ahead. Nathan rode a good ten miles before finding a decent place to make camp for the night. There was water from a seep that had pooled at the foot of a ridge, concealed by a heavy growth of willows. First Nathan unsaddled his grulla and unloaded the packhorse, allowing the weary animals to roll. He then quickly gathered wood, knowing it would be dark before he could boil coffee and broil his bacon, but he needed the food and hot coffee. Whatever the reason, a fire after dark—in Comanche country— could be the death of a man. Nathan chose a low place in the ground, kept the blaze small, and doused it when the coffee was hot and his rashers of bacon ready. He shared the bacon with Cotton Blossom and drank the coffee from the pot. There was little else to do except turn in for the night, so Nathan rolled in his blankets, his head on his saddle, a Colt near to his hand. He could count on Cotton Blossom alerting him to any approaching danger, but weary as he was, sleep wouldn't come. His mind drifted back to the afternoon shooting, to Vern Tilton, and he recalled something Wild Bill Hickok had once told him.

"When a man pulls a gun on you, always shoot to kill. Let him live, and the first chance he gets, he'll show his gratitude by shootin' you in the back."

"Bill was right, Cotton Blossom," Nathan said. "Even if he fails to bushwhack me, he can always claim that my hand wasn't steady or that I was afraid of him . . ."

As he had done so often, Nathan allowed his mind to wander back over the years, to that bleak day in January 1866. Ragged, hungry, afoot, he had returned to his fire-ravaged home near Charlottesville, Virginia, following two long years in Libby Prison in Richmond. Old Malachi, an aged Negro, had lived long enough to describe and name the seven renegades who had murdered Nathan's mother, father, and sister. Swearing a vow of vengeance on his father's grave, Nathan had taken the trail of the killers, following it west. His constant companion had been Cotton Blossom, the only living reminder of a past that had been lost to him forever. Reaching St. Louis, Nathan had become involved with young Molly Tremayne, only to lose her when he had again taken up the vengeance trail. While he had never gotten over Molly, he had never tried to reclaim her, for their parting had been bitter. So he had never learned that pretty Molly had died less than a year after his leaving, having given birth to his son. . . .

In a little Missouri town, Nathan had found and had killed the first of the seven men on his death list. In Waco, Texas, dealing faro, he had found himself in an uncomfortable position when the three unwed daughters of the saloon owner had set out to trap him. He had escaped, only to find himself pursued by Eulie, the eldest of the trio. Unable to rid himself of her, he had made the best of it. Eulie had dressed as a man, had called herself Eli, and had proven her ability to ride, rope, and shoot. Nathan's manhunt had led him to New Orleans, and there Eulie had so impressed Barnaby McQueen with her horse savvy that McQueen had persuaded her to remain at his ranch, gentling a horse. Nathan had begun spending his time in New Orleans saloons, seeking some word of the men on his death list.

On a New Orleans street, Nathan had gone to the aid of a stranger, and as a result, had gunned down two killers employed by Hargis Gavin, owner of a New Orleans gambling empire. Byron Silver, the stranger whom Nathan had befriended, had been associated with French Stumberg, owner of his own gambling houses and archenemy of Gavin. Stumberg, from what Nathan had learned, harbored two of the killers on Nathan's death list, so when Byron Silver had persuaded Stumberg to hire Nathan, Nathan had taken the job. But Nathan quickly learned three things. The first and most disturbing had been Stumberg's involvement in white slavery, the selling of young women in Mexico. Second, Nathan had found Stumberg intended to win a horse race—a race in which Eulie was determined to ride a McQueen horse—by ambushing certain riders. Finally, Nathan had learned Byron Silver was an undercover agent from Washington, seeking to trap French Stumberg. The day of the horse race, Eulie had been shot out of the saddle and had died. Byron Silver had been wounded, leaving only Nathan to prevent the escape of Stumberg and his killers, and Nathan had accomplished that by blowing up Stumberg's steamboat, with the gambler and his killers aboard.

Nathan had left New Orleans, having learned that one of the killers he had believed was with Stumberg was riding with the notorious Cullen Baker. Baker and his gang had been reported in Arkansas, and Nathan had ridden to Fort Smith. Offered the badge of a deputy U.S. marshal, Nathan had accepted it, awaiting Baker's next foray into Arkansas. Eventually he had confronted the Baker gang, killing two of the outlaws. One of them was a killer from Nathan's death list.

Returning to Texas, five men still to be found, Nathan had paused in Lexington, where he had become friends with Viola Hayden and her father, Jesse. Viola had been set to ride Daybreak, her big gray, in a race with odds against him of twenty-to-one. On impulse, Nathan had bet five hundred dollars on the horse, but after collecting his winnings—ten thousand dollars— had been forced to shoot his way out of an ambush. While in Lexington, Nathan had met Texas Ranger Captain Sage Jennings. From the ranger, Nathan had learned that two of the killers he sought had left Texas, apparently bound for Indian Territory. Following, Nathan had gunned one of the men down, taking from him a young girl, Lacy Mayfield. From Lacy Nathan had learned that the man he had killed had been on his way to Colorado. Nathan, taking the girl with him, had ridden to Colorado. Reaching Denver, he found that the killer he sought had ridden south to Ciudad de Oro, a mining town. Leaving Lacy at a Denver boarding-house, Nathan had ridden south, finding and gunning down one of the killers on his death list. There, however, Nathan had been given a false lead that had taken him to Austin, Texas, while the killer he sought had gone to Fort Dodge and eventually to Denver.

Reaching Austin, Nathan had found Viola Hayden working in a saloon, destitute, her father dead at the hands of the man who had lost ten thousand dollars to Nathan just a few months before. Despite Nathan's efforts to save the girl, she had shot the man who she believed had killed her father and had then shot herself. Returning to Colorado, Nathan had found Lacy Mayfield involved with the owner of a saloon, a man Nathan had learned was one of the killers on his death list. In the fight that followed, Lacy had been gunned down by the outlaw when she had come between him and Nathan's gun. Thus it had been a bitter victory, the killing of this fifth man, for he had taken Lacy with him. While in Denver, Nathan had become friends with Wild Bill Hickok, and when Hickok had ridden east to Hays, Kansas, Nathan had ridden with him. Nathan had spent a few days with Hickok, until he had been elected sheriff. Nathan had then ridden to Kansas City, uncertain as to how and where he would find the last two men on his death list.

In a Kansas City newspaper, Nathan had seen a re-

ward dodger that had been widely circulated by the
Pinkertons on Frank and Jesse James. Among the
names of men who had ridden with the infamous outlaws, Nathan had found the name of one of the killers
he sought. Following a bank robbery by the James
gang, Nathan had found the hideout of the outlaws
and had led a sheriff's posse to it. While Frank and
Jesse had escaped, Nathan had confronted the man he
had sworn to kill and had forced a shootout. At loose
ends, not knowing where he might find the seventh
man, Nathan answered an advertisement in a Kansas
City newspaper and took a position with the Kansas-
Pacific Railroad between Kansas City and Hays. It had
been his duty to repair telephone lines torn down by
Indians or outlaws and to warn train crews of damaged
track. After serving with distinction for a few months,
Nathan had resigned because he had seen nor heard
nothing of the seventh and last man he had sworn to
kill. Riding south into Indian Territory, he had been
taken prisoner by the ruthless El Gato and his band of
thieves and killers.

Nathan had soon learned that the killer he sought
was not among the renegades, and as he plotted his
escape, he had learned that El Gato had a girl he
planned to sell into slavery in Mexico. Talking to her,
Nathan had learned that her name was Mary Holden
and that she longed to escape. But before Nathan could
make a move, he had been forced to ride with El Gato
and his outlaws on a winter raid into Kansas. Slipping
away during a blizzard, Nathan had returned to El
Gato's camp, overpowering the two men El Gato had
left behind. He had then taken Mary south, to Fort

Worth, Texas. Nathan had been in Texas often enough to have become friends with the post commander, Captain Ferguson, and the officer, assuming Mary was Nathan's wife, had assigned them a cabin. By the time Nathan and Mary had left Fort Worth, riding north, Nathan Stone had done the very thing he had vowed never again to do. He had become involved with a woman, more committed than he had ever been, but still burdened with his oath to kill the last of the seven renegades who had murdered his family in Virginia.

While at Fort Worth, Nathan had learned by telegraph that Texas outlaw John Wesley Hardin had been involved in shootings in several south Texas towns and was believed to be riding north. One of several men who had been riding with Hardin had been identified as Dade Withers, the seventh and last man on Nathan's death list. He and Mary had ridden to Fort Dodge and then to Hays without finding a trace of Hardin. Fifty miles east of Hays, on their way to Abilene, they had ridden into a holdup involving a Kansas-Pacific train. As he had traded lead with the outlaws, Nathan had been seriously wounded. But the train crew had remembered him from his Kansas-Pacific days, and taking Mary and the wounded Nathan aboard, had reversed the train and backed it to Abilene. The railroad, grateful for Nathan's daring, had paid all his medical bills and presented him with a reward. When he had recovered, he had been offered the task of taking a posse after the outlaws, for they had become an expensive nuisance, destroying track and stopping trains bearing army payrolls. But Nathan had declined, determined to find that seventh man, so the Kansas-Pacific had hired other men to trail the train robbers.

Again Nathan had taken Hardin's trail, and he had found evidence that the outlaw and his companions had reached Wichita with a trail herd. But there the men had split up, and Nathan had trailed Dade Withers west, knowing only that the man rode a horse with an XIT brand. Reaching Fort Dodge, Nathan and Mary had learned that a lone outlaw had robbed the mercantile at Dodge City, just west of the fort. At the mercantile, Nathan had learned the outlaw had ridden south on a horse bearing an XIT brand. He had not been followed, for he had struck exactly at sundown, so when Nathan had taken the trail the next day at first light, it had been easily followed. But the lone rider had traveled less than a mile when he had been surrounded by others. He had ridden away with the larger band and Nathan had followed them all south until they had crossed the Cimarron, into Indian Territory. Thus the seventh man on Nathan Stone's death list had become part of El Gato's band of renegades.

Riding to Kansas City, Nathan had agreed to pursue the outlaws on behalf of the Kansas-Pacific Railroad, but learned something that stopped him in his tracks. Mary Holden was expecting his child, and he had set aside everything else to marry the girl. But Mary had refused to remain safely in Kansas City, insisting on staying at Fort Dodge until Nathan and his posse had captured the band of renegades. But the outlaws always escaped into Indian Territory, leaving Nathan frustrated. Unknown to Nathan, El Gato had been sending a man to Fort Dodge to look and listen, and the outlaw chieftain had learned that Mary—his former captive—was there. Nathan had become fed up with railroad methods and had ridden to Hays. From there he had taken a train to Kansas City to resign from the railroad posse. Awaiting just such an opportunity, that very morning El Gato's men had stolen Mary away from the fort and had taken her into the wilds of Indian Territory, to the outlaw stronghold. Only Cotton Blossom, Nathan's hound, had followed.

Learning that Mary had been abducted, the post commander at Fort Dodge had telegraphed the Kansas-Pacific office in Kansas City. Nathan immediately had engaged a locomotive and tender for an emergency run to Hays. From there, he had ridden to Fort Dodge, arriving after dark. He had learned that a party of soldiers had gone after Mary, only to be ambushed. Nathan had then ridden out alone, to find Cotton Blossom awaiting him near the Cimarron. With the dog guiding him, he had ridden into Indian Territory and had found the outlaw camp. In the darkness of El Gato's cabin, he had killed the outlaw leader in a knife fight, only to learn that the renegades—a dozen strong—had already ravaged and murdered Mary. Grief and rage had taken control of Nathan Stone, and he had burst into the outlaw bunkhouse, his Winchester blazing. He had gunned down ten of the outlaws—including Dade Withers—but had been so severely wounded he had been in danger of bleeding to death. He had been saved only because Cotton Blossom had returned to the fort and had been able to attract the attention of the soldiers.

Healed in body but sick to his soul, Nathan had ridden to Kansas City, only to learn the newspapers had created for him an unwanted reputation as a fast gun, a gunfighter. The Kansas-Pacific had released an etching of him, and his reputation seemed to have spread throughout the frontier. In one town after another, he had been forced into gunfights to save his own life, with each new killing adding to the deadly legend. Finally, in the fall of 1872, he had managed to drop out of sight. Riding south to New Orleans, he had found refuge with Barnaby and Bess McQueen, who had befriended him and Eulie so long ago. There he had remained until the last week in February 1873. Finally he had ridden away, hopeful of escaping his past, only to find it stalking him like the pale horse. There in the street of this little Texas town he had been forced to face up to the awful truth. He was a marked man. While he had fulfilled his promise to his dead father, it now seemed a hollow victory, as he thought of what it had cost him. His vendetta had led to a bitter parting with Molly Tremayne, in St. Louis. He had been hell-bent on going to New Orleans, and it was there that Eulie had been shot. His winning—and taking—ten thousand dollars had cost Viola Hayden her father, driving her to murder and suicide. Lacy Mayfield had been gunned down trying to save one of the very men Nathan had sworn to kill. Poor Mary had suffered a horrible death in Indian Territory only because she had wished to be near him. He groaned, for their faces seemed to have been burned into his mind with a hot iron, and he couldn't escape them. Sensing his anguish, Cotton Blossom came near. He scratched the dog's ears, thankful for his faithfulness, feeling even that was more than he deserved.

For a long time Nathan lay looking at the silver stars

in the purple of the sky, until he finally slept. Sometime after midnight something awakened him, and he realized it had been the rattle of dry leaves, as Cotton Blossom had gotten to his feet. It was in the small hours of the night, when every sound was magnified many times, and it was all the warning Nathan Stone had. With the snick of an eared-back hammer, he was moving, rolling away from his saddle, palming a Colt. There was a roar from the surrounding thicket and two slugs slammed into Nathan's saddle. He fired three times. Once at the muzzle flash, once to the left, and once to the right. There were no more shots, and there was a rustle of leaves as Cotton Blossom trotted toward the thicket. Nathan followed, and taking the dead man by the ankles, dragged him out into the clearing. The moon had risen, and with the starlight Nathan had no trouble identifying the man.

"Damn you, Vern Tilton," Nathan said bitterly. "Damn you . . ."

Also available from
National bestselling author

RALPH COMPTON

THE BLOODY TRAIL
SHADOW OF THE GUN
DEATH OF A BAD MAN
RIDE THE HARD TRAIL
BLOOD ON THE GALLOWS
THE CONVICT TRAIL
RAWHIDE FLAT
THE BORDER EMPIRE
THE MAN FROM NOWHERE
SIXGUNS AND DOUBLE EAGLES
BOUNTY HUNTER
FATAL JUSTICE
STRYKER'S REVENGE
DEATH OF A HANGMAN
NORTH TO THE SALT FORK
DEATH RIDES A CHESTNUT MARE
RUSTED TIN
THE BURNING RANGE
WHISKEY RIVER
THE LAST MANHUNT
THE AMARILLO TRAIL
SKELETON LODE
STRANGER FROM ABILENE
THE SHADOW OF A NOOSE
THE GHOST OF APACHE CREEK
RIDERS OF JUDGMENT
SLAUGHTER CANYON
DEAD MAN'S RANCH
ONE MAN'S FIRE
THE OMAHA TRAIL
DOWN ON GILA RIVER

"A writer in the tradition of Louis L'Amour and Zane Grey!" —*Huntsville Times*

Available wherever books are sold or at
penguin.com

S543

Charles G. West

"THE WEST AS IT REALLY WAS."
—RALPH COMPTON

Way of the Gun
(Coming March 2013)

Even at seventeen years old, Carson Ryan knows enough about cow herding to realize the crew he's with is about the worst he's ever seen. They're taking the long way around to the Montana prairies, and they're seriously undermanned. They're also a bunch of murdering cattle rustlers—and now the law thinks he's one of them...

Frank Leslie

DEAD MAN'S TRAIL

When Yakima Henry is attacked by desperados, a mysterious gunman sends the thieves running. But when Yakima goes to thank his savior, he's found dead—with a large poke of gold amongst his gear.

THE BELLS OF EL DIABLO

A pair of Confederate soldiers go AWOL and head for Denver, where a tale of treasure in Mexico takes them on an adventure.

THE LAST RIDE OF JED STRANGE

Colter Farrow is forced to kill a soldier in self-defense, sending him to Mexico where he helps the wild Bethel Strange find her missing father. But there's an outlaw on their trail, and the next ones to go missing just might be them...

DEAD RIVER KILLER

Bad luck has driven Yakima Henry into the town of Dead River during a severe mountain winter—where Yakima must weather a killer who's hell-bent on making the town as dead as its name.

REVENGE AT HATCHET CREEK

Yakima Henry has been ambushed and badly injured. Luckily, Aubrey Coffin drags him to safety—but as he heals, lawless desperados circle closer to finish the job...

BULLET FOR A HALF-BREED

Yakima Henry won't tolerate incivility toward a lady, especially the former widow Beth Holgate. If her new husband won't stop giving her hell, Yakima may make her a widow all over again.

Available wherever books are sold or at penguin.com

S0096